A Question of Identity

JUNE THOMSON

This low-priced Bantam Book
has been completely reset in a type face
designed for easy reading, and was printed
from new plates. It contains the complete
text of the original hard-cover edition.
NOT ONE WORD HAS BEEN OMITTED.

A QUESTION OF IDENTITY

*A Bantam Book / published by arrangement with
Doubleday & Company, Inc.*

PRINTING HISTORY

Doubleday edition published November 1977
Bantam edition / May 1980

ISBN 0-553-13407-8

PRINTED IN THE UNITED STATES OF AMERICA

0 9 8 7 6 5 4 3 2 1

For Mark and Paul

Chapter 1

As George Stebbing climbed over the gate into the lower meadow, he could see the members of the archaeological society still hard at work, despite the heat of that August afternoon. The trench they were digging now stretched almost half the width of the field, approaching close to the boundary hedge where his land ended and his neighbour's, Geoff Lovell's, began, while in the centre a large rectangle had been marked out from which the turf and top-soil were being removed. Girls as well as men were shovelling and digging, wheeling the excavated material away in barrows or painstakingly sifting it through sieves.

He had to admit everything looked all right. There was no litter, not even near the tents where some of the younger ones were camping during the dig, and they were taking care to keep the top-soil, as he'd told them.

Not that this was the real reason for his visit, although it wouldn't do them any harm to think he was checking up on them every so often. He was really looking out for the girl, the one with the brief shorts and the long, brown legs. She had smiled and waved to him the first morning.

There's life in the old dog yet, he told himself, with a shame-faced yet half-approving grin. And there's no harm in looking, although if I was twenty years younger, it'd be a damn sight more than a look I'd be after.

He was glad now that he'd agreed to let them come. It made a bit of a change from the normal daily routine on the farm, although at first he hadn't been too keen. It was his son's idea. He was the one who had noticed the broken pieces of pottery, turned up when the ditches were being re-dug, and who had taken them along to the local museum to have them dated. They were early Saxon, he had been told, and could indicate the site of a settlement or homestead. Would he allow some test diggings to be done?

George Stebbing had finally agreed. The field was a scrubby bit of pasture, too small for cultivation, although he was planning to have the hedges grubbed out and turn it into part of the adjoining field, ready for putting under the plough the following autumn. There seemed little harm in letting them make their dig before this was done, especially when it was pointed out to him that ploughing could destroy forever any archaeological remains.

Besides, as a relative new-comer to the district, it might do him a bit of good socially to be on friendly terms with the society that included a few local dignitaries on its committee.

"All right. Let them come," he had said at last.

He wasn't quite sure himself what he had expected. Long-haired students, most likely, making a damn nuisance of themselves by playing guitars and trampling down his corn; certainly not these hard-working men and women, some of them quite elderly, who had given up their summer holidays and were prepared to slog away hour after hour in the sun.

He started off down the slope, his blue eyes moving restlessly as he looked out for the girl. But it was Mr. Rose, an earnest, middle-aged history master from the grammar school, normally a fussy man about his appearance but dressed now in a filthy khaki shirt and shorts and an old, floppy linen hat, who scrambled out of the trench to meet him, his face glistening with sweat. It was the first time he had been in charge of a dig and, knowing Stebbing's initial reluctance to let them on his land, he was desperately anxious that nothing should go wrong.

Stebbing watched him approach with dismay. He had been hoping to avoid Rose but, under the circumstances, there was nothing much he could do except stay and talk to him for a time, before finding an excuse to wander off on his own.

"Found anything yet?" he asked.

Secretly he had set his heart on their discovering something really valuable, like a hoard of buried treasure or, at least, some gold coins but so far they had turned up nothing more exciting than a lot more broken pottery and some fire-blackened bones.

Rose's face lit up.

"Yes, indeed we have, Mr. Stebbing! This very morning, as a matter of fact. Some post-holes! It's all very thrilling!"

"Oh, really?" Stebbing asked, trying to sound interested, although the discovery of post-holes didn't strike him as being particularly exciting. "Is that important?"

"Dear me, yes. It could be very important. Judging by the size of them, they could indicate a building of some significance. A barn, for instance. Or even the house itself. And then, goodness knows what we might find. Grain-storage pits! Perhaps even the original hearthstone!"

Stebbing gazed about him uncomfortably, embarrassed by Rose's enthusiasm and pedantic style of speech, which always made the farmer feel at a loss as to what to say in reply.

Suddenly his attention was caught by the figure of a man, standing a little distance off in the adjoining field and watching them with apparent interest. He was a short, powerfully built man, with heavy shoulders and, with his back to the sun, he gave the impression of a strong, dark, hostile shape against the light.

"There's Lovell," Stebbing remarked.

Rose looked in the same direction and seemed uneasy.

"Who is he?" he asked. "I've noticed him watching us on several occasions over the past few days."

Stebbing laughed.

"It's the farmer who owns the land next to mine. A funny devil. Probably thinks you're going to start digging up his field next. I'll call him over and explain."

Cupping his hands round his mouth, he shouted, "Hi, Lovell! Come over and take a look if you want to."

Geoff Lovell heard him but he made no reply and, after a few seconds, he turned and began walking away, trying to appear nonchalant and unhurried but inwardly cursing himself for having been such a bloody fool to come in the first place. He should have waited until later in the evening when most of them had packed up and gone home, although even then it wasn't entirely safe. A few of them were camping in the field; he had seen lamps alight in the tents until quite late. But, at least, there'd be less chance of running into Stebbing. Seeing him standing there, he hadn't dared go too close to the hedge and get a good look and all he had been able to make out was the trench was being extended, although he couldn't see its exact line.

Should he go back and complain to Stebbing, get him to call a halt to the digging, making as an excuse that, if they came too close to his land, they might mess up the drainage?

Then he decided against it. Stebbing was looking for an excuse to strike up an acquaintanceship and by going and talking to the man, he'd be playing straight into his hands. He'd be round at the house, wanting to discuss it and that would be even worse. Better to risk them digging in the field, for the chances of them turning up anything must be a thousand to one, although he didn't count on it. There had been too much bad luck over the past few years for him to believe that things would ever go his way again.

He came to the last meadow behind the farm-house and stopped at the gate, reluctant to go any further. The land here sloped gently down on all sides so that the house and outbuildings were clustered in a hollow and he remembered, as a child, stopping at this same place, particularly in the evening when dusk was falling and the lights were shining out from the windows, and thinking how safe, how protected it seemed, held between the folds of earth as between a pair of hands. Then home-coming had been a special and secret delight. There had been a deep sense of belonging. Now, he saw the same scene with different eyes. It seemed to suck at the very roots of his strength.

Christ, if only I could get out of it! he thought. Stebbing would buy it for that son of his. That's what was at the back of his seeming friendliness. And if I'd sold out to him three years ago, none of this would have happened. I'd get rid of it like a shot now, only it's too bloody late.

As he stood there, he saw the figure of a woman in a blue dress emerge from the house and turn to look in his direction, putting her hands over her eyes as a shield against the sun. It was Betty. She must have seen him, silhouetted against the sky at the top of the slope, for she waved tentatively. He made no answering gesture. From that distance, he saw her hesitate, look back towards the house and then, after a few moments of uncertainty in which she stood irresolute in the yard, she started towards him, disappearing for a time behind the trees that surrounded the farm. Still he didn't move. Presently she came into sight again and began climbing the slope towards him, stopping a little short so that the gate formed a barrier between them.

Always this space between us now, he thought bitterly. This holding back from any contact.

She was smiling at him nervously as she faced him; not a proper smile, more like wincing. In the bright sunlight, she looked ill. The shadows under her eyes were dark, like bruises, and he saw how thin and transparent her skin was, stretched across the delicate bones that seemed to shine through it.

She reminded him of a bird, fearful, fragile, light in the hands, and she roused in him the same instinct for protection and the same despairing sense of his own clumsiness.

He looked down at his hands as they lay on the top bar of the gate; a farmer's hands; strong and muscular; short-fingered; the nails broken and dirty; fit for work and that was about all, and he felt a sudden contempt and revulsion for his own body.

"You've been up there?" she asked, putting up a hand to hold back a piece of hair that had fallen across her forehead.

Despite the estrangement, he knew what she meant. There had never been the need for many words for them to understand each other.

"I had a look," he admitted reluctantly.

"And it's all right?"

"I reckon so."

Feeling her eyes on his face, he dropped his own glance, knowing that he had never been any good at lying to her.

"What are they doing now?" she asked.

"Still digging," he replied, trying to sound off-hand. "It's all right, I tell you. They're working in the middle of the field. They won't come anywhere near the hedge."

Better not tell her about the trench, he decided. There was no point in frightening her needlessly.

"You're sure?"

No! he wanted to shout. I'm not bloody sure! Not about anything anymore. Instead, he tried to smile at her reassuringly.

"You worry too much," he told her but he had

struck the wrong note; too light; too intimate. He saw her draw away.

"Don't go up there, though," he went on. "Stebbing's hanging about. He might see you."

"He saw you?" she countered quickly.

"No," he said, lying again. "I made sure he didn't. The man's a damned fool."

He meant it as a bit of a joke between them, a shared amusement at Stebbing's thick-skinned stupidity but the remark came out with all the bitter anger and contempt that he really felt towards the man. And having once started to release his anger, he found it difficult to control, although he realised that Stebbing was only a scapegoat.

"Where's Charlie?" he asked, opening the gate.

He saw her back away at his approach, although he pretended not to notice.

"I don't know. Behind the barn, I think, seeing to his pigs."

"Well, keep him away from the house. I don't want him talking to anybody."

"You think someone might come?" she asked, sounding frightened.

His anger finally broke.

"I don't bloody think anything!" he burst out. "Just keep Charlie away. And make sure the dog's off the chain."

"It's my fault," she said in a tone of flat assertion that was not expecting any answering denial.

His anger drained away, leaving him ashamed and awkward. Despite her frailty, there was this steely quality in her that he had never known how to deal with, that baffled him and made him helpless.

"It's no-one's fault," he muttered, turning away to fumble with the gate fastening.

She didn't answer but began walking away from him down the slope towards the farm. He let her go, following only when she was half the field's length from him and then walking slowly so that there was no chance that he should catch her up.

Stebbing, who had watched Lovell leave, turned

back to Rose, his face flushed and his blue eyes hot
with anger.

"Surly bugger," he said, half to himself. Lovell had
deliberately ignored him, an insult he found hard to
take in front of other people.

Well, that's the last bloody time I'll speak to him,
he decided. He can go to hell as far as I care.

Rose, aware of a certain tension and anxious that
no disagreeableness should attach itself to him and
his party, put in brightly:

"I don't know if you'd like to have a look at the
post-holes, Mr. Stebbing? As I was saying, they could
be an important find. The proportions . . ."

"Ah, yes, proportions," said Stebbing, walking away
from him. He had caught sight of the girl, the one he
was looking out for, a little distance away, kneeling
down by a small pile of pottery fragments that she
was washing in a bucket of water, and he felt his
good humour return as he stood over her, looking
down into the cleft between her breasts, revealed by
the scanty sun-top she was wearing.

"Warm work?" he asked, grinning appreciatively.

Behind him, Rose, who had trotted after him, was
saying with maddening persistence:

"The post-holes are over in this direction."

Stebbing winked at her, indicating that he would
much prefer to stay talking with her, and turned to
follow Rose.

As it happened, he was not to see the post-holes
that afternoon.

A sudden shout away to their left made them both
turn. A young man was standing up in the trench on
the far side of the field, waving his arms to attract
their attention.

"Mr. Rose!" he was shouting. "Over here!"

"My word!" said Rose, pushing up his glasses ex-
citedly on his nose. "I believe young David's discovered something."

He set off at a brisk lope, Stebbing following him
and wondering if, perhaps, at last, the excavations
had turned up the treasure he had been hoping for

and speculating how much of it, if any, he could claim for it having been found on his land.

The young man had climbed out of the trench to meet them. One look at his face was enough to tell Stebbing that whatever it was he had discovered, it wasn't something pleasant. He was a deathly, greenish-white colour and he pointed wordlessly down into the trench where he had been digging before turning aside with a muttered apology to be sick in the grass.

Stebbing and Rose stood on the mound of earth at the edge of the trench and looked down into the newly dug section where the young man's spade lay abandoned at the bottom. At first, neither of them could see anything unusual. The excavated sides were studded with stones, some of them quite large, and threaded with the fibrous roots that had spread out through the sub-soil from the trees that grew along the edge of the field.

Then Stebbing saw it and, taking Rose by the arm, pointed. At the far end, protruding from the loose clods of earth that had not yet been cleared away, was a foot. Or what remained of a foot, clad in the mouldering fragments of a boot, the leather rotting and falling away to reveal . . .

Stebbing averted his eyes.

"I think we'd better get the police," he said gruffly. "That's no bloody Saxon corpse down there. And," he added, looking at the young man who was still retching miserably into the grass, "I'll get him fixed up with a drop of brandy at the same time. Do you want to come for a swig yourself? You look as if you could do with it."

"No, I'll stay here," Rose replied, with surprising firmness. "I'm in charge of the site and it's my responsibility to see no-one touches anything. Evidence, you know. Besides, I wouldn't like any of the women to see it. It's not a pleasant sight."

"You're bloody right there," agreed Stebbing and, thankful for the excuse to get away, he set off across the field, accompanied by the young man, while Rose, his back to the trench, stood on the mound of earth, shooing away with flapping gestures of his arms those members of the society who, realising something unusual was happening, had begun drifting down from the main excavation site.

Chapter 2

He was still there three quarters of an hour later when Detective Inspector Rudd arrived, accompanied by his detective sergeant, Boyce, and a contingent of uniformed and plain-clothes men.

Rudd saw him as he walked down the field towards the site, taking in with a few, quick, interested glances not only the small, dejected figure of the history master, now sitting cross-legged on the grass, a handkerchief draped over the back of his neck to keep off the sun, but the whole view.

The field was small and roughly triangular, bounded on one long side by a ditch and a hedge, on the shorter side by a coppice of trees near which some tents had been erected and on the third side by another hedge with a gate in it that gave access to the large wheatfield round which they had walked on the way from Stebbing's yard where they had parked their cars.

Across the field a line trench and a partly excavated area in the centre, marked by mounds of excavated earth, showed where the archaeological society had been working. Wheelbarrows and tools lay abandoned here and there, for the digging had been called off and the members had retired to the tents to drink tea and wait for the arrival of the police. Only Mr. Rose remained on duty, hot and miserable and feeling obscurely guilty, as if the discovery of the body were, in some inexplicable way, his fault.

He scrambled to his feet as he saw the group of men approaching, a little cheered by the appearance of the man who seemed to be in charge of them. He looked less like a policeman than a farmer, with a frank, open face and the slow, easy walk of a countryman.

"Mr. Rose, isn't it?" Rudd asked. "I gather from Mr. Stebbing you're in charge here."

"That's right," Rose replied. "And I assure you I had no idea . . ."

Rudd looked him over with a friendly eye. The man looked ready to drop.

"I think they're brewing up tea over by the tents," he told him. "Why don't you get yourself a cup? I'll have a chat with you later."

"Thank you," Rose said gratefully and Rudd watched sympathetically as he stumbled away.

"Poor devil," he commented to Boyce, his burly, deep-voiced sergeant. "He's dug up more than he bargained for here. Well, let's have a look at what's been found. Pardoe, you'd better come in on this."

Pardoe, the police surgeon, a brisk man with heavy horn-rimmed glasses and a no-nonsense air about him, detached himself from the group of men and came forward.

Together with Pardoe and Boyce, Rudd approached the edge of the trench and peered down into it. They contemplated the foot in silence for a few moments and then Rudd and Pardoe clambered down for a closer look.

"About four feet down," Rudd commented, "so it's a relatively shallow grave. The ground's dry, too. We shouldn't have too much trouble getting him out."

"How long's he been down there?" asked Boyce. The trench was too narrow for the three of them and he remained on the top.

Rudd squatted down to examine the foot in close-up.

"Hard to say," he admitted. "What do you think, Pardoe?"

Pardoe touched the boot with a fastidious finger.

"A fair time. The leather's well rotted. But I can give you a better idea when we've uncovered the rest of him."

"Right!" said Rudd. "We'll get started on it straight-away."

He climbed out of the trench, slapping his trouser legs to rid them of the clinging crumbs of earth, and began giving orders for the erection of a canvas screen round the site.

"Then I want a thorough search made of the field," he added. "Stapleton, you're in charge of that. Take the uniformed men and collect up anything you find."

Stapleton moved off and Rudd turned to McCullum, a tall, laconic Scot who, while awaiting orders, had seated himself on the grass and was slowly rolling a home-made cigarette.

"I'd like some photographs taken of the trench as it is now and then a series at successive stages as he's dug out. Get a few general shots, too, of the field."

McCullum nodded and moved off, carrying his equipment, towards the screen that was being erected.

"And when McCullum's finished taking the first shots, I want you, Moody, to get your coat off and start digging him out," he told a large, powerfully built, young constable. Turning to Boyce, he added, "See that every scrap of soil's saved, so get those plastic sheets spread out and make sure everything that's dug out goes onto them. Denny had better take over from Moody when he's about three feet down. Barker and Frome can sift the soil as it comes out. I don't want anything missed, not even a shirt button. I'll leave you in charge, Tom, while I have a word with Stebbing."

"Right," said Boyce and, beckoning to Moody, disappeared inside the screens. As he walked away, Rudd heard with some amusement Boyce shouting, "For God's sake, man! It's not a pick and shovel job! You're not digging up the High Street. Get those turves off clean!"

Stebbing, who was waiting a little way off, had been craning his neck, torn between an anxiety to see what was going on and yet not observe too closely anything that might be unpleasant. Rudd had already summed him up in the walk from the farm-house where Stebbing had met them. He was a large, paunchy man, with a florid complexion and a bustling, self-assertive manner that, the Inspector guessed, covered up a much less confident personality beneath it.

"Nasty business," he said as Rudd approached.

"Yes," Rudd replied and added, "The land's yours?"

"Up to the hedge."

"And beyond that?"

"Belongs to a man called Lovell. He farms it with his brother."

Rudd turned to contemplate the further field. About half a mile away the roof of a house and its surrounding buildings was just visible below a gentle slope of grassland.

"That his place?" he asked.

"Yes," Stebbing replied and added quickly, "About that dead man they found. I swear to God I know nothing about it, Inspector. It came as a complete shock them finding it."

"An archaeological society, isn't it?" Rudd asked, ignoring the man's remark.

"That's right," Stebbing said. He seemed eager to explain. "We'd found these bits of pottery and we thought—that is, my son suggested—they might like to have a look at the field this summer. It's due to go under the plough in the autumn . . ."

"So they had your permission?"

"Oh yes," Stebbing said and laughed a little too loudly. "So it's hardly likely, is it, that I'd give them the go-ahead to dig, if I'd put the body there myself?"

Rudd, who was well used to the overanxiety of the completely innocent to establish their guiltlessness, said blandly, "It never crossed my mind, Mr. Stebbing. Have you noticed at any time that the earth in the field had been disturbed?"

"No, I haven't. Mind you, it's the tail end of my land and, as you can see for yourself, it's not much use at the moment, so I haven't bothered with it. It could be months before I'd walk down this far."

Long enough, Rudd thought, for the grass to grow again, especially if the turf had been replaced over the grave and well pressed down.

"Is there any nearer access to the field, apart from the road that runs past your place?"

Stebbing shook his head.

"No path or cart-track?"

"No."

Rudd looked across the fields to where a distant line of telegraph posts marked the road along which he had driven a little while earlier.

"It's a fair way off," he mused.

"Nearly a mile," Stebbing replied.

"Have you noticed anything unusual over the past, say, couple of years? A car parked in the road, for instance, or strangers about?"

"I can't say I have. As you saw for yourself, the road's pretty quiet. There's only my farm and Lovell's along it. But that's not to say someone couldn't have parked there and come across my land without me seeing him, especially at night."

"I'll check with Mr. Lovell," Rudd replied. "He may have noticed something."

Stebbing hesitated, as if about to say something, and Rudd cocked his head inquiringly, inviting the man to speak.

"Yes?" he asked.

Stebbing wetted his lips.

"It may mean nothing, Inspector, but Lovell's been

hanging about since they started digging. I saw him myself this afternoon. In fact, I shouted to him to come across and have a look but he ignored me and walked off. Then Mr. Rose remarked he'd seen him, too, on a couple of occasions. I'm not saying there's anything to it . . ."

"Just curiosity?" Rudd suggested easily.

"That's right," Stebbing agreed. He seemed relieved that Rudd had put forward this explanation. "Or he might have thought they'd move onto his land without asking his permission. He's a funny bloke, Inspector. Since I bought the farm three years ago, I've tried being neighbourly but he doesn't welcome visitors. I thought his wife and mine might get together, too, for a bit of a chat but he made it clear he wants to keep himself to himself. Quite rude he was when I called. Mind you, that brother of his must be a bit of an embarrassment."

"Oh?" said Rudd. "In what way?"

His face had relaxed into the friendly, listening expression that his colleagues would have recognised as part of his interviewing technique. It fooled Stebbing as it had fooled many others. Encouraged to go on, the farmer tapped his forehead significantly.

"A bit short up here. Simple. I'm not saying he ought to be put away or anything like that. The chap seems harmless enough. But I can see, with a brother like that, Lovell may not want many people calling."

"Difficult for him," agreed Rudd. "But I'm afraid I'll have to drop in on him and ask a few questions— about cars seen in the vicinity, that sort of thing. I suppose I could walk across the fields to his house?"

"I'd go round by the road, if I were you," Stebbing advised him. "He's got a dog that's kept loose in the yard so you'd be safer going in by the front way. It's pretty fierce; went for me when I called. I wouldn't like it to take a lump out of you."

"Thanks for the warning," Rudd said and, nodding pleasantly, turned back to the trench. The canvas screen had been erected and, inside it, Moody was carefully removing the earth, throwing it to one side onto the large plastic sheets that were spread out on the grass and over which two constables were squatting, sorting it over with trowels.

The heat, trapped inside the screen, was stifling.

The makeshift grave, which lay roughly at right angles to the trench dug by the archaeological society, had now been partly uncovered. The turf that had covered it had been cut into squares and was lying separate from the mound of loose earth. Rudd contemplated them with his hands in his pockets.

"See those turves are parcelled up," he told Boyce. "The forensic boys may want to have a look at them. One thing's certain, he's been down there long enough for the grass to take root over him again."

They watched in silence for a few more minutes until the soil had been dug out to a depth of three feet and then Rudd moved forward.

"All right," he said to Moody. "You can take a rest. It's a trowel job from now on. Denny, you take over. You're the expert. I want him brought out as whole as possible."

Moody retired gratefully, mopping his streaming face, and Denny, a thin, bright-eyed man, squatted down at the edge of the grave and began carefully removing the earth with a small trowel. Rudd had seen him at work before and admired his patience. He would pick away, if necessary for hours, with the same delicate precision as an expert restoring an old master.

Rudd drew Boyce outside.

"There's not much I can do here until he's properly uncovered and Denny's going to take at least an hour. Besides, I want to go over to the neighbouring farm."

"Something interesting?" Boyce asked inquisitively.

"Possibly," Rudd replied. "According to Stebbing, the man who owns it, a chap called Lovell, has been hanging about watching them digging on the site. It could be nothing more than curiosity but he's an obvious person to call on anyway. It's his land on the other side of the hedge. Stebbing has noticed nothing unusual but Lovell may have done. Whoever put the body there must have carried it either across Lovell's land or Stebbing's."

"Seems an odd place to choose," Boyce remarked. "Why take the trouble to bring it this far? If I'd killed somebody, I wouldn't want to go humping it across the fields, looking for a place to bury it."

"That's assuming it was murder," Rudd pointed out.

"I think it's a fair enough assumption," Boyce replied. He was feeling hot and tired and argumentative. "If it was a suicide or a natural death, why bother to try and get rid of the body? The man didn't bury himself, that's for sure, but whoever did wanted him well hidden. If this archaeological society, or whatever it is, hadn't started digging, he might never have been found. Even then, it was just chance they uncovered him. If the trench had been dug a few feet to the left, he might still be down there and no-one the wiser."

"He might have died or been killed near here," Rudd replied, "which would explain why he was buried in this particular field."

"Then either the man who buried him happened to have a spade handy to dig the grave, in which case it suggests, if it was murder, it was planned beforehand or he was able to get hold of one fairly quickly, unless he was willing to run the risk of leaving a corpse lying about until he could come back later and get it under the ground."

"It's a point worth following up," agreed Rudd. "I'll check with Stebbing and Lovell if they've noticed any tools missing from their farms. They're the two nearest places likely to have spades. He's been down there too long for someone to borrow the equipment the archaeological society brought with them."

He glanced across at the tents, where there were signs that the society was already striking camp.

"I'd better have a word with Rose before he leaves," he added. "Not that I expect he can tell me much."

As he strolled over in that direction, Rose came forward to meet him, his face anxious.

"We're moving out, Inspector, I hope only temporarily. You see, we've found these post-holes . . ."

"You'll be allowed back," Rudd interrupted to assure him. "I'll let you know when, Mr. Rose. It should be within a couple of days."

"Most distressing. Most distressing. And just when we were making such excellent progress. It's an early Saxon site, you see, which could be very important archaeologically and some of my members have only a limited time to work on the dig."

"You haven't noticed anything unusual yourself while you've been working here?" Rudd asked.

"In what way?"

"Well, for example, an old spade left lying about?"

"No, I can't say we have. Everything that's found is most carefully preserved. All the earth is sifted and the pieces of pottery are washed, numbered and put to one side. You can examine those if you wish."

It was clear Rose had no interest in anything on the site that wasn't of archaeological significance and Rudd decided to leave it there. His own men, under Stapleton, were systematically searching the field. If anything of relevance to the dead man had been left behind, they would find it.

He put the next question with careful casualness.

"Fascinating these archaeological digs. I gather Mr. Lovell's been to have a look."

"Not exactly to look at the site," Rose corrected him. "He's been watching us from the next field. I've noticed him myself several times."

"Perhaps a bit worried you might start digging on his land?" Rudd suggested lightly.

But Rose took it as a personal affront.

"I can assure him we would do no such thing," he replied stiffly. "We are a responsible society. At no time would we excavate a site without first getting the owner's permission."

Rudd smiled and, thanking him, walked away. The interview hadn't been very productive, except to confirm that Lovell had been watching the excavation from his own land on the other side of the boundary hedge.

Had it just been curiosity? he wondered, as he skirted the wheatfield. It was certainly worth following up and he found himself looking forward to the interview with Lovell, Stebbing's unfriendly neighbour, who kept himself to himself.

Meanwhile it was a glorious day, one to be enjoyed. Beside him, the wheatfield stretched away, the pale gold ears stiffly erect on their short stems, rustling as they rubbed together, under a sky of indeterminate hazy brightness that seemed to have had the colour bleached out of it by days of continual heat. A scent of warm grain filled the air, Mediterranean in its intensity, while, far off, a combine harvester droned lazily as it worked some unseen field.

Chapter 3

Reaching Stebbing's yard, Rudd collected his car and turned out of the farm entrance, heading for Lovell's place, about three quarters of a mile down the road. He drove slowly, noting as he went the features of the area.

The road was narrow and tree-lined, little more than a hard-surfaced lane, with barely room for two cars to pass abreast. On either side were grass verges, heavy with cows' parsley and meadow sweet, and behind them hedges, broken here and there by gates, through which he caught glimpses of fields growing wheat and potatoes mostly. Beside one, a narrow neck of trees ran down to the edge of the road. At no place, he noticed, was the field where the body had been found visible from the road.

As he had been driving, he had a growing conviction that his sergeant had voiced and that he himself had felt from the beginning, that the location of the grave was in itself significant. Why had the body been carried so far off the road? He could understand why the nearby fields had not been chosen as a burial site. They were cultivated and therefore likely to be disturbed at some future date when they were ploughed. But the wood was easily accessible and a body buried there could remain forever without being discovered.

On a sudden impulse, he stopped and, drawing the car onto the verge, walked a little way between the trees. In places they grew closely together and, after only a few minutes' walk, he saw, on glancing back, that his car was no longer visible between the dense foliage. Stooping down, he picked up a handful of the leaf mould that lay inches thick under the trees and let it trickle out between his fingers. It was soft and light. And yet, whoever had buried the body had chosen a field at least half a mile away from the road where the earth was tighter packed and covered with turf that would first have to be removed before the grave could be dug.

Why? Because of its inaccessibility? Or was there some other more positive reason?

Thoughtfully, he walked back to the car and drove on down the lane.

A little distance further on, a gravelled opening on his left indicated the entrance to Lovell's farm and, parking the car at the side of the road, he got out and walked back towards the five-barred gate, fastened with a padlock and chain, that shut off the end of the drive.

As he put his hand on the gate, a dog came tearing up the slope from the farm-yard and flung itself against the bars, snarling and barking savagely, its lips drawn back to expose sharp, white teeth.

Rudd kept his distance as he contemplated it. It was a large black dog, a mongrel but with a lot of Labrador in it and quite clearly it was not going to be appeased with a few kind words and a pat on the head.

Beyond the gate, a rough, wheel-rutted drive led down an incline to a yard and outbuildings at the bottom. The house itself stood at right angles to the road, presenting a blank gable end, its windows looking out across the yard to the huddle of sheds and barns that faced it. It was an old building, with plastered walls and a roof of uneven, weathered tiles that was curiously shaped, the back of it sweeping down lower than the front to cover the first storey. Beyond the house, the ground sloped upwards again towards a meadow that would lead, Rudd guessed, in the direction of the field where the body had been found.

There was no-one about. The yard was deserted. Meanwhile, on the other side of the gate, the black Labrador kept up its hysterical onslaught against the bars and it was clear to Rudd that, unless he was prepared to be savaged, there was no way of approaching the house. It seemed to be stale-mate.

Behind the barn, Geoff Lovell heard the dog barking and guessed the reason. In a way, he had been half expecting it. His luck had run out years before and he realised, with a morose fatalism, that he almost welcomed this final down-turn of events as a kind of relief. The waiting was over. The worst had come.

All the same, he stood irresolute, wondering what to do. It was Charlie who decided it for him. He had grown increasingly uneasy as the dog's outcry continued, glancing alternately in the direction of the road and then towards Lovell, his round face anxious.

"There's someone a' the gate," he said at last.

Geoff Lovell ignored him, thrusting the fork into the straw and carrying it over to the heifer pen where he stood at the fence to watch the soft-eyed animals trample it underfoot. A fine, sweet-smelling, golden dust rose in the sunlit air.

Behind him, Charlie touched his arm.

"Geoff, there's someone a' the gate," he repeated. "The dog's barking."

"I know," Lovell replied impatiently. "Leave it be, Charlie."

"Shall I go, Geoff? Shall I see what they want?"

Lovell stifled his rising anger. It was no good, he realised. Charlie would go on and on about it until he went to silence the dog. Besides, whoever had called was evidently going to stand his ground until some-one came.

Thrusting the pitch-fork into the straw-pile, he turned to his brother.

"Listen, Charlie," he told him. "You stay here. Understand? I don't want you coming out. Whoever it is, I'll get rid of him as quick as I can. You finish seeing to the heifers."

He saw the familiar, stubborn look pass over Charlie's face, his mouth drooping sulkily.

"Why can't I talk to him, too, Geoff? Nobody comes to see us these days."

"Stay here," Lovell said shortly. "I'll be back in a few minutes."

"It ain't fair," Charlie replied, turning his face away. "I don't ever get to talk to anybody."

Lovell looked at him with a mixture of baffled anger and pity. It was hard on Charlie. He had few pleasures and, like a child, he welcomed any diversion but he could not be trusted. God knows what he might say if allowed to talk.

"Listen," Lovell said to him, trying to keep the impatience out of his voice. "You stay here, like I told you, and I'll give you a game of cards later this evening. All right?"

"All right, then," Charlie agreed reluctantly. "But I still think it ain't fair," he added, raising his voice as Geoff walked away round the end of the barn.

Rudd, who had stayed where he was at the gate, letting the dog bark itself hoarse, watched Lovell approach up the drive. He was stockily built, broad-shouldered and, Rudd estimated, in his forties. Although not bad-looking, there was a dark, surly air about him, accentuated by his sun-burnt skin and thick, black hair, turning grey over the ears, that hung low on his forehead. He gave the impression of strength and masculinity and smouldering energy that was kept banked down, apparent in his heavy, deliberate walk and the deep crease between his eyebrows.

"Mr. Lovell?" Rudd asked pleasantly, over the gate.

The man didn't acknowledge the greeting but shouted at the dog that cringed immediately and came to heel.

"What do you want?" he asked belligerently. "This is private land."

"I'm a police Inspector," Rudd replied. "I'd like to ask you a few questions."

He saw the expression on Lovell's face close over.

"What about?" he asked.

Rudd regarded him with a cool eye. He had no intention of conducting the interview across a five-barred gate. It was time, he decided, that Lovell, too, should be brought to heel.

"If you'll tie that dog of yours up, we'll talk in the house," he said. "Otherwise we can go into headquarters for a proper interview. It's up to you."

Lovell stared at him for a few seconds and then his gaze dropped.

Not so tough after all, decided Rudd, once his bluff's been called.

"All right. Wait here," Lovell said in a surly voice.

He dragged the dog off by its collar down the slope into the yard where he fastened it up to a piece of chain attached to the wall of the barn. Like its master, the fight had gone out of it. Or so it seemed. But, as Rudd climbed over the gate and strolled down the track towards the farm, the hair round its scruff and along its spine rose and its lips drew back in a threatening snarl. The Inspector gave it a wide berth as he walked past it.

Lovell was standing at the door of the house, his hand on the latch, wondering whether to open it or not. The Inspector was alone and it was evidently an informal visit. Lovell could see that, if he kept his head, it might be possible to get rid of the man fairly quickly. To ask him inside would show some willingness to co-operate and, besides, Charlie was less likely to see them and come out to join them than if they were standing outside in the yard.

"You'd better come in," he said shortly, pushing open the door, and Rudd followed him into the house.

The door led directly into the room beyond that was long, low-ceilinged and shadowy after the dazzle of the sunlight outside. Rudd, pausing in the doorway, took in its features in a few rapid glances as his eyes got used to the dimmer light. On his right, an oval, gate-legged table stood under one of the small casement windows, with four round-backed, Victorian chairs drawn up to it, while against the nearby wall an old-fashioned oak dresser stood beside a door that led presumably into an adjoining room. A sofa and a pair of arm-chairs, covered in worn cretonne, faced a coke-burning stove of mottled enamel, the only modern-looking object in the room, that was placed in the deep alcove of what was probably the original fireplace opening, for the smoke-blackened beam was still in position above it and the high mantel-shelf. A door next to the fire-place stood ajar, giving a glimpse of the two bottom treads of a narrow, boxed-in staircase that extended upwards, Rudd guessed, alongside the chimney breast.

But what struck him most about the room was its neatness and cleanliness. There was none of the comfortable clutter that most farm-houses collect. The furniture, although old and well-used, was highly polished, the ornaments and pieces of china on display over the fire-place and on the dresser shelves were neatly arranged and, apart from some bills tucked in behind a vase and a pair of Wellington boots standing tidily on a sheet of newspaper in the hearth, there were few signs of family occupation. A shot-gun propped up in the corner near them seemed out of place.

"Well?" asked Lovell.

He had taken up a position in the centre of the room with his back to the circle of chairs, blocking the Inspector's approach. It was obvious he had no intention of asking Rudd to sit down.

"Just a few questions, Mr. Lovell," Rudd said casually. The man seemed more at ease although it was, he guessed, largely a pose. He was standing with his hands in his trouser pockets but the powerful fore-arms, bare below rolled-up shirt sleeves, were still tense. Rudd could see the bunched muscles under the dark skin.

"I believe you own the land next to Mr. Stebbing's?" Rudd continued.

"That's right."

"And yours and Mr. Stebbing's are the only farms along this road?"

"Yes. What of it?"

"You haven't seen or heard anything suspicious in the past couple of years, have you?"

Lovell's reply came a little too quickly.

"No, I haven't."

"No cars parked late at night? No strangers about on your land?"

"No."

"You seem very sure, Mr. Lovell."

"I've a right to be," Lovell replied. "That dog of mine's loose day and night in the yard. No-one could set foot on my land without him letting me know about it. That's why I keep it."

It was a reasonable answer, as Rudd had to admit to himself. The dog had been quick enough to notice him and give warning as soon as he approached the gate. Under the circumstances, it seemed futile to put the next question but Rudd asked it all the same.

"No tools missing from the farm?"

The query seemed to disturb Lovell for some reason. He had become more relaxed and confident as the interview continued. Now the old bristling, suspicious manner returned.

"Tools? What tools?" he asked sharply.

"Any tools. But I was thinking specifically of something like a spade or a garden fork."

Lovell was about to speak when the sound of the door opening distracted both of them. Turning, Rudd saw a man standing in the doorway, blinking as his eyes got accustomed to the subdued light. It was difficult to tell his age. He had the round, moon face and soft, unformed features of a child, but, judging by his height and build, was probably in his thirties. As he stood there, peering at them from the threshold, his hands dangling loosely in front of him, Rudd guessed he was Lovell's simple-minded brother of whom Stebbing had spoken.

Lovell's face had darkened and his voice when he spoke to him was angry and yet, underneath his impatience, Rudd thought he heard a certain gruff affection.

"What do you want, Charlie?"

Charlie looked from his brother to the Inspector with a shy smile, as if hoping to be introduced, but Lovell quickly recalled his attention.

"I said, what do you want?"

"Cup o' tea," Charlie replied.

"Go through to the kitchen, then," Lovell said, jerking his head in the direction of the door at the far end of the room.

Charlie crossed the room slowly, his boots scraping on the floor. As he passed Rudd he ducked his head to give him a bashful, sideways look and grinned up at him.

"Hurry up," Lovell told him.

He still seemed reluctant to go.

"There's men up there diggin'," he told them, indicating vaguely with his thumb somewhere outside.

Lovell made an impatient sound and, opening the door, bundled him into the further room that Rudd only caught a glimpse of. It seemed to be a kitchen for he noticed saucepans on a shelf before Lovell shut the door on the pair of them.

"I thought I told you to stay away," Lovell said furiously to Charlie, as soon as the door closed behind them.

Betty Lovell, who was mixing pastry at the table, looked up, her eyes troubled.

"What's the matter?" she asked. "I heard the dog barking and then you talking in there with someone. Who's come?"

"The police," Lovell replied briefly, pushing Charlie in front of him, "and *he* has to come nosing round."

"I only wanted a cup o' tea," Charlie protested. "It's hot work, Geoff, humpin' that straw about. The dust'd got down my throat."

He coughed unconvincingly.

"Make him one, will you, and see he keeps in the kitchen?" Lovell asked Betty. She had remained standing at the table, motionless, her hands still in the bowl. Her face had a rigid expression that he knew meant she was fighting against panic.

"What have they come for, Geoff?" she asked. "What have they found?"

He shook his head in warning and glanced significantly in Charlie's direction. She understood and, for a brief moment, in that silent interchange, there was greater intimacy between them than there had been for a long time. She had even called him by his name.

Christ, he thought bitterly. It takes something like this to bring us together.

"It's nothing," he said, making it sound unimportant. "And there's only one of them, a Detective Inspector. All he's done is ask questions about who owns the land round here."

The moment of intimacy had passed. She turned away, wiping her hands, and with lowered eyes brushed past him to put the kettle on to boil.

"I suppose I'd better get back to him," Lovell said awkwardly, and to Charlie he added with more anger than he intended, "Stay here. You understand? Don't you move a foot out of here until I tell you to."

"Can we still have that game o' cards?" Charlie asked appealingly. He had pulled a chair out from the table and was sitting obediently, like a good child, his hands grasping his knees.

Lovell looked down into his round, anxious face.

"Yes, Charlie," he said in a softer voice. "We'll have that game of cards."

On the other side of the closed door, Rudd could hear Lovell's deep voice, although he couldn't distinguish the words, and then a woman's lighter tones answering him. For the first time since his arrival, he remembered Stebbing had referred to Lovell's wife and assumed she was keeping deliberately out of the way. Stebbing had said they didn't welcome visitors and it could have been this natural dislike of strangers that had prevented her from coming out to speak to him. All the same, he was intrigued and he began walking casually towards the door in the hope that, when Lovell came out, he might catch a glimpse of her. But the farmer re-entered the room unexpectedly, shutting the door so quickly behind him that Rudd saw nothing more than the same shelf of saucepans and the end of a wooden table on which a blue and white mixing bowl was standing.

"I was asking if you'd noticed any tools missing from the farm," Rudd reminded Lovell, picking up the conversation where it had been broken off.

"I've missed none," Lovell replied shortly. He remained standing with his back to the door, as if to prevent Rudd from entering the kitchen or someone from leaving it.

"You're quite sure?"

"I'd've noticed."

The interview seemed to be over. And yet Rudd lingered. It struck him as strange that Lovell hadn't asked why these inquiries were being made, although, given Lovell's natural taciturnity, it might not be in his character to do so.

"The men your brother was referring to are probably mine," he continued, dropping into his easy, gossipy style, although he doubted if it would have any softening effect on Lovell. "There's been a body of a man discovered in that field of Mr. Stebbing's. You know, the one where the archaeological society has been digging. I believe you've been along to have a look a few times."

He was hoping the remark might provoke some reaction in Lovell but he merely shrugged and said, "What of it? I was checking up they didn't come trespassing on my land."

Rudd waited, giving Lovell the opportunity to question him about the dead man, as most people would have done but, as Lovell said nothing, Rudd felt compelled to ask, "It doesn't interest you that a body's been found there?"

"Why should it? It's none of my business. It's on Stebbing's land, not mine."

It was said with an air of triumph, as if Lovell knew he had scored a point, and Rudd had to agree that, in a strange way, he had. After all, why should Lovell concern himself about a dead body that wasn't even on his property? The man was perfectly entitled to shrug his shoulders and dismiss it as nothing to do with him.

"Has Mrs. Lovell been to have a look at the dig?" he asked pleasantly, unwilling to let the subject drop.

"No," Lovell replied.

"Not interested either?"

The slight emphasis that Rudd put on the last word wasn't lost on Lovell. He scowled.

"She's got better things to do with her time," he said abruptly. "And so have I. So if you've finished . . ."

As he spoke, he had begun walking towards the front door, which he opened pointedly. He clearly considered the interview at an end. All the same, out of some irrational perversity, Rudd was determined to have the last word. On the doorstep, he paused to say in his official voice, "There are no more questions for the moment, Mr. Lovell, but I may have to come back to make further inquiries."

A strange expression passed over Lovell's face as he confronted the Inspector across the threshold. It was a look of unutterable weariness and defeat and, seeing him in the strong sunlight that flooded the yard, Rudd was aware that the strain was not of a recent origin. It had settled in his eyes and round his mouth; the look of a man who has been carrying an intolerable burden for too long.

He's close to breaking point but he's covering up well, he thought.

The next instant, the expression had vanished and Lovell was looking at him jeeringly.

"Look out for the dog, then," he said. "Don't blame me if it's off the chain and sets on you."

With that, he went back into the house, slamming the door shut behind him. As if on a signal, the dog, which had been lying quietly in the yard, began

barking again, leaping forward the length of its chain
and falling back, choking and snarling.

Rudd walked away slowly. If Lovell thought he
was going to be frightened off, then he had picked
the wrong man. In the centre of the yard, he paused
deliberately, ignoring the dog, which strained and
snarled a few feet behind him, and, turning to face
the farm-house, looked it over with a calm and interested scrutiny.

It was a long, low building, probably only one
room deep, with plastered walls, once painted cream,
that showed discoloured patches where they had been
amateurishly repaired. The paintwork on the door
and windows was shabby, too, and the outbuildings
across the yard also showed signs of poor repair. A
tractor, standing by the barn, looked old.

Was this the burden that Lovell was carrying? A
run-down farm that was a constant struggle to keep
going?

It might account for his lack of neighbourliness that
Stebbing had commented on. Pride, combined with a
lack of money, might make Lovell wary of mixing
with his more prosperous and successful neighbours.
Or was there some other reason that had forced
Lovell to retreat from the world, shutting himself and
his family away from any contact with outsiders?

With these thoughts in his mind, he strolled up to
the gate and, as he climbed over it, he looked back.
Lovell, without so much as a glance in his direction,
had emerged from the house and was crossing the
yard. Stooping down, he unfastened the chain, and
the dog, set free, came racking up the track towards
the Inspector, barking furiously as it came.

The inference was obvious. Lovell had had the last
word after all and was seeing him off.

Damn the man! Rudd thought with exasperation, as
he got into the car and started the engine. Any further inquiries he might have to make at the farm
were not going to be easy. There would be no dropping in for a casual gossip. At the same time, as he
admitted to himself with a rueful grin, there was
something he had to admire, however reluctantly,

about Lovell. The man possessed a certain strength and hardness, as well as sheer bloody-mindedness, that the Inspector found himself responding to. He was no fool, either. Unlike Stebbing, it wouldn't be easy to trick him into giving anything away.

Chapter 4

Stebbing himself came out of the house as Rudd drove into his yard and strolled over, eager for a chat.

"Any luck?"

"Not much," admitted Rudd.

"You saw Lovell?"

Rudd hesitated, half inclined to make some pleasant but non-committal remark that would discourage Stebbing's curiosity. But Lovell intrigued him and he was curious himself to find out more about the man. There might be some piece of gossip that Stebbing had picked up about his neighbour and would be willing to pass on, even though he admitted knowing little about him.

"Yes, I saw him," he said, "although I didn't find him very forthcoming."

"I did warn you," Stebbing said with a grin. He seemed to be enjoying the idea of Rudd's possible discomfiture. "The dog go for you?"

"Lovell chained it up eventually."

"It'll have somebody one of these days," Stebbing commented. "No wonder no-one goes near the place. The postman won't deliver at the house anymore; leaves the letters, when there are any, in a box by the gate, or so I've been told."

"Has Lovell always been like this?" Rudd asked.

Stebbing shrugged.

"I can't really say. I've only been in the district myself for the past three years, when I bought this place and, like I told you, I had a couple of tries at being friendly. I don't bother now."

A man crossed the yard at this moment and Stebbing broke off to shout at him.

"Hi, Len! Come over here a minute, will you?"

To Rudd he added, "That's Len Wheeler. He'll know a bit more. He used to work on Lovell's farm a while back."

Wheeler came reluctantly towards them. He was a man in his fifties, with a small, brown face and wary eyes. Years of hard, outdoor labour had pared him down to essential muscle and sinew so that he gave the impression of the tough, well-weathered strength of leather or whip-cord.

"The Inspector'd like a word with you," Stebbing told him.

Rudd silently cursed Stebbing's bluff and unsubtle introduction. Wheeler was clearly put on his guard.

"Oh ah?" he said carefully. He came no nearer, remaining a few feet away from them.

Keeping his distance, Rudd thought disgustedly. In his own way, he's as bad as Lovell.

Stebbing stood by, smiling, pleased at having effected the meeting and quite unaware that a silent confrontation was taking place.

"I've just called at Mr. Lovell's farm," Rudd began. Wheeler made no reply and Rudd, rarely at a loss, felt uncertain how to continue in the face of his obvious reluctance to talk.

"Mr. Stebbing tells me you used to work for him."

Wheeler's eyes flickered momentarily in Stebbing's direction. Then after a long pause, he said slowly, "That's right."

"How long ago was this?"

Again the pause before Wheeler replied, "About twelve, thirteen years."

It's like getting blood out of a stone, Rudd thought angrily but he kept his expression bland as he put the next question.

"You left?"

"I got given me cards."

It seemed a promising opening and Rudd pursued it.

"Oh, really? Why was that?"

"Not enough work."

There was an odd under-tone of sarcasm in Wheeler's voice as he said it and Rudd looked interested. Wheeler was unbending but it was a slow process.

"Or so he said," Wheeler added, without any prompting this time. The sarcastic note was stronger, too, or perhaps Rudd's ear was better tuned to picking it up. He felt Wheeler was hinting at something more than the mere words implied and he cocked his head inquiringly.

"Who works the farm now?"

"Lovell and that brother of his, seemingly. They've not taken on anyone else as I know of."

"Seemed a run-down sort of place when I saw it," Stebbing interrupted. "Not enough capital put into it if you ask me."

Wheeler immediately looked blank, withdrawing from the conversation, and Rudd, sensing this, turned a shoulder deliberately against the farmer, excluding him. He doubted if Stebbing would notice. He was too thick-skinned. But the gesture wasn't lost on Wheeler. For a moment, something like amusement showed in his eyes.

There's a streak of malice there, thought Rudd, if only I can get at it.

"I shouldn't think Charlie could do much," he commented, fishing for an opening. But it wasn't the right one. Wheeler merely shrugged indifferently.

"Charlie's all right. He's strong and he's willing and that's something these days."

So it evidently wasn't Charlie who had aroused Wheeler's spite. Rudd tried another tack.

"Does Mrs. Lovell help much on the farm?" he asked off-handedly.

The gleam was back.

"She looks after the poultry and the garden. Least-ways she did when I was there," Wheeler replied with a half-grin that implied some hidden animosity but whether directed at Mrs. Lovell herself or women in general Rudd couldn't tell. But quite clearly the mention of her name brought back some old bitterness.

"I didn't see her this afternoon," Rudd went on, with seeming casualness.

He had the feeling that he and Wheeler were playing some verbal game, the rules of which he wasn't yet sure about, although he was beginning to understand them a little better. But he realised there would be no shortcuts. Wheeler would play it out under his own terms.

Beside him, Stebbing opened his mouth as if he were about to interrupt again and Rudd plunged on, overriding him.

"How long have they been married?"

He asked the question more for the sake of something to say to keep Stebbing out of the conversation than in expectation of any significant answer but Wheeler's reply was surprising.

"Who?" he asked.

"Why, Lovell and his wife, of course."

"She ain't his wife," Wheeler announced with a look of triumph.

Rudd was silent for a moment, nonplussed by the unexpectedness of the remark, and Stebbing took the opportunity to come in himself at this point. During the conversation, he had been fidgeting at Rudd's side, feeling excluded and anxious to play his part. Now he said sharply:

"Not his wife? But you never said."

"You never asked," Wheeler retorted. He seemed to get a perverse pleasure out of scoring this point off his employer.

"But when I spoke of her as 'Mrs. Lovell' you didn't put me right," Stebbing said angrily. "Damn it all, when I went to call on the man, I referred to her as 'Mrs. Lovell' to his face and *he* didn't say anything either."

He was clearly annoyed that no-one had taken the trouble to acquaint him with this particular piece of local knowledge and Rudd guessed that, under it, lay a deeper resentment that, although he had bought land in the district and invested money, he was still treated as an outsider.

Wheeler looked amused.

"Maybe that's because she is Mrs. Lovell."

"You mean she's Charlie's wife?" Stebbing asked incredulously.

Wheeler laughed out loud at this.

"Is it likely?" he asked. He was ready to go on playing Stebbing for some time yet, teasing the man into guessing his way into the truth but Rudd, who had had enough, had no intention of letting him do so.

"Whose then, Mr. Wheeler?" he asked with quiet authority.

Wheeler turned a cool glance on him.

"Ronnie's," he said.

Stebbing, on whom the subtlety of the game was lost, opened his mouth to ask another question but Rudd silenced him with a warning gesture of one hand.

"Go on," he told Wheeler.

Their eyes met and Wheeler, with an almost imperceptible flicker of his eyelids, acknowledged that the time for fooling was over.

"Ron Lovell," he explained sullenly. "Geoff Lovell's younger brother. Cleared off and left her about fifteen years ago."

Was that the reason for Wheeler's malice? Rudd wondered. Did the man resent, or perhaps disapprove of, the Lovell household? It was an interesting line of inquiry that might be worth following up, provided he could talk to Wheeler on his own, without Stebbing's presence.

"Local girl?" he asked. He put the question because it was possible Wheeler had known her before her marriage to Ron Lovell and perhaps resented the fact that, by marrying into a local farming family, Wheeler's employers, she had risen above what the man considered to be her station.

"No," Wheeler replied. "From Dorset. Ronnie met her when he was doing his National Service in the fifties. Geoff Lovell got exempted. Old man Lovell was alive then but ailing and Geoff was needed on the farm. But Ron got called up and came back after doing his two years with *her*."

Rudd was doing some rapid mental calculations.

"So they were married how long before he left? A couple of years?"

"Nearer three."

"And then he left her. Do you know why?"

"No, Lovell took me on after he left; said he needed someone else to help him on the farm. Old Lovell had died by then, so there was only him and Charlie left to run the place. But Ronnie was always a bit wild and seemingly he couldn't settle down to the life after the army."

"What's she like?" Rudd asked.

Wheeler lifted his shoulders indifferently. The game being over, he seemed to have lost interest in the subject.

"Quiet," he said. "One of them women who don't say much. Maybe too quiet for Ronnie."

Turning to Stebbing, he added, "If that's all, I've got work to get on with."

Rudd nodded, letting Stebbing dismiss him. There would be other opportunities to talk to him later. Meanwhile, Stebbing was saying as Wheeler walked away, "I don't understand it. Nobody told me. I thought they were married. I could have put my foot right in it when I was talking to Lovell."

"You saw her when you called?" Rudd asked.

"Yes, but not for long. She was in the yard and went into the house almost as soon as I arrived. Fair-haired woman. Thin. Not my type. Looked nervous."

A brooding look came into his face as he recalled the encounter.

"Do you know, Lovell didn't even ask me inside the house? Kept me out in the yard. I don't call that friendly."

Lovell's lack of neighbourliness evidently rankled with him still. Rudd, his thoughts elsewhere, grunted a reply. An idea was beginning to take shape in his mind but he needed time and a little peace in which to think it out more fully.

"I'd've been willing to help the man out, if he'd've met me half-way," Stebbing continued, still pursuing his own particular obsession. "Lent him equipment or one of my men for half a day, if he was short-handed. But I'm not putting myself out now."

It was with relief that Rudd saw Boyce approaching and, making this his excuse, he walked away, leaving Stebbing standing alone in the yard.

"Denny's nearly uncovered him," Boyce announced as Rudd came up. "Are you coming to have a look at him or shall I tell them to hang on?"

"No, I'm coming," Rudd replied abstractedly.

Boyce looked at him inquiringly.

"Found out something at Lovell's farm?" he asked.

"Not from Lovell himself," Rudd replied. "He claims he noticed nothing unusual."

"Claims?" echoed Boyce. "You mean he may not be telling the truth?"

"I don't know," confessed Rudd, moving his shoulders uncomfortably. "Lovell's an odd bloke. According to Stebbing, he's frightened off any visitors to the farm, including the postman, and I certainly wasn't welcomed with open arms. I got the impression, too, that Lovell was deliberately keeping Charlie, that's his subnormal brother, and his wife from meeting me. At least, I thought she was his wife, and so evidently did Stebbing. But I've been having a chat with a man called Wheeler who used to work on Lovell's farm and, according to him, there was a third brother, called Ronnie, who was married to Betty and who cleared off and left her about fifteen years ago. So that means she's Lovell's sister-in-law. But why all the secrecy? And why, if Lovell left her all those years before, has she stayed on at the farm? Most women would have gone home to their own family long ago. It can't be easy for her, running a house for her husband's two brothers."

He paused for a moment, wondering how to put into words the other impressions he had picked up at the farm: Lovell's expression of strain; his anxiety to hustle Charlie out of the way; even the excessive tidiness of the living-room. They were all significant, he felt, of something more than their surface appearance, in much the same way as Wheeler's remarks had hinted at more than the mere meanings of the words.

"Sounds a funny set-up," Boyce was saying, without a lot of interest, and Rudd decided to leave it there.

"There's another thing," he went on. "I'm more than ever convinced that whoever buried that body was a local man who knew the field. It can't be seen from the road and, anyway, there's a wood on the way to Lovell's farm that would make a much better place to dump a body, supposing the man who did it was a casual visitor, looking for somewhere to get rid of an unwanted corpse. So, assuming he's a local man, it's more than likely that the dead man was in some way connected to this area, too; somebody known to him; somebody whose body he had to get rid of because it could be recognised as having links with him. And it crossed my mind, after Wheeler had told me about the other brother, that the body we've dug up might be Ronnie Lovell's."

"What's the theory?" Boyce asked, looking interested. "He returns after fifteen years? There's a family quarrel? Lovell kills him and . . . ?"

"Buries him on Stebbing's land," Rudd concluded for him. "That bit doesn't make sense, does it? In fact, Lovell more or less said the same thing himself. Of course, I hadn't heard then from Wheeler about the third brother, Ron, but when I told Geoff about the dead body being found, he said he wasn't interested as it was none of his business. It was on Stebbing's land, not his; as if that proved something."

"Well, it could," Boyce pointed out, not unreasonably. "It could mean the body had nothing to do with him."

"I'm not sure," Rudd replied. "He showed very little reaction—too little, if you get my meaning, as if he was prepared for the news. And yet he's under some enormous strain. I could see it in his face, although, to be fair to him, it could simply be money worries. That farm of his looks on its last legs. But if he *did* kill his brother, and we've got no proof that he did, I know what I'd do in Lovell's place—put him under my own ground where I know he'd not be disturbed."

Boyce was silent for a few seconds.

"I don't know," he said, at last. "It might still hold up as a theory. That field doesn't look as if it's ever been cultivated. It was pure chance that Stebbing got that society in to start digging."

"According to Stebbing, it's due to go under the plough in the autumn."

"Lovell may not have known that."

"True enough," agreed Rudd. "All the same, it'd be taking a risk. He's got fields of his own. Assuming it is his brother's body, why not bury it where he knew it'd be safe?"

Boyce lifted his broad shoulders in an indifferent gesture. He wasn't much interested in human motivation, which, according to his way of thinking, didn't come into the category of factual evidence and was therefore merely speculative.

"People do funny things," he remarked casually. "Maybe he just didn't like the idea of it being on his land."

"Superstition?" Rudd asked quickly.

He thought of Lovell's dark, brooding face. He had struck the Inspector as a man of close and secretive temperament, not easily roused but nevertheless possessing deep passions. Supposing Lovell, having killed his brother, felt that to bury him on his own land was to sully it in some way? Perhaps bring bad luck? Or had it been a motive more twisted even than that? It was on Stebbing's land, after all. Supposing Stebbing had aroused in Lovell not just antipathy but such a deep-rooted hated that Lovell had scored off him by burying the body on his property? But that suggested madness and Rudd wasn't sure that Lovell would act in such a crazy way. He was a man under strain, certainly. But was he insane? Rudd wasn't sure.

"Do you know what Ronnie Lovell looks like?" Boyce was asking.

Rudd roused himself to answer.

"No, but I could ask Wheeler. He evidently knew him and I expect he could give us a description. All he said was Ronnie got called up into the army in the fifties, met a girl from Dorset, married her and left a couple of years later. But we'll have to be damned careful. We've got no proof yet who the dead man is and I don't want to start any rumours going round the village."

He paused, thinking of the other things Wheeler had said or hinted at; for instance, that Betty Lovell was perhaps too quiet for Ronnie. Had he been suggesting there was another woman?

"Well, whoever he was, there's not much left of him now," Boyce remarked. "I doubt if his own mother would recognise him."

They had skirted the large wheatfield while they had been talking and were approaching the gate that led into the smaller meadow that lay beyond, across which a line of men was moving as they carried out the search. More men were coming and going from the canvas screen that had been erected round the grave. On the opposite side of the field, the tents belonging to the archaeological society had already gone.

Rudd, who had begun to climb over the gate, paused on the top of it to glance in the direction of Lovell's farm. From that elevated position, he could see the roofs of the house and its surrounding buildings, which seemed, at that distance, to be huddled closer together. No smoke emerged from the chimneys but he caught a glimpse of sunlight striking off glass on the tiled slope of the back of the farm-house roof; a sky-light, no doubt, to an attic under the steep pitch.

He tried to imagine the life that went on under that roof; Lovell left to run the farm with only a subnormal brother to help him and a woman who had been deserted by her husband years before; a funny set-up, as Boyce had remarked.

Boyce, who had dropped down into the field, asked, "You stuck up there?"

"No," Rudd replied, climbing down. "Just thinking."

"The light'll be going soon, if we don't get a move on," the sergeant pointed out.

Rudd noticed, then, that the sun was setting behind the trees, casting long shadows across the grass.

"I'm coming," he replied and, joining Boyce, they set off together for the far side of the field where a cluster of men were waiting outside the screen.

Inside, the heat was intense in that enclosed space and the air smelt strongly of hot canvas and crushed grass. Mingled with it was another odour, more subtle and less easy to define; the smell of earth and decay coming up from the oblong hole in the ground, six feet long and four feet deep, by the side of which Pardoe and Denny were kneeling. Rudd joined them, squatting down on his haunches to look into the open grave.

Chapter 5

There was, as Boyce had said, not much left of the man. The skeleton appeared to be intact, to which scraps of decayed flesh and tattered, dirt-soiled cloth were clinging. Only the boots had survived relatively whole but even these were falling apart. What remained of the head grinned up at them in the dreadful, fixed and mirthless grimace of death.

But it was the position of the corpse that interested Rudd most of all. It was lying on its back, it arms neatly folded across its chest, the hands resting near the shoulders. Someone, it seemed, had taken the trouble to lay the body out before burial. It hadn't been roughly tumbled into its makeshift grave.

"Is this how you found it?" he asked Denny.

"Exactly," Denny replied. "Nothing's been shifted,

45

except the soil round him. And I know what you're thinking. The same thought struck me as I uncovered him. Look at this as well."

He pointed to an object that was caught against the chest. Rudd bent down to examine it more closely. It was a large safety-pin, rusted and almost unrecognisable.

"I came across four more of them," Denny went on. "They'd dropped to one side, the length of the body, the first being up near the head, the last by the feet. McCullum's taken photographs so you'll be able to see the exact positions for yourself."

Something else caught Rudd's attention, as he was bending forward. The body was covered with the rotted remains of fabric, the exact colour of which was indistinguishable from the surrounding earth, although its closely woven texture and relative thickness were still discernible. It was, he guessed, probably wool, which might suggest the man had been wearing an overcoat. But an overcoat, however long, does not extend as far up as the head or down to the feet, as this clearly did, for pieces of the same fabric were clinging to the skull and some lay close to the boots.

He touched one of the scraps with a finger-tip and then turned to Pardoe.

"A blanket?" he asked. "It could be. And five safety-pins. Do you know what that suggests to me? A shroud. Whoever buried him laid him out and then wrapped him up, fastening the covering together with pins to stop it from falling off."

Pardoe nodded.

"I noticed that myself. The cloth's too far gone for me to say exactly what it was but I agree, it could be a blanket. Forensic will be able to come up with more details on it and, once we've got him out, I'll be able to tell you if there's any more of the same material under him."

"Anything else about him?" Rudd asked.

"Not much at this stage," admitted Pardoe. "He's been down there at least a year, possibly two, but that's only a guess. One thing I can tell you though—you won't get any finger-prints off him. He's too far goñe for that. And you'll be disappointed if you're counting on identifying him from his dental records."

He pointed with the stem of his pipe at the head.

"I'd say he'd had most of his teeth removed to have dentures fitted . . ."

"None were found?" Rudd asked quickly, turning to Boyce, who shook his head.

"Not so far."

"Height?" Rudd went on, turning back to Pardoe.

"I'm not committing myself on that either," the doctor replied. "Not until I've got him back in the lab and can re-assemble the bits and pieces more accurately. Even then, I can't guarantee an exact measurement."

"Hair colour? Age." Rudd suggested hopefully. But Pardoe refused to be drawn.

"I'll need to do some tests on him first. And I can't give you any idea either how he died, so it's no use asking. There's no obvious signs of violence that I can see, such as a fractured skull, and, with so little left of him, it's not going to be easy. If he was shot, we might find the bullet still in the body or at least marks of it on a bone. Stabbing's a bit trickier unless, again, the knife marked a bone. If it was suicide or a natural death, it may be even more difficult to prove. But I'll do the tests and see what they produce."

"And nothing personal found on him?" Rudd asked, turning back to Boyce. "A signet ring, for instance, or a watch?"

Boyce looked a little uncomfortable.

"There was this," he replied and, bending down, picked up a small, blackened lump that was lying on one side of the plastic sheeting that had been spread out to receive the excavated soil. Rudd took it and, holding it in the palm of his hand, examined it carefully. It was a cross and chain, so corroded together that it formed an almost solid mass of metal.

"Barker found it in one of the spadesful of earth that Moody dug out, so we don't know exactly where it was in relation to the body," Boyce explained. "It was covered with dirt and looked like a piece of stone. But it wasn't all that far down. About six to eight inches, Moody reckons, so it may have nothing to do with the dead man."

Rudd rubbed it between his fingers, loosening the soil that clung to it. As far as he could see, the links in the chain were small and fine.

"It looks like something a woman might wear," he remarked.

"Could be," Boyce agreed. "In which case, it might have been dropped accidentally."

Rudd contemplated it thoughtfully. It was a damned nuisance that Moody hadn't noticed it at the time and pin-pointed its exact location in relation to the body.

"But what's it doing under the earth?" he asked. "This field's never been cultivated. If someone had dropped it accidentally, it would still be lying on the top or, at most, trodden down into the grass."

"Fell down a crack?" suggested Boyce. "We've had two hot summers now. Last year in particular was very dry. Do you remember the farmers were complaining about lack of rain? If the ground dried out and opened up, it's possible it slipped down a hole and got covered over."

"I suppose so," Rudd agreed but without much enthusiasm. "I'll check with Stebbing to see if he's noticed this field drying hard out at any time and we'll make inquiries locally in case anyone's lost a cross and chain—plated, by the way it's corroded. Solid gold or silver wouldn't have gone like that. In the meantime," he added, addressing Pardoe, "we'd better get him out. I'll leave you and Denny to deal with that."

Pardoe nodded agreement and Rudd, beckoning to Boyce to follow him, walked outside the screen where he took deep breaths of fresh air.

"When Pardoe and Denny have moved him," he said, "I want you to make a thorough search of the grave itself. Collect up anything that's left and keep your eyes open for a pair of false teeth. They may be essential in proving identity. Otherwise . . ."

He raised his shoulders in a gesture that Boyce had come to recognise as expressing a complex mood, partly exasperation, partly perplexity. The sergeant said nothing but tried to look encouraging.

"There's something odd about this case," Rudd went on, after a few minutes' silence in which he stared down moodily at the grass. "Apart from the choice of the site itself, which I still think is strange, there's this question of the body being prepared for burial—the arms folded across the chest; the shroud, if that's what it is; even the missing false teeth could be significant . . ."

"Of what?" Boyce asked, looking perplexed himself.

"Of the body being laid out."

"It could be, I suppose," Boyce said, sounding unconvinced. "Or it could be they just dropped out."

"And then there's the cross and chain," Rudd went on, ignoring him and pursuing his own train of thought. "I know it may have nothing to do with the dead man but I can't help feeling . . ."

Again he hesitated to put into words the vague impression he had in his mind. It was not so much a definite idea as a series of words that had begun to collect together. Superstition. Sacrament. Concern for the dead. Burial rites.

And for some reason that he could not explain, he kept coming back to Wheeler's story of Ron Lovell's wife, deserted after a few years of marriage; the farm, isolated from the outside world with the dog on constant guard; the shot-gun propped up in a corner of the living-room; and Lovell's dark, brooding, hopeless look as he stood on the threshold of the house.

He saw Boyce looking at him and he made an effort to rouse himself, switching his mind back to the immediate present.

"Proof," he said briskly. "We need proof. It's too late to do much today but we'll check on that cross and chain in the village tomorrow. I want a house-to-house done on it, but leave out Wheeler and Lovell. I'll question them myself. At the same time, find out if any strangers have been seen about the village in the past couple of years—a tramp, or someone looking for casual farm-work. Judging by the boots, the man was used to doing outdoor, manual work. And ask if anyone's disappeared from the village—left home for any reason. I don't want Ron Lovell's name mentioned at this stage but if anyone brings it up, then get them chatting about him. He's a possible lead but we've got to tread damned carefully over that one. The question of identity, though, is going to be crucial to this case. Until we know who the dead man is, we've got nothing much to go on."

Behind them, Pardoe and Denny were emerging from the screen, carrying a coffin shell between them.

"It looks as if they've finished," Rudd remarked. "Take a couple of men with you, Tom, and get the grave searched. I want to have a last look round before we leave."

Boyce nodded and moved off, collecting up Moody and Kyle as he went, while Rudd walked away across the field, following in the wake of the line of uniformed men who had almost reached the far side.

What was he hoping they would find? Nothing of much significance, he imagined; only the assorted rubbish that fields and hedgerows always seem to yield in such astonishing quantities: old shoes, tin cans, bits of paper and plastic; all of which would have to be examined and none of which would be likely to have any bearing on the case.

At the corner, he turned, walking round the perimeter of the field, looking for any gap leading to a path or bridleway along which the body might have been carried but, apart from the gate leading into the wheatfield, there was none. The field was enclosed on two sides by thick, well-maintained hedges. On the third side, along which ran the boundary between Stebbing's land and Lovell's, the hedge looked older and could have been planted, Rudd guessed, a long time ago, possibly at the time of the initial enclosure of the land, for it contained some large, well-grown trees. Here and there, the bushes were sparse, with gaps between them, but on Stebbing's side there was a wide ditch that looked as if it had been recently re-dug, surmounted by a three-strand barbed-wire fence, supported on posts that also looked comparatively new. Rudd paused and thoughtfully pulled away a piece of loose bark from one of the posts, revealing the wood beneath that was still clean and un-weathered. He could check with Stebbing when the fence had been erected but, Rudd reckoned, it had been put up a year, if that. So, before the fence had been built, it would have been relatively easy to carry a body to the field, over Lovell's land and through one of the gaps in the hedge, before burying it a few yards inside the boundary on Stebbing's land.

Stebbing's land. Always he came back to this crucial question. Why this particular field? And there appeared to be no rational answer; not yet, anyway.

He turned away, his shoulders humped, and started back across the field. The light was going fast now. The sun had disappeared completely, leaving behind a nimbus of brightness, streaked with rose-coloured clouds. Red sky at night. It was going to be another hot day tomorrow. In the coppice, a colony of rooks was settling down for the night, cawing hoarsely and flopping down with heavy wings into their untidy nests in the top-most branches of the trees. The men who had been searching the field were moving off towards the gate, their task finished. There was a feeling of completion; of the day ending.

Boyce, emerging from the screen, came across the field to meet him.

"Any luck?" Rudd asked.

The sergeant shook his head.

"Apart from some more of that fabric, which we've collected up, there's nothing except a hole in the ground."

"Damn!" Rudd said softly. Without the man's false teeth, identification was going to be more difficult.

"I've covered it over with a tarpaulin," Boyce went on. "Do you want the screen left up?"

"No, it's not necessary. The site's been cleared. We shouldn't need to make another search."

He turned to Stapleton, who had been in charge of the uniformed men.

"You've finished, too?"

Stapleton nodded.

"Then we'll pack up," Rudd said. "It'll be dark

soon. I'll get a Panda car to patrol the lane but I doubt if anyone from the village will bother to come sight-seeing."

"There's nothing to see, anyway," Boyce replied gloomily, glancing round at the gathering dusk. He hated the countryside after dark, with its silence and atmosphere of indefinable menace, and was longing to get back to the lights and the cheerful bustle of head-quarters.

"You coming back now, sir?"

"Later," Rudd replied.

He had an inexplicable desire to linger, now that the light was going, and, as the others tramped away, he remained behind in the field alone, feeling the silence and the dusk settle round him.

The great, rounded heads of the trees, massed with leaves, were merging into the sky and the contours of the land were fading, too, although he could still just discern the long mounds of excavated earth left behind by the archaeological society. They reminded him of photographs he had seen of mass war graves, dug to accommodate the countless, anonymous dead. The image stirred his imagination but he could make no connection between it and the oblong pit, the length of a man, that lay at his feet, except for the obvious metaphor of death and burial. But he felt instinctively that there was something more that linked them; something to do with the darkening trees, the falling twilight; the very air that still held the heat of the day and was breathing back a gentle exhalation of warm grass and earth from the ground beneath his feet.

Away to his right, a faint light showed where Lovell's farm-house stood among its surrounding trees and he gazed speculatively towards it.

Did another link exist there? He wasn't sure and yet he felt, with a strong sense of intuition, that somehow it all made sense and that the broken pieces could be brought together to form a pattern, if only he could find the beginning of it.

Chapter 6

It wasn't until late the following afternoon that Boyce returned from the house-to-house inquiries in the village, looking tired and hot. Lowering himself gratefully into a chair, he bent down to loosen the laces in his shoes, commenting, "Thank God that's over."

"Any luck?" Rudd asked eagerly.

He had remained behind in the office working on the preliminary reports on the case, leaving Boyce in charge of the men who were carrying out the inquiry.

"Not much," Boyce replied. "Nothing on the cross and chain. No-one in the village has lost one. I still think it could have been dropped accidentally by someone from outside—picnickers, say."

"That's not very likely," Rudd objected. "From what I've seen of people picnicking, they stay fairly near the road, where they've parked the car, or make for an obvious beauty spot. No-one's going to hump packets of sandwiches and flasks of tea that far across the fields."

Boyce lifted his shoulders wearily.

"What's the theory, then? That it's got something to do with the body? But it wasn't found on him. In fact, it wasn't even found near him. My guess is it's a waste of time as far as this case is concerned."

"You may be right but it'll have to be followed up, all the same, as soon as forensic have come up with a few more details on it. Then we can start making inquiries at jewellers' . . ."

"You mean, *I'll* make the inquiries," Boyce corrected him. "It'll be me who'll be hoofing it round the shops, I know that. And a fat lot of good it'll do, if you ask me. That cross and chain's cheap, mass-produced stuff. You'll probably find any Woolworth's stock them and sell hundreds of them every year. Still, I suppose it could be evidence."

He didn't sound very convinced.

"Anybody reported missing from the village?" Rudd went on to ask. "Any husband or son left home?"

"Not much on that either, although at one stage I thought we'd struck lucky—a husband who'd left his wife for somebody else's. It was the right timing, too; about two years ago. But as someone saw them together in the local Odeon the other Saturday night, he's presumably still alive and well and living in sin over at Little Fenny. So that was a wash-out. No-one else has gone missing and there was no report of any strangers seen about the place, except for one old tramp who's well known in the village; turns up at regular intervals, it seems. But as he's been seen in the past couple of months, it can't be him either."

"That needn't rule out some outsider turning up," Rudd replied. "I've been having a look at a large-scale map of the area. . . ."

Walking over to the desk, he spread it out again for Boyce's benefit and the sergeant, with a martyred look, heaved himself up from the chair to cross the room and look at it.

"The village is here," Rudd said, pointing with a finger, "and this is the main road that leads to Harlsdon, the nearest market town. It's also the bus route, so anyone arriving in the village from the Harlsdon direction would come along that road."

His finger traced along it, turning off to follow the secondary road that led, by a circuitous route, past the fields, the boundaries of which were marked in, and the two farms belonging to Stebbing and Lovell.

"I see what you mean," said Boyce. "Anyone coming by bus from Harlsdon and making for Lovell's place would get off before the village and walk down the lane to the farm."

"Exactly," Rudd replied. "He needn't show himself in the village at all."

"Any good checking with the bus conductors on that route?"

"We can try it but I doubt if we'll come up with anything definite. It's at least two years ago, too long for anyone to remember one individual passenger."

"This the place where the body was found?" Boyce asked suddenly, noticing a small pencilled cross in one of the fields.

"Yes. I marked it in," Rudd replied. "And I checked the distances on the scale while I was at it. It's roughly equidistant from both farms; a little over half a mile."

"Half a mile?" mused Boyce. "It doesn't sound far but it's still a hell of a long way to carry a body. Whoever did it must have been a pretty powerful man."

"Yes," agreed Rudd. He thought of Geoff Lovell's broad shoulders and muscular arms. Could he have managed such a burden? There was Charlie, of course, who could have helped him to carry it but Lovell would have been taking a great risk in involving his brother, knowing his tendency to talk. But perhaps that explained why Lovell had been so anxious to keep Charlie at a distance when the Inspector called at the house, to prevent him from blurting out anything incriminating.

"The name of the field's been marked in," Boyce

was saying, bending low over the desk to read the tiny writing. "Hollowfield, is it?"

"Yes. I rang up Stebbing to ask him if the field had a name. They often do and it seemed better to have something to refer to in our reports. It's probably called that because the land slopes down there from the meadow higher up."

"You can see how far it is from the village," Boyce continued, still studying the map. "It must be all of four miles. I can't imagine anyone lugging a dead body that far."

"Which would support the theory that it was carried there from this direction," Rudd added, jabbing a finger at the road with its two farms.

Boyce straightened up.

"That reminds me, Ron Lovell's name was mentioned twice during the door-to-door this afternoon."

Rudd, who had been folding the map, looked up with quick interest.

"Yes?"

"One old girl who Johnson interviewed brought his name up. Hang on a sec., I've got some notes on it."

Getting out his notebook, he ruffled over the pages, looking for the right place.

"Here we are. It's not much but it might be useful. According to Johnson, when he asked about people missing from the village, she said, 'There's only Ron Lovell and he's been gone a long time. Used to live with his brothers on one of the farms down Hallbrook Lane. Married a girl he met when he was in the army and then left her. Leastways, that's what I've heard. But then, he never was much good, not even as a youngster. Roaring round the village on that motorbike of his and spending half his time over at Harlsdon; in the public houses, I shouldn't wonder.' After that, she veered off into a moan about young people generally; no respect for their elders; that sort of thing. Johnson heard her out. It lasted a good twenty minutes he told me," Boyce added with a grin. "Any good, is it?"

"It adds a bit more detail," Rudd replied. "The stuff about him marrying a girl he'd met when he was in the army I'd already got from Wheeler. But the bit about the motor-bike and the possible drinking in Harlsdon could be quite useful. It gives us a better picture of him—the local tear-away, by the sound of it. It might also be worth checking on the pubs. Did she come up with a description?"

"No. You said not to ask too many questions about him and I'd warned the men to play it down, so Johnson didn't like to press it too far. The other time his name cropped up was when I was talking to the man who runs the local garage, name of Tidyman. His place also specialises in repairs to farm machinery and it seems Ron Lovell used to work there as a lad out of school hours and at week-ends. He was quite good, too, with machinery, according to Tidyman; good enough for Tidyman to offer him a job there after he'd left school, which Ron Lovell wanted to take up. But his father wouldn't let him; insisted he join his brother working on the farm. Old man Lovell was a bit of a tyrant, as far as I could make out; ruled those boys with a rod of iron. Tidyman went into a lot of detail about old Lovell which probably isn't of much use . . ."

"Let's hear it all the same," Rudd interrupted him. "It could add to the picture."

"Well, evidently he was something of a local Scrooge; wouldn't spend a ha'penny if he could get away with a farthing, and thought twice about parting with that—I'm giving you Tidyman's words, by the way—and it's one of the reasons for Geoff's present difficulties. Old Lovell let the farm go downhill and when Geoff came to take it over, it needed a hell of a lot doing to it and there just wasn't the money to put it right. He worked those sons of his hard, too. Towards the end, he had a bad heart and was supposed to take things easy but he dropped dead in the fields one day, checking up that Geoff was doing his work properly. None of them ever mixed much, except Ronnie, who tried to make a life for himself away from the farm; and, according to Tidyman, there was a bit of feeling in the village against Charlie. Tidyman agreed that he's quite harmless but some of the locals didn't like seeing him about and there was talk that he should have been put away in a home. So the Lovells have never been good mixers or exactly popular."

"Did he say anything else about Ronnie Lovell?"

"Not a lot. I got the impression that Tidyman felt sorry for him because he'd never had a proper chance. He did say something about him being a bit wild and wearing his hair in what he called 'them sideboards.' I've got a note here, by the way, of one comment he made that's worth quoting."

Referring to his notebook, he read out in a dead-pan voice, " 'I know he was a bit of a telly boy but that ain't to say there was no good in him.' "

" 'Telly boy' ?" Rudd asked, mystified.

Boyce grinned.

"I think he meant Teddy boy."

"It would fit, I suppose," Rudd said, "assuming he's talking about the time he knew Ron Lovell before he went into the army. It'd be the fifties, the Teddy boy era."

"That's the nearest he got to a description of him, I'm afraid," Boyce added, a little apologetically.

"It all helps," Rudd assured him. "We've got a much clearer picture now of what Ron Lovell was like; a bit wild; a natural mechanic who's forced to work on the family farm; escapes once into the army but comes back; escapes for a second time, leaving behind a young wife. If we carry that a bit further, I think we can make a guess as to where he went. My bet is he made for a town. He sounds the type who'd be drawn by the bright lights of a city and I'll bet, too, that he got himself a job in a factory or garage. It's what he was good at. I know it's not much to go on but it narrows the field a little if we have to go looking for him."

"Assuming we haven't already found him," Boyce pointed out, "four feet down."

"That's still to be proved," Rudd replied, "and for that we need a description."

"Tidyman?" suggested Boyce. "He obviously knew him quite well."

"If we have to, but I'd prefer somebody who was in touch with him more recently, since his army days. Wheeler's the obvious choice. He knew the Lovell family well and worked on the farm for a time after Ron left, so he may have picked up a few interesting bits and pieces of information."

He glanced at his watch.

"It's gone six o'clock so he should have knocked off work for the day. I want to see him at home, not at the farm. He's more likely to talk freely without Stebbing hanging about, sticking his oar in."

"You know his address?" Boyce asked.

"Yes. I looked it up on the electoral register at the library and checked it on the map. If I see him this evening, we should have some details to compare with what Pardoe can tell us about the body."

At the door he added, "Get today's house-to-house down in a report, will you, Tom? We'll need it for the file."

He left, ignoring Boyce's gusty sigh that followed him out into the corridor.

Wheeler's cottage was one of a brick-built pair, with a heavy, slated roof and narrow, sash windows, standing on the main road into the village, not far from the turning that led to the farms. There was a depressed, mean look about them, oddly out of keeping with the rural setting, as if they had been transported there from the Victorian terrace of some inner-city suburb.

Rudd pushed open Wheeler's gate and, disregarding the front door with its forbidding, dark green paint and heavy, iron knocker, tramped round to the back of the house where a long kitchen garden, given over mainly to the growing of potatoes, stretched down to a ramshackle chicken house and wired-in run at the bottom.

The back door was set open with a half-brick and, as he knocked, Rudd saw beyond into a dimly lit and not very clean kitchen, with a deep, old-fashioned sink and wooden draining-board and a table covered with worn American cloth that was stacked with dirty dishes.

Wheeler came out of an adjoining room in answer to his knock, chewing, his braces hanging loose, his shirt unbuttoned, showing a thin chest, knobbed with small bones and surprisingly white below his sunburnt face and neck.

"Oh, it's you again," he said in greeting. There was a small, self-satisfied grin on his face, as if he had been expecting the visit.

"Just a few more inquiries, Mr. Wheeler," Rudd replied in his official voice, wondering how he was going to introduce the subject of Ron Lovell into the conversation without it appearing to be the main reason for his call.

Wheeler jerked his head, inviting Rudd to enter, and the Inspector followed him into a further room where Wheeler had evidently been eating his evening meal, for the round table in the centre was roughly set with a cloth laid across part of it on which were standing a plate of cold meat, a jar of pickles and an opened packet of sliced bread.

"Cup of tea?" Wheeler suggested, and when Rudd accepted, he went back into the kitchen to get another cup. While he was gone, Rudd took the opportunity to look about.

It was a small room, crowded with heavy, dark, ugly furniture of the period that belonged, Rudd guessed, to Wheeler's parents, an impression borne out by the framed photographs that stood on the sideboard; one of a wedding group in which the bride wore a huge hat, which looked like a platter full of flowers, and veiling; the other a stiff, studio portrait of a young man in the army uniform of the First World War, standing to attention in front of a painted backdrop of rocks and a waterfall.

The thick, cotton-lace curtains muffling the window, the array of vases and ornaments on every available horizontal surface, the patterned wallpaper of large leaves and flowers that age and dirt had darkened to an all-over sepia tone gave the room an oppressive, claustrophobic atmosphere.

There was no sign that a younger woman had influenced it and, as Wheeler's occupation of it seemed to be of the makeshift quality of a solitary male making temporary camp, apparent in the hurried preparations of the meal and the clothes scattered about the room, Rudd guessed his situation: that of a middle-aged bachelor who had gone on living in his parents' home after their death.

Wheeler came in, carrying a cup and saucer, still wet from being quickly washed under the tap, and poured Rudd a cup of tea. It came out as the same colour as the tea-pot, a thick, dark brown, that tasted strongly of tannin. Rudd kept the grimace off his face as he drank it down, although it left a wry taste in his mouth.

"Well?" Wheeler asked abruptly. He had seated himself at the table, opposite Rudd, and had started to eat again, cramming the food into his mouth.

Rudd began with his official questions. Had Wheeler noticed any strangers about? Had there been any tools missing from the farm? To both, Wheeler answered "No."

There was a forced, unnatural quality about the opening of the interview, as if both men knew that this was a mere preliminary formality that was to lead up to something much more crucial. Above his energetically chewing mouth, Wheeler's eyes were watchful and, Rudd thought, amused.

Damn the man, he thought. He knows perfectly well why I'm here. There seemed to be no solution to it except to plunge in.

"We've been making inquiries in the village," Rudd began, "about any local men who have left home for any reason and Ron Lovell's name was mentioned."

He paused, inviting Wheeler to speak but he merely nodded and shovelled more meat into his mouth.

"It places me in rather a difficult position," Rudd confessed with pretended naïveté. "In any inquiry like this, we're obliged to follow up every possible lead, however unlikely. So I've come to you, Mr. Wheeler. You knew Ron Lovell and I'm sure I could rely on your discretion not to gossip is I asked you a few questions about him."

Wheeler watched him speculatively for a few seconds. He wasn't entirely taken in by the flattery and he realised Rudd was setting up his own rules for the interview. In return for the Inspector's confidence, Wheeler would be expected to answer the questions in a straightforward and factual manner and not to talk about it afterwards.

"All right," he conceded reluctantly at last, pushing his empty plate away. "What do you want to know?"

"When Geoff Lovell took you on at the farm, did he give any reason why his brother had left home?"

"No. He just said, 'Ronnie's gone so I'm left short-handed.'"

"No mention of a quarrel?"

"Not that I heard of."

"Did Charlie ever say anything about it?"

"Charlie!" Wheeler looked scornful. "You've seen him, have you? Well then, you know what he's like. Given half a chance, he'd talk your ear off. Most of it's rubbish anyhow. I didn't bother listening to him."

It was clear that Wheeler regarded Charlie and what he had to say as beneath contempt. But Rudd wasn't entirely convinced. Even if Wheeler hadn't paid much attention to Charlie, he must have picked up some of his remarks. After all, Wheeler wouldn't have been human if he hadn't been interested in his employer's private life and Rudd guessed that, although Wheeler might consider himself above passing on gossip, he had a malicious enough interest in other people's business to listen to it.

"How did Mrs. Lovell seem to be taking it?" Rudd asked, deciding to drop the subject of Charlie for the time being and circle back to it again later when Wheeler was less on his guard.

The spiteful glitter that Rudd had seen before in Wheeler's eyes returned.

"Her? She didn't say much but then she never does. She kept to the house a lot of the time so I didn't see her all that often."

"Shy?" suggested Rudd. He had finished the bitter tea and sat back relaxed in his chair.

"Shy?" Wheeler repeated, tasting the flavour of the

word with a small, ruminative movement of his mouth.

"Maybe," he admitted, without much conviction.

"Stuck up?" Rudd offered as an alternative. Wheeler tasted that, too, and seemed to find it more to his liking.

"Didn't mix and didn't want to mix," he said with more warmth and then added, without any prompting, "She were a bloody good cook, though. I'll give her that."

It was said with an odd mixture of genuine admiration and personal animosity that revealed more than Wheeler intended and Rudd thought he could guess what it was. Had Wheeler, a bachelor living alone, taken a fancy to Betty Lovell? It was worth testing out.

"She's never thought of remarrying?" he asked casually.

Wheeler's face closed over.

"Not that I know of," he said shortly. "She's still there, ain't she?"

"Funny she didn't go back to her own family after the marriage broke up," Rudd continued in a gossipy voice.

"Maybe she didn't want to. Maybe she reckoned she was better off as she was," Wheeler replied. The half-grin was back and with it the jeering undertone of innuendo.

Rudd looked interested. The interview had reverted to Wheeler's rules but the Inspector was prepared to tolerate this provided he learned something useful as a consequence. His difficulty was in finding the right question to ask that would provoke the response he was looking for. He decided to open tentatively.

"Can't be easy for her, though," he suggested.

"Easier, maybe, than it was," Wheeler replied.

Without Ronnie? Rudd thought. Is that what he's driving at? Or does he mean something more than that?

"Happier on her own?" he hinted.

A complex expression passed over Wheeler's face, secretive and yet knowing. It was accompanied by one of his small, derisive smiles that had a twist of bitterness in it this time.

"You'd need to ask *her* that, wouldn't you?" was his reply.

It was an evasive answer, committing Wheeler to no opinion of his own, and yet the wry emphasis he put on the word "her" convinced the Inspector that Wheeler meant something by it.

"Perhaps I'll do just that," he countered, hoping by this bolder, frontal attack to draw Wheeler out into the open.

His remark had some effect. Wheeler looked triumphant.

"Take my word, you'll get nothing out of her," he told Rudd. "Nor out of him neither."

The last comment was made after a pause so tiny that if Rudd hadn't been straining to pick up every nuance of Wheeler's conversation he might have missed it altogether or passed it over as being of no significance.

You'll get nothing out of her—nor out of him neither.

And then suddenly Rudd understood, although he kept his expression bland.

"You're probably right," he agreed equably. "I'd be wasting my time. Now, Mr. Wheeler," he went on, more briskly, "there's a couple more questions I'd like to ask you, just for the record. You've no idea where Ron Lovell went to after he left the farm?"

"No," Wheeler said sulkily. He knew that the game had passed out of his hands and he was aware, also, that he might have said too much. The Inspector's face gave nothing away but, all the same, the man was no fool.

"Or if he's been in touch with his wife or his brother since he left? Written to them for example?"

"Not that I know of."

"Or visited them?" Rudd asked cheerfully, dropping in the suggestion as a perfectly natural thing Ron Lovell might do.

Wheeler shook his head.

"I shouldn't think so."

"But you have no proof?"

Wheeler took it as a rebuke.

"No, I ain't got no proof. But it ain't likely, though, is it?" he replied, looking angry.

Rudd ignored his anger, although he understood the cause of it. Wheeler had lost out, not only in the question and answer game but also in the situation at the farm which he had hoped to exploit. The roots of his malice and bitterness went a long way back, Rudd decided.

"I'd like a description of Ron Lovell," he went on.

"Just for the record?" Wheeler asked, with a flash of his former sarcasm.

"Exactly," Rudd replied, ignoring that, too.

"It's been a long time since I saw him," Wheeler said reluctantly. It was clear that, as a last throw, he was going to try blocking any of the official questions. However, Rudd had no intention of letting him do so.

"Height and build don't alter all that much," he replied promptly.

"I ain't much good at judging height."

Rudd countered that one.

"Well, was he taller or shorter than his brother Geoff? Or about the same height?"

"A bit taller," Wheeler admitted.

"The same build?"

"No. Ron was thinner. Not so broad in the shoulders."

Rudd gave him an encouraging smile that Wheeler resented. He was sitting hunched up at the table, among the debris of his supper, in an attitude of angry defeat.

"Hair colouring?"

"Not so dark."

"Brown rather than black hair?" Rudd suggested.

"Maybe. Yes, all right, it was. Dark brown."

"Eyes?"

But Wheeler had been driven too far.

"I never looked," he said, jeering. "And if that's all you want . . ."

"One more question," Rudd said. "When you were working on the farm, did Geoff Lovell keep a dog?"

"Yes. A collie."

"Was it allowed to run loose?"

"No. It were kept chained up except at night."

"So he's got the Labrador since you left?"

"Yes."

"Any idea when?"

"No, I ain't."

"That's all," said Rudd jauntily, rising from the table. "Thank you, Mr. Wheeler, for being so patient."

Wheeler looked up at him, his narrow face tight with dislike and resentment.

"You can see yourself out," he said.

It wasn't so much a question as a statement.

Rudd saw himself out, allowing his face to relax into a smile only when he reached the safety of the back door.

He was in the same jaunty mood when he got back to the office where Boyce was still at work, laboriously typing out, letter by letter, the report on the house-to-house inquiry.

"You look pleased with yourself," he commented, as Rudd entered. "Did Wheeler tell you anything useful?"

"Not *tell*," Rudd replied. "Wheeler doesn't work that way. He throws out a few hints and leaves you to draw your own conclusions, if you can. I did manage, though, to squeeze something more direct out of him—a description of Ron Lovell. Not a very detailed one but it'll do to be getting on with. But Wheeler did come up with something interesting which, if I interpret it right, could suggest a possible motive, assuming it's Ron Lovell's body we've found. He hinted that Geoff Lovell and Ron's wife, Betty, might be lovers. It could be pure spite, of course. He's obviously got it in for the Lovells and I think I know why. He fancied Betty Lovell himself; at least, he fancied her cooking and my guess is she showed him he wasn't welcome. It could have been the reason why Geoff Lovell dismissed him; he was making a nuisance of himself hanging round Betty. But supposing there is something in what he hinted? After all, it isn't all that far-fetched. They're still comparatively young. Betty's alone and available now that her husband's cleared off and I can't imagine Geoff Lovell finding it easy to get a woman. He's too . . ."

He paused, searching for a word that would convey to Boyce the air of brooding unhappiness that Lovell conveyed. Not finding one, he left the sentence unfinished and went on.

"The farm's isolated. Even if they welcomed visitors, which they don't, they can't meet many people, so they'd be thrown together. It'd follow naturally that they'd develop some kind of close relationship. It could be another reason why Geoff Lovell got rid of Wheeler; he was afraid he'd notice that he and Betty were a bit more to each other than brother and sister-in-law. And it could be the reason, too, why they've cut themselves off from the outside world, with that dog virtually on guard. According to Wheeler, when he worked on the farm, Lovell had a collie but it was kept tied up during the day. He's acquired the Labrador since. Now Stebbing mentioned that, when he called at the farm soon after he arrived in the district three years ago, the dog was loose then. So Lovell was actively discouraging visitors at least a year before Ron Lovell could have come back."

"In case they'd see something they shouldn't?" Boyce suggested.

"Yes, and in case Charlie talked. Wheeler spoke of him wanting to chat and I noticed, when I called there, that Charlie seemed eager to start up a conversation with me, only before he could say much, Lovell hustled him out into the kitchen."

"So the theory now is," said Boyce, "that Ron Lovell comes back, finds his wife and his brother are sharing a bed, there's a quarrel over it and . . ."

"Ron Lovell gets killed," Rudd put in. "Not necessarily murdered. It could have been an accident. Supposing Geoff Lovell hit him and he fell and broke his neck? But, whatever way it happened, he's left with the dead body of his brother on his hands. He can't admit to it. There'd be an inquiry and awkward questions would be asked, such as, 'What was the quarrel about?' So he says nothing, largely to protect Betty Lovell."

"But it's not a crime, sleeping with your sister-in-law, is it?" Boyce objected.

"It's not incest, if that's what you mean," Rudd agreed. "But I can understand someone like Lovell not wanting it known. Country morals are still quite a bit different to a city's. If the truth came out, you can imagine the gossip. Besides, he must have felt an enormous amount of guilt about it. So must she."

"Come to that, if we go along with your theory, why couldn't Betty Lovell have shoved him down the stairs?" Boyce asked. "She'd have as much motive as Geoff for seeing he kept his mouth shut."

Rudd was silent. The idea hadn't occurred to him.

"It's possible, I suppose," he agreed at last, with a reluctance he couldn't have explained.

"You didn't meet her when you went to the farm?"

"No. She was in the kitchen; keeping out of the way, I suspect. But Wheeler hinted that her marriage to Ron might have been a failure and she was happier without him."

"That would give her an even stronger motive," Boyce pointed out. "She's glad to see the back of him and then he turns up again, upsetting the apple cart."

"It's all theory," Rudd put in. "We mustn't forget that. What we've got against the Lovells is pretty thin so far. A body's discovered near his land; not on it; we mustn't lose sight of that. Lovell is seen watching the archaeological society digging in the same field. His brother left home fifteen years ago and hasn't been seen since, as far as we know. It's nothing more than straws in the wind."

"But at least they show which way the wind's blowing," Boyce said. "What'll you do now? Go back to see Lovell again?"

"Sometime," Rudd agreed. "But not yet. I'm inclined to leave him alone for the time being. Let him stew for a bit. Besides, I haven't really got a good enough reason for going back to call on him. I'll wait until Pardoe comes up with something more positive on the corpse and see how far it tallies with Wheeler's description of Ron Lovell. If it fits, I'll have a little more to go on. And I'll make damn sure I see Betty

Lovell the next time I call there. Meanwhile, we'd better get stuck into the routine stuff; check through the missing persons' files for a start and draw up a list of possible names. Get our liaison officer at the Yard to go through those outside the area. We can tackle the more local ones here."

"Oh, God!" Boyce said mournfully. "There'll be ruddy hundreds of them."

"Not that many," Rudd told him. "We'll begin with those reported missing two years ago and work forward from there. We know from the boots, it's not likely he was a professional man; an accountant, for example. Nor a teen-ager run away from home. He'd lost most of his teeth so he must have been an older man. That'll shorten the list a bit. I'll chase up Pardoe, too. He may be able to give us something of a description of the body which will help."

"It's still going to mean hours of bloomin' work," Boyce said, only partly mollified.

"It'll keep you busy," Rudd replied cheerfully. "And at least you'll be sitting down."

Chapter 7

But it was two days later before Pardoe was able to supply the evidence that Rudd was waiting for. He was in the office, going over the reports of the case with Boyce when the door opened and the brisk, upright figure of the police surgeon entered. The Inspector broke off what he was saying and looked up eagerly.

"You've got something?" he asked.

"Not a lot," Pardoe admitted. "You'll have to wait until the experts at the Yard come up with the more detailed stuff, such as the clothing. It's too far gone for me to be able to tell you much about it except this—the boots he was wearing were a size eight. And we were right about the body being wrapped up. There was quite a lot more of the same material under the corpse, including the head. It looks like a woollen blanket but, again, I'm not committing myself on that either."

"A shroud," Rudd remarked, half to himself.

Pardoe looked at him quizzically under bushy eyebrows in a manner that put the Inspector in mind of a fox-terrier: alert, intelligent, but with a sharp edge to him that he didn't bother to conceal.

"What conclusions you draw from it is your business," he replied. "All I can do is give you the facts as I find them. The cross and chain I can't be much help on either. It's silver-plated and there's some kind of pattern etched into the crucifix but I can't raise it in detail. The Yard may have better luck. As to the body itself, he seems to be a man between forty and fifty. I can't get nearer than that. Medium build. Height about five feet ten inches. Dark brown hair, going thin on top. There were a few grey hairs mixed in with it but not a lot."

Rudd looked quickly at Boyce, who nodded in agreement at his unspoken question. The details that Pardoe had described agreed broadly with the description that Wheeler had given of Ronnie Lovell. But only in very general terms and, although it was sufficient to keep Ron Lovell in the running as a possible victim, it wasn't enough to prove positive identity.

"Any distinguishing features that might help us prove who he was?" he asked hopefully. Pardoe shook his head.

"Finger-prints are out. I did warn you of that. So is the possibility of finding any scar tissue that could be checked on. He's been under the ground too long for that. You've not found his dentures?"

"No," Rudd replied.

"Well, without them, you're not going to get much joy out of dental records," Pardoe said brusquely. "As I pointed out to you when the body was first uncovered, he'd had most of his teeth removed. There were a few back ones left but they're in such poor condition, I doubt if he ever made regular visits to a dentist. If you want some idea of what he looked like, the best I can do is take measurements of the skull and get a police artist to draw up a sketch from them but all you'll get is an outline of the general structure of the face. It can't provide details such as the exact shape of the nose or mouth."

He paused and looked questioningly at Rudd.

"There is another way, assuming you've got a candidate for the dead man. Have you?"

"Perhaps," Rudd replied guardedly.

"Could you get a photograph of him?"

"I might. But that's not going to be much help, is it, if he's that far gone?"

"Not for normal identification, I agree. But there's another method. Ever heard of the Ruxton case?"

"Wasn't that the doctor who was hanged in the thirties for the double murder of his wife and her maid?"

"That's right. I've taken a special interest in it because of the medical evidence brought forward at the trial. If you remember, the dismembered bodies of two women were found in a ravine in Scotland and the prosecution had to prove that the bits and pieces belonged to Mrs. Ruxton and her maid, Mary Rogerson, who were missing from their home in Lancaster. It wasn't easy because whoever killed them had done a pretty thorough job of getting rid of any physical characteristics that could have proved identity; finger-tips, facial features; even down to a piece of skin that might have shown a birth-mark on Mary Rogerson's right arm. But when the case came to trial, the prosecution were able to prove who the bodies were with some very clever forensic evidence; the final, crowning proof being a positive identification they made between one of the skulls and that of the doctor's missing wife. They got hold of a photograph of Mrs. Ruxton in which she was wearing some kind of tiara, measured the actual piece of jewellery which they found, blew up the photograph until the measurements were exactly the same and then compared the facial details in the photograph, which was now life-size, with the head of the dead woman. That way they were able to prove by the jaw-line the position of the nasal root and so on that it was Mrs. Ruxton's skull. Fascinating case!"

His eyes were bright with the same kind of lively interest that Rudd had seen in Rose's face when he talked about the Saxon site he was excavating.

"But I needn't go on about it," Pardoe added. "The point I'm making is this—if you could get a photograph of your candidate for the dead body and have it blown up to life-size, I could do a similar comparison between the two heads and tell you straightaway whether you'd got the right man. It'd have to be exactly life-size, of course. McCullum will be able to advise you on that. He's the photographic expert. Well, I'll leave you with it."

After he had gone, Rudd turned to Boyce.

"What do you think?" he asked.

Boyce looked doubtful.

"It's a hell of a long shot but I suppose it's worth a try. Where are you going to get hold of a photograph of Ronnie Lovell?"

"Betty Lovell?" Rudd suggested. "She's almost certain to have a picture of him somewhere about the house. Failing that, there's army records or someone he knew after he left the farm, if we can find out where he went. He must have been living and working somewhere. Any luck with the missing persons' lists?"

"Not yet," Boyce replied. "I'm still working through the Home Counties ones with Kyle. The Yard haven't come up with anything either. Something may come of it, I suppose, providing he was reported missing. You'll be going back to see Lovell?"

"Yes, this afternoon probably, after I've had a word with McCullum about this photographic evidence. But what Pardoe was able to give me on the dead man is close enough to Wheeler's description of Ronnie Lovell for me to ask a few more questions. Besides, I've been looking for an excuse to meet Betty Lovell. If we're right in thinking Ron came home and that's his body we've found, she could be a possible witness."

"What about the other brother—Charlie, isn't it? He

might know something, too, and from what you've
told me about him, he seems more likely to talk."

"Too likely," Rudd replied. "I don't want to make
use of him unless I have to. He's got the mind of a
child. You can imagine what a defence counsel would
make of his testimony if we based a case on his evidence alone. It'd be thrown out of court. No, we've
got to find something more reliable than that. And the
first step is to prove that it *is* Ronnie Lovell we've
dug up. Until we've done that, we're running about in
circles. Pardoe's suggestion about the photograph is
one way we may be able to do it. I think I'll go and
have a chat with McCullum about it now."

He found McCullum downstairs in the darkroom,
developing the last of the photographs that he had
taken at the site of the grave.

"Aye, it could be done," he agreed, after Rudd had
explained Pardoe's theory to him. "But I'd need one
of two things in any photograph you came up with;
either some detail in the clothing that could be
measured, similar to the piece of jewellery in the case
you were talking about. With a man, it's not going to
be so easy. They don't dress themselves up with gew-
gaws as a woman does, but something like a tie-pin or
a watch might do. Or, failing that, I'd need a specific
detail in the background that I could re-photograph
and measure."

"What sort of thing?" Rudd asked.

"Almost anything could do. I'll give you an example. Supposing it was a snapshot taken of the person
standing against a gate. If you could identify the
gate, then it could be measured, photographed and I
could use it as a scale to make a life-size enlargement
from the original snapshot."

"I see," said Rudd thoughtfully and, thanking
McCullum, he went back to the office, where he sent
for Boyce.

"McCullum sounded hopeful," he announced, "so
I'll be off to Lovell's farm later this afternoon to see if
I can lay my hands on a photograph of Ronnie
Lovell. By the way, I'd like to meet you afterwards at
Stebbing's place, say about six o'clock. We ought to

get that grave filled in and there's one more measurement I want to take—the distance from the grave to the main excavation site where Rose said he found the post-holes. Somebody forgot to take it and I'll need it for the large-scale plan of the field. I meant to mention it to you earlier when we were going over the reports but Pardoe came in and it slipped my mind. So bring spades and the tapes with you and a couple of men, then we can get the job finished today and Rose and his merry band of diggers can move back into the field as soon as they like."

"Right you are," Boyce replied. "I'll round up Kyle and one or two others."

He left the office and Rudd settled down at his desk to complete the reports on the case.

Later he set off for Lovell's farm, parking the car near the opening. As he approached the gate, the dog came racing up as it had done on the first occasion and stood menacing him through the bars. But this time he didn't have to wait so long before it was called off. A woman appeared in the doorway of the house almost at once, looked briefly in his direction and then hurried out of sight round the corner of the barn. Shortly afterwards she returned, accompanied by Charlie, and stood watching from the doorstep as her brother-in-law hastened up the drive with an ungainly stride.

So Lovell must be out, Rudd thought.

He had the feeling, too, that both of them were carrying out instructions, for the woman remained standing at the door, as if on guard, while Charlie slipped a leather strap that he had ready in his pocket through the dog's collar and dragged it off, without speaking to Rudd or waiting for him to climb over the gate.

By the time he had done so, they were already waiting for him in the yard below, Charlie by the dog that he had now chained to the barn wall and the woman on the doorstep.

Rudd, who had come to a halt a little way off, stood looking at the pair of them with amused interest that he didn't allow to appear on his face. Charlie was ob-

viously ill at ease and Rudd got the impression that
he wasn't supposed to remain there, for he avoided
their eyes and looked down at his boots, which he
was scuffling about in the dust.

"Charlie!" the woman called and he looked at her
from under his eyebrows and then walked away with a
sulky air.

He wants to stay and see what happens, Rudd
thought, but he's under orders not to. What's he been
told to do? Fetch Lovell as soon as I appear? It
seemed a possibility.

It struck him then that Charlie might be suffering
more than the other two from the self-imposed isola-
tion. He seemed childishly eager to welcome anyone
who called and perhaps he did not understand or
share the sense of guilt or shame that kept Geoff and
Betty Lovell apart from their neighbours.

Rudd watched his retreating figure thoughtfully
and then turned to Betty Lovell.

She was a slightly built woman in her thirties who
probably had been pretty when young but whose
fragile looks had been worn away by years of anxiety
and work. Her hair, once fair, now faded to an indeterminate light brown still streaked with blond, was
tied back at the nape of her neck, although shorter
pieces had escaped and clung round her forehead,
softening the shape of her face. It was a drawn,
harassed face, wide in the forehead, narrow at the
chin, that still possessed a little of the child-like, elfin
charm that in her teens would have been her best fea-
ture.

Had that been what had attracted Ron Lovell to
her? Rudd wondered as he walked towards her,
smiling and holding out his hand.

He felt as if he were approaching a nervous animal
that had to be soothed and quieted. Absurdly, he
wanted to stroke her hair and thin hands. Her face
was laid so dreadfully bare, with all the years of
worry and exhaustion stamped too vividly in its
drawn lines and hollows. He felt an immediate compassion and tenderness, not just for her but for some-

one she put him in mind of but who exactly he couldn't at that moment recall.

"Mrs. Lovell?" he asked pleasantly.

She backed towards the door, putting her hands against its surface as if for reassurance.

"You wanted to see Geoff?" she asked in a breathless voice. "He's up the fields. Charlie's gone for him."

"I see," said Rudd. "You don't mind if I wait for him?"

"No," she replied. "But I've got work to do inside."

"I'll come in, too, if it doesn't bother you," Rudd said quickly, seizing the opportunity. "It's hot standing out here in the yard."

She hesitated but hadn't the courage to refuse him and he followed her through the cool, dark living-room into the kitchen, of which he had caught only a glimpse on his previous visit.

It was better lit than the living-room for, being at the end of the house, it had two windows, one overlooking the yard, the other in the end wall opening out at the side of the building.

Like the living-room, it was spotlessly clean; simply equipped with a deep, white-glazed sink, a few cupboards and shelves and a two-burner oil stove that suggested that, although the house had electric light, it wasn't wired up for power. A large deal table occupied the centre of the room; on it lay some shirts that she had evidently been mending, for a raffia sewing basket stood beside them and one of the shirts was spread out with a needle threaded through the collar, close to a frayed patch that she had been darning with tiny, neat stitches in white cotton.

She drew a chair out at the table and sat down but made no attempt to pick up the sewing and Rudd had the impression that she was waiting anxiously for something, possibly for Lovell's arrival.

He stood watching her, for one of the rare occasions in his life uncertain how to proceed.

It would be so easy to question her before Lovell arrived. Too easy. Perhaps that was why he shied away from it. Her vulnerability gave her a powerful shield. Besides, he had remembered who her face reminded him of. Years before he had tried to dissuade a man from jumping from the fifth floor of a building. He, too, had worn the same exposed expression, as if all the nerve ends were too close to the surface of the skin, and his upper lip had lifted in the same ghastly parody of a smile, a rictus of pure fear.

Perhaps she, too, was close to that extremity, and he did not want to be the one who drove her beyond the edge.

Drawing out a chair next to her and sitting down, he began talking in an easy, chatty way, trying to get her to relax.

"How very quiet it is here, Mrs. Lovell. No noise. No traffic. It must be nice and peaceful."

She didn't reply but he went on nonetheless.

"Not many neighbours, have you? I suppose Stebbing's is the nearest farm?"

He forced her to answer this time, by cocking his head on one side and looking at her with a bright, interested expression.

"Yes" was all she said, but it was a beginning.

"Seemed a friendly sort of man when I met him," Rudd continued. "A good sort to have as a neighbour, I should imagine."

"We don't . . ." she began and then broke off. Geoff Lovell could be seen coming across the yard, almost at a run, struggling to put his shirt on as he came, with Charlie, looking breathless and excited, stumbling after him.

There was a brief altercation between them, visible through the window. Charlie seemed to be protesting. Rudd could see his long arms swinging, his slack mouth opening and closing. Then Lovell took him by the shoulders and, turning him about, pushed him towards the outbuildings.

"I told you, get them pigs seen to!" he shouted after him.

Then he came striding towards the house. They heard the front door slam shut and a few seconds later he burst into the kitchen.

Rudd got to his feet and said equably:

"Good afternoon, Mr. Lovell. I'm sorry to come bothering you again."

The man was clearly in a temper, but whether with Charlie or on account of his own visit, Rudd could not tell. His face was flushed and he was breathing heavily, the thick barrel of his chest rising and falling deeply under his unbuttoned shirt. But he had powerful self-control. Tucking his shirt into the top of his trousers, he said with a gruff attempt at politeness:

"I'm sorry if I've kept you waiting. I was up the top field."

"No matter," Rudd replied. "There's no hurry. I was chatting to Mrs. Lovell."

He watched for Lovell's reaction. It came in the swift glance he gave her that she answered with a small, deprecatory movement of one hand. They knew each other well enough for words not to matter, which was only to be expected. They had shared the same house, the same closed-in life, possibly the same bed for long enough for them to know each other as well as any married couple. But, at the same time, he was aware of a tension between them, although Lovell seemed more relaxed after their wordless exchange. Betty hadn't said much and this pleased him. He was prepared to be more open and friendly himself in consequence.

"Fancy a cup of tea?" he asked Rudd. "I know I could do with one. Put the kettle on, Betty. You can take a cup across to Charlie. He's seeing to the pigs."

Rudd looked at Lovell with renewed respect. The ploy was not lost on the Inspector. The suggestion of tea was a device to get Betty out of the house and to keep Charlie away from it as well. The man, for all his apparent heaviness, had got that move worked out neatly enough.

Rudd sat back, prepared to watch and wait. An opportunity would come. If need be, he could make one himself. But, for the time being, he was content just to sit there, absorbing the atmosphere of the place and feeling his way into the relationship between the two of them.

Betty Lovell moved quietly about the kitchen, filling the kettle, removing the mending from the table and setting out cups and saucers in its place. There was something self-effacing about her, as if she were perfectly happy to remain in the background. Lovell rolled himself a cigarette while Rudd made a few remarks about the weather and the state of the harvest.

The tea was made and poured and Betty Lovell carried one of the cups out of the kitchen. Lovell waited until he saw her crossing the yard before he spoke.

"You've come about that man they found on Stebbing's land?"

It seemed a curious way of framing the question, as if Lovell were reminding the Inspector that the body had nothing to do with him, although Rudd was prepared to admit he might be reading more significance into it than was justified.

"Found out who he is yet?"

Rudd shook his head.

"The man's been dead for over a year. It's not going to be easy but we're making inquiries."

"In the village?" Lovell asked, his eyes very bright. "They'll tell you anything there."

"They told me no-one has been reported missing recently," Rudd replied. "No-one who's left home, at least not for a long time."

Lovell was silent and Rudd let the silence continue for a few moments before he added quietly, "Someone did mention your brother Ronnie."

There was no outburst of anger or bitterness as he had expected. Instead, Lovell went on stirring his tea before he finally looked up, a strange, crooked, half-smile on his face, and said:

"So they're still on about that, are they, after all these years?"

"You must understand my position, Mr. Lovell," Rudd replied, in his negative, official voice. "I have to follow up every possible line of inquiry."

"Even one that's fifteen years out of date?" Lovell interrupted him to ask. "What's on your mind? That Ron turned up here after all these years? That I killed him, I suppose, and buried him on Stebbing's land? I ask you, does it make sense?"

It was so near to the theory that Rudd had indeed worked out, including the main objection to it, that he was nonplussed for a moment by Lovell's directness. There was, too, a new boldness about the man that he hadn't seen before. The sullen air was gone. He was almost triumphant.

"I have to follow it up, even though it may seem unlikely," Rudd replied, a little on the defensive. "I'd prefer to question you, rather than your sister-in-law. However . . ."

He left the threat unspoken. Lovell looked at him, weighing him up. The heavy look had returned to his face and Rudd realised he was close to losing his temper. Then he lifted his shoulders in a gesture that expressed contempt.

"You enjoy stirring things up, don't you?" he asked.

"I'm trying to avoid it," Rudd replied stiffly.

"All right." Lovell had come to a decision. "Ask what questions you want."

"I'd like a description of your brother. Better still a photograph."

"I can tell you what he looks like. We haven't kept any photos."

It came a little too pat.

"None?" Rudd asked.

"None. When he cleared off, I told Betty to burn everything, his letters, the photos, the lot."

"Why?"

"Why d'you think?" Lovell countered with a sneer. "He was no good. She was better off forgetting all about him."

"Why did he leave?"

"I told you. He was no good. Never had been. The army made him worse. He'd never liked farm-work much anyway and he couldn't settle. He wanted to move on, so he left."

"And that was the only reason?"

"It's the one he gave me himself."

Rudd crossed his legs. The interview had settled down to the quick give and take of question and answer that he was used to. But he remained on the alert. Lovell was no fool. He was more quick-witted than Rudd had first given him credit for. Or he had his story well worked out.

"Do you know where he went?"

"No idea," Lovell replied indifferently. "He didn't say. He just packed a few things and went."

"On his motor-bike?"

"Oh, so you've heard about that?" Lovell said with an amused grin. "You have been busy asking questions, haven't you? Yes, he left on his bike."

"Have you ever heard from him since he left?" Rudd asked, ignoring the contempt in the man's voice.

The question was unexpected. Lovell hesitated, at a loss as to how to reply.

"How do you mean?" he asked.

"Has he ever written? Sent money?"

"No."

"So how do you know if he's still alive or not?"

"I'd've heard if he was dead," Lovell said quickly. "Somebody would have let us know."

It was acceptable as an answer, although Rudd had the impression that Lovell had grasped it on the spur of the moment. He was certain of this when Lovell added:

"They'd've put it on the radio, an S.O.S. message, wouldn't they?"

Is he trying to convince himself as well as me? Rudd wondered. But he decided to leave it there. It was a possible weak spot in Lovell's story that he might be able to exploit on another occasion. Meanwhile, he preferred to give Lovell the impression that he had been taken in by it. .

"I suppose so," he replied. "Could you give me a description of your brother?"

"The man you've found isn't Ron," Lovell said with conviction. "You're barking up the wrong tree there."

"Then you won't object if I go ahead and prove that it isn't?"

"All right," Lovell said sulkily. "What do you want to know?"

"Height. Colouring. Details like that."

"Well, he was a bit taller than me; round about five feet ten, I'd say, and not so dark. More Charlie's colouring."

"Any distinguishing marks?"

"If you mean moles or scars, no, he hadn't none."

"Shoe size?" Rudd asked.

"How the hell should I know?" Lovell replied angrily. "I don't know the size he took in shirts, either, so it's no good asking."

"Any of his clothes still about the house?"

"After fifteen years?"

"What happened to them?"

"He took his best stuff with him. What was left, Charlie wore. They fitted him; good enough for working in, leastways."

"Including his boots?"

Lovell laughed as if he were beginning to find the interview amusing.

"No, not his boots," he replied with a derisive look. "They didn't fit. I think Betty chucked them out."

"Who was his dentist?" Rudd went on to ask.

The question threw Lovell. The smile, Rudd noticed, quickly disappeared from his face.

"Dentist?" he repeated blankly.

"Yes, dentist," Rudd said, watching his face closely.

He took his time before replying.

"I don't think he went to one, not after he came out of the army. He may have seen a dentist then. I wouldn't know."

"So his army records should have the details?"

The remark seemed to take Lovell by surprise.

"Do they keep them that far back?" he asked.

"I imagine so," Rudd said briskly. "His dental records could be extremely useful, you see, Mr. Lovell, in proving identity."

He made the remark deliberately, to test out Lovell's reaction. The man didn't reply but looked away quickly, frowning, as if he were suddenly aware of unknown and dangerous areas of investigation, or so it seemed to Rudd.

"What regiment was your brother in?" Rudd asked.

"What did you say?" Lovell replied abstractedly.

Rudd repeated the question.

"The Royal Engineers."

"And I believe it was while he was in the army that he met and married Mrs. Lovell?" Rudd went on.

Lovell nodded. The sarcastic, jeering air had gone, leaving him subdued.

"Can you tell me where and when they were married?"

Lovell roused himself to ask sharply. "Why? What need is there to know that?"

Rudd had no intention of explaining that, with this information, there was a possibility that he might be able to get hold of a photograph of Ronnie and Betty Lovell taken on their wedding day, if the photographer were still in business and kept a back file of pictures he had taken. It was a slim chance but one worth trying.

"Just a line of inquiry we might need to check on," he replied vaguely.

"I don't know the details," Lovell mumbled.

"He didn't write to tell you?"

"Only that he was married and would be bringing Betty home after his demob."

"I'll have to ask Mrs. Lovell then," Rudd said, getting to his feet.

Lovell was on his feet, too, standing in front of the Inspector as if to bar his way.

"Do you have to?" he asked. His manner was almost supplicatory and there was a grave and touching dignity about it that made Rudd realise the depth of affection he must hold for his brother's wife. Lovell was not a man who would find it easy to ask a favour of another.

"I need to know the date and the place of the wedding," Rudd insisted.

"Then can I ask her myself? I'd rather it came from me. She's been upset enough . . ."

He left the sentence unfinished and, when Rudd nodded, went out of the room abruptly and Rudd saw him striding across the yard.

Chapter 8

As soon as he had disappeared round the corner of
the barn, Rudd moved swiftly into the living-room.
He had at most, he reckoned, a few minutes. Lovell
would have to ask Betty for the information and
would probably spend a little while longer explaining
why it was needed. All the same, knowing him, he
wouldn't be gone for long. A man as suspicious by
nature as Lovell wouldn't leave Rudd much time to
be alone in the house.

In a few quick strides, he was at the door beside
the fire-place, had opened it and was going up the
steep stair-case, so narrow that his shoulders brushed
the walls.

At the top, it ascended onto a tiny, square landing
with a dormer window that overlooked the back of

the house. A brief glimpse through it showed him the steep fall of the tiled roof and beyond it a kitchen garden.

Two doors opened off the landing. The one on his right gave onto a bedroom, simply furnished with a deal chest of drawers and a single iron bedstead, bedside which stood a rush-bottomed chair with a man's jacket hanging over the back rail and some comic books with brightly coloured covers lying on the seat.

Charlie's room, thought Rudd, shutting the door quickly, but not before he had noticed another door at the opposite side of the room that led, presumably, to a third bedroom, situated over the kitchen. There was no time, however, to examine it.

The door on his left opened into another bedroom, larger than Charlie's and better furnished although, like his, the back wall sloped sharply, following the angle of the roof. He took in the details swiftly. The floor boards, on which lay some rugs, were polished to a high gloss. A vase of garden pinks stood on the deep window-sill. Against the far wall was a heavy, old-fashioned oak wardrobe, also highly polished, with a chest of drawers of the same period standing across the corner near the window that held a small, oval mirror on a wooden stand, a brush and comb and a plastic bottle that looked as if it might contain hand-cream. There was no sign of any photographs and Rudd knew he didn't have time to search through the drawers.

Immediately inside the door was a double bed with a cover of flowered chintz that matched the curtains, faded but still pretty.

The room had the same neat, spotless look of the other rooms in the house, oddly untouched and impersonal, and yet softened by the gentler touches of femininity in the flowers and the patterned fabric.

From the doorway, Rudd could just reach the double bed. With one hand he pulled down the coverlet far enough to expose the pillows. On one lay a nightdress of pale pink cotton, on the other a pair of striped pyjama trousers, both neatly folded.

He had seen enough. Twitching back the cover, he closed the door and scrambled down the stairs in time to appear at the front door just as Lovell approached it from the yard, as if he had anticipated his arrival and had come to meet him.

His presence at the door didn't strike Lovell as suspicious. Rudd wore a bland expression and, with his hands in his pockets, he looked unhurried and relaxed. Besides, Lovell had other things on his mind. The hasty, snatched conversation with Betty had left him disturbed and anxious. They had spoken in undertones so that Charlie could not overhear them. But, although Lovell had sent him sharply about his work, he had hovered nearby, clearly curious to know what they were talking about.

His presence about the place was a continual threat but there was nothing that could be done about it, except to try to keep him away from the house whenever the Inspector called, although Lovell could see it wasn't going to be easy. It no longer looked likely that Rudd was going to restrict himself to a few, infrequent visits.

Suppose he insisted on talking to Charlie?

Lovell wasn't sure what his rights would be in such a situation. Could he refuse to let him be questioned? After all, Charlie wasn't normal. Even Rudd must realise that. He could, of course, deny anything that Charlie might say, pleading that he'd got confused over what had really happened.

Betty, too, was another source of anxiety. He knew he could count on her silence. There was no problem there. *She* would give nothing away. But the longer the investigation went on, the more strain she would suffer and God knows she had already been through enough. He could see it in her face when he asked the questions about her marriage that Rudd wanted the answers to.

She told him and then asked quickly, "What does he want to know for?"

"I don't know," Lovell replied. "He's just nosing about, that's all. It doesn't mean anything."

It was better, he decided, to say nothing about the

other inquiries that Rudd had spoken of making; into Ron's army records, for instance. That was another source of worry that was best kept to himself.

How far back would the police be prepared to go? Not that they'd found out much, he told himself. Nothing that would be of any use to them in proving who the dead man was. Unless they got hold of a photograph.

Christ! He had forgotten the Inspector had asked about photos of Ron. He turned away, eager to get back to the house before Rudd had time to start looking about. Downstairs was all right. There were no photos in the living-room, not even in the dresser drawers. But he could get a search warrant, Lovell supposed, and turn the place over.

And, God, if that happened . . .

Charlie delayed him, tugging at his sleeve to hold him back.

"Can I come to the house with you, Geoff?"

"No, stay here," Lovell told him.

"But I fancied another cup o' tea. I always have a second cup."

"Then you'll bloody well have to wait for it!" Lovell shouted.

Betty came forward, her lips set and disapproving at his outburst, to lead Charlie off, coaxing him as a mother might do to distract the attention of a difficult child.

"Not yet, Charlie. I'll make a fresh pot later. Come on, now. I want you to help me collect up the eggs."

They walked off together, Charlie looking back over his shoulder at his brother with a sullen expression.

Lovell watched them both with a sense of angry and yet defeated despair before turning abruptly and walking rapidly back to the house where Rudd met him at the door.

"You've not been gone long, Mr. Lovell," he remarked cheerfully. "Were you able to find out what I wanted?"

"They were married at Bidderton registry office," Lovell said shortly.

"And the date?"

Lovell told him.

"Bidderton," Rudd remarked chattily, as he made a note of the details. "That's in Dorset, isn't it?"

"Yes."

"Nice part of the country, Dorset," Rudd added.

"Is that all?" Lovell demanded.

"For the moment," Rudd replied. But he seemed in no hurry and remained standing on the doorstep, looking about him with a frankly interested gaze.

"If you've finished . . ." Lovell reminded him.

"Yes, of course," Rudd replied. "I mustn't keep you talking Mr. Lovell. I'm sure you've got work to do. And so have I."

It was said pleasantly enough and he was smiling in a friendly manner, but his eyes were cool and watchful and Lovell thought he could detect a warning note in the final remark. Rudd was telling him that the inquiries were not yet over. And behind it, Lovell sensed something else. It was almost as if the Inspector were trying to provoke a response and, if that was what he was after, it was a game that two could play at.

"If you're leaving, then I'll let the dog off the chain," he replied in an amused, drawling voice.

Rudd's smile widened.

"As long as you let me get to the gate first," he countered easily.

He didn't hurry, however, and went strolling off up the drive, his hands still in his pockets, as if he had all the time in the world. There was something exasperatingly confident about his back and the set of his shoulders that tempted Lovell to release the dog before he had climbed to safety over the gate. But he didn't and it was with a feeling of defeat and anti-climax that he finally freed the dog, after he heard Rudd start up his car.

What was the point in it, after all? He couldn't hope to win. All he could do was postpone the final reckoning. Or trust to a miracle. And that wasn't likely to happen.

But, at least, there was something positive he could

do, right now, while Betty and Charlie were safely out of the way and, with sudden decision, he entered the house and went up the stairs to the room with the double bed in it, where he began jerking open the drawers in the chest. The top one contained Betty's clothes, folded with the neatness that he had come to realise was almost obsessive, although he understood it, even sympathised with it in a strange way. A white blouse lay on the top. Next to it was a petticoat patterned with tiny blue flowers. At the sight of them, his resolution drained away. Their pristine, bridal freshness intimidated him and his hands hovered over them incapable of pillage.

"What are you looking for?"

It was Betty's voice behind him. He turned to find her standing in the doorway, her face taut, but whether with anger or anxiety he couldn't, in his own confused and guilty state of mind, decide.

"Nothing," he muttered.

She crossed the room and he stood aside to let her pass. For a moment, she stood without speaking, looking down into the open drawer. Then she closed it quietly.

"You were looking for something," she said.

There was a coldness in her voice, as if he were a stranger, an interloper who had no right to be there and he felt his anger return.

All right! Let her know the truth, he thought. I've done with lying to protect her.

"Photos of Ron," he told her.

"Why?"

"Because *he*'s been asking for them."

He jerked his head towards the window, to indicate the world outside, Rudd's world.

She kept her eyes on his face as she asked the next question.

"What does he want them for?"

He made a helpless gesture with one hand.

"I don't know. He's heard gossip, that's all. He's checking up on anyone from the village that's gone missing."

"Missing!"

There was an hysterical note in her voice and he looked at her with quick anxiety, frightened that he had said too much.

"Don't, Betty," he pleaded.

He saw her stiffen at his concern.

"Oh, don't worry," she told him coldly. "I shan't break down, if that's what's bothering you."

Averting her face, she went over to the wardrobe and, taking down a cardboard shoe-box that was hidden behind a suitcase on the top shelf, she handed it to him.

"If it's photos of Ron you want, you've been looking in the wrong place," she said.

He opened it awkwardly and found it full of letters and photographs, held together in neat bundles with elastic bands.

"Is that the lot?" he asked. "There's no more?"

"No. You've got them all." Her voice was contemptuous. "What are you going to do with them?"

"Burn them," he said and added quickly, "It's safest."

She didn't reply, merely lifted her shoulders in a gesture that expressed weary acceptance before leaving the room.

He waited until he heard the stair-case door close behind her and then, putting the box down on the bed, he began taking out the bundles and, removing the elastic bands, shuffled quickly through their contents, telling himself he ought to check to make sure they contained nothing that need not be destroyed. All the same, he was aware of a certain voyeurism, a jealous need to pry into the life she had shared with his brother.

The letters, few in number, were written on blue, lined paper in Ron's pointed scrawl. He caught sight of the words "Darling Bet" on the first one before, overcome with shame and anger, he thrust the letter back.

The photographs were mostly of Ron; snapshots of him taken in army uniform; several of a trip to some unknown beach: Ron in swimming trunks with his arms round the shoulders of two friends; Ron sitting propped up against a rock with a cigarette in his mouth. In all of them, he had assumed the characteristic pose that Lovell remembered with an odd mixture of bitterness and affection; the head flung back in that cocky, challenging manner; the swaggering look of self-confidence.

He could not bring himself to look at the wedding photographs, easily distinguishable from the others by their size and their white covers stamped with silver bells. He merely laid them on one side with the rest.

The box was now empty, apart from a few snapshots of Betty on her own, taken long ago, it seemed, before her marriage. He looked at them sadly. Betty at fifteen. Or thereabouts. Long before he had known her, anyway. Smiling, with her hair loose. Virginal.

Thrusting the lid on, he carried the box back to the wardrobe where he replaced it on the shelf before gathering up the scattered letters and photographs into a bundle and making for the door.

At the bottom of the stair-case he paused, listening. From the kitchen he could hear the rattle of crockery. Nearly half-past six. Betty would be preparing the evening meal. He heard the rush of water as she turned on the tap and then the knock of metal, as if she were placing a saucepan on the stove.

He crossed the room silently and, opening the front door, ducked round the far side of the house, so that she should not see him passing the kitchen windows.

The rubbish heap was at the end of the garden, behind a row of currant bushes and, as he squatted down and spread the letters and photos out in a loose pile, he could smell the hot, pungent odour of their leaves. Still crouching, he lit a match and, sheltering it in the palm of his hand, carried it down to the papers. The flame, almost invisible in the bright light of the late afternoon sun that flooded the garden with a level, golden radiance, touched the corner of a snapshot and ran quickly across the glazed paper. As he watched the smiling face char and buckle, he felt a sense of pleasurable satisfaction that at the same time shocked him. His decision to burn them wasn't, he realised, merely to prevent them falling into the hands

of the police. Much stronger were his own motives of
personal revenge, as if by burning the pictures and
letters he could finally rid himself of the man. And
that was as pointless as trying to beat Rudd at his
own game.

He got to his feet, staring moodily down at the
burning fragments. The flames had almost finished
their work, flickering across the last scraps of paper in
little, licking spurts, smokeless in the still, warm air.
The cover of one of the wedding photographs began
opening slowly in the heat, as if turned by an unseen
hand but he didn't wait to see it. Instead, he began
walking back along the path towards the house,
remembering the contempt in Betty's voice when she
had asked him what he was going to do with them.

Perhaps she was right. Perhaps he was contempt-
ible. But whatever she thought, they were bloody
well gone now. Too late to get them back. Too late to
salvage anything from the God-awful mess.

He pushed open the door into the kitchen with a
feeling of angry resentment. Charlie was already
there, washing noisily at the sink, throwing drops of
water over the floor as he swilled his face and arms.

"What you been doin', Geoff?" he asked, looking
up, his hair wet and spiky.

"Nothing," Lovell replied roughly. "Move over."

He washed his own face and hands quickly, taking
the towel from Charlie before he had finished with it.

"Here! I ain't done drying myself," Charlie protested.

"You take too bloody long," Lovell told him.

Going over to the table, he jerked out a chair and
sat down. Betty was placing a dish of potatoes in the
centre of the table and he looked deliberately into her
face.

"It's done," he told her, watching for her reaction.
Her face remained inscrutable. The lowered eyes,
veiled by her lashes, gave nothing away. Perversely,
he wanted to provoke a response, as Rudd had tried
to do with him.

"I said it's done," he repeated in a louder voice.

"I heard you the first time," she replied flatly and,

moving away from the table, began getting out plates from the rack over the sink. He watched her covertly out of the corner of his eyes.

From the back, she still looked young, with her thin body. He saw the bony elbows jutting out from the rolled-up sleeves of her dress and the child-like upper arms, so small that he could span them with his finger and thumb. Her hair, which was tied back anyhow, had begun to spring back into waves in the steam from the boiling saucepans and he suddenly remembered the photographs of her as a girl, with her hair loose.

Christ! And she had to go and marry *him!*

Weren't there plenty of other women he could have taken and left her alone? That girl in Harlsdon, for instance. Nancy. He'd been knocking about with her before he went into the army and even after he'd come back, married to Betty, it hadn't taken him long to pick up with her again. And he knew Ron had been writing to her after he'd been called up.

God! Photos! Could he have given her a photograph of himself? Perhaps one of the snapshots he'd had taken. It hadn't occurred to him before but it was possible. It was the sort of thing Ron would do.

Supposing the police found out he'd known her? From what Rudd had said, they'd evidently made inquiries in the village about Ron. It only took one person to mention that he'd been going out with a girl from Harlsdon to put the Inspector on her trail. Bob Deal and Frankie Cotter knew about her, for a start. They were two of that group who had been youngsters then, roaring off on their motor-bikes evening after evening into the town. . . .

He had a sudden, vivid memory of Ron standing in front of the sink, ducking slightly at the knees in order to see himself in the little, square mirror that hung on the wall above, combing back his hair with long sweeps of the comb and then turning round, settling the collar of his jacket and asking with that bloody, pleased grin of his:

"Well, d'you reckon they'll fancy me tonight?"

Lovell thrust his chair back and got up from the

table, aware of the startled expressions on the faces of Betty and Charlie at his abrupt movement.

"I'm going out," he announced.

This time he did get a reaction from her.

"But I'm just going to serve up the supper," she protested.

"Then stick it back in the oven," he replied over his shoulder, as he made for the door.

It was how Ron would have spoken to her, confident, uncaring, selfishly absorbed in his own needs, and it gave Lovell a certain shameful and guilty satisfaction that, for once in his life, he could find the courage to behave to her in exactly the same way.

Chapter 9

When Rudd arrived at Stebbing's farm, he found
Boyce already waiting with Kyle and two other constables, equipped with spades and measuring tapes.
Boyce raised his eyebrows to indicate interest in how
the interview with Lovell had gone but Rudd shook
his head. It wasn't something he wanted to discuss in
front of the other men.

They walked to the field where Rudd set the two
constables to the job of filling in the grave. It had
been measured, photographed, thoroughly examined.
There was no more evidence that it could possibly
yield and yet he watched them throw in the first few
spadesful of earth with regret. A man's body had lain
there. Soon it would be nothing more than an oblong
patch of raw earth and that, too, wouldn't remain for

long. The grass would take over again and by next summer there would be no sign that it had ever existed. It seemed to him the dead man should have had a more permanent memorial, although there was a rightness about it, too, that he recognised.

He turned away, leaving the men to their task, and began walking across the field to where Boyce and Kyle were measuring the distance from the grave to the excavation, the tarpaulin cover of which had been rolled back.

"Sixty feet five inches," Kyle called out and Boyce, having made a note of it, began winding in the tape.

Rudd strolled over and stood looking down at the site, his hands in his pockets. There wasn't much to see. For a few square yards, the turf and top-soil had been removed, revealing a yellowish layer of more densely packed earth in which several darker patches, roughly circular in shape, were clearly visible. Squatting down, he gently poked at the soil in one of them with a finger. It was finer in texture and more granular than the surrounding clay.

"Know what these are?" he asked, looking up. Boyce shrugged indifferently. Kyle, more anxious to create a good impression on a superior officer, frowned heavily as if trying to recollect some temporarily forgotten knowledge.

"Post-holes," Rudd told them. "According to Rose, this could be the site of some Saxon building, a farmhouse, say. Interesting to think people were living here all that time ago."

Expressing the thought out loud only partly exorcised the impression the field gave him. Besides, it was something more than a mere sense of history. If he had to define it, he would have explained it as a feeling of brooding presence, a weight in the atmosphere that wasn't, strangely enough, an unpleasant sensation, although there was a solemnity in it and an air of waiting. It reminded him of an occasion when, as a child, he had explored the empty rooms of a large, derelict house on the outskirts of the village where he lived. Like the field, they were full of sunlight so there was nothing sinister about them and he had felt no fear as he walked through them, only a sense of loss, even though he had never lived there, and the same feeling of sad withdrawal as if those who had once occupied those rooms had vacated them only temporarily and were waiting somewhere, he didn't know exactly where, to re-occupy them. It had been the first occasion that he had been aware of the concept of time; an endless chain of years, it seemed, stretching in front and behind him, which was probably why the memory and its attendant emotion had remained so vividly with him to be stirred into life again by the evocation of a similar response that, for some inexplicable reason, this area of rough grass with its surrounding trees and mounds of earth had roused in him.

"Saxons?" Boyce was asking. "Aren't they the lot with the horns on their helmets?"

"You're thinking of Vikings," Rudd corrected him.

"Oh, well," Boyce replied, lapsing once again into indifference.

"Angles, Saxons and Jutes," Kyle announced unexpectedly. Boyce and Rudd turned to look at him in surprise. "Came from the continent. First started raiding along the east coast before the Romans left. Stayed on to settle and farm. Took over from the Celts. Big, blond people. Good warriors. Pagan."

He tailed off, looking embarrassed.

"Well done, laddy," Boyce remarked with heavy humour. "Come and sit in the front."

Kyle coloured up.

"We did the Saxons once at school," he explained defensively. "I don't remember much more about them except they used to build timbered halls where they met to drink mead."

" 'The flight of a sparrow,' " Rudd said half to himself. He was struggling with a school memory of his own but it was too vague to put into words. Something to do with life being like a bird flying from the darkness into a lighted hall and out again at the far end, into darkness again. Who had said it? He couldn't remember but he felt sure it had some Saxon connection. Perhaps Rose would know.

"What . . . ?" Boyce began but Rudd was spared the embarrassment of trying to explain by the arrival of the two constables, who had finished filling in the grave and were coming towards them, wiping their faces.

"We'll push off then," said Rudd. "We've done all we can here. Better get the site covered over before we go."

When Boyce and Kyle had rolled the tarpaulin over the excavated area, they set off to walk back to Stebbing's farm, skirting the cornfield, rich gold now in the drying sun, and then striking across the pasture beyond to the yard where Stebbing was waiting for them, exuding curiosity.

"Any news?" he asked.

"Inquiries are proceeding," Rudd replied in his best official voice and saw Boyce cough and cover his mouth to hide a smile. "You can tell Mr. Rose, by the way, that we've finished with the field so he and his society can move back into it any time they like."

"Right. I'll tell him," Stebbing replied. He was obviously on edge, fidgeting from foot to foot as he stood in front of them, his eyes roving across their faces, searching for any give-away expression, and Rudd wondered if Wheeler hadn't been stirring things up by dropping a few of his sly little hints in order to whet Stebbing's inquisitiveness.

"Mrs. Stebbing would be only too glad to offer you a cup of tea," the farmer went on. He seemed anxious to keep them there, no doubt in the hope of pumping them further. "There's beer but I suppose as you're on duty . . ."

Rudd thought longingly of beer, cool and bitter, but even tea would be better than nothing. He saw the men's faces light up at the thought of something to drink and he was about to accept reluctantly for their sake when Stebbing glanced quickly over his shoulder towards the gate where a battered grey van was just passing the farm entrance.

"Funny," he remarked. "That's Lovell. I wonder where he's off to at this time of the evening."

Rudd made a rapid decision. Looking at his watch,

he said hurriedly, "I'm sorry, Mr. Stebbing. I've just remembered a conference at headquarters. Boyce, you'd better come with me. Kyle as well. You other two can make your own way back."

As they walked towards the car, Boyce asked, "What conference? First I've heard of it. I was dying for a cup of tea, too."

He sounded aggrieved.

"Get in the back and don't argue. I don't want Lovell to see either of us," Rudd told him. "Kyle, you take the keys and drive. You're to follow the van that's just passed. Don't get too close but, if you value your head, don't lose him."

As he climbed into the back with Boyce, the sergeant asked, "What's the idea?"

"Lovell's up to something. I don't know what but I think it's to do with my visit this afternoon. I must have got him rattled enough to leave the farm and I reckon he wouldn't do that without good reason."

They had driven up the lane and were turning left onto the main road, in the direction of Harlsdon. Lovell's van, hidden from them round the bends of the lane, was now visible ahead of them on a straight stretch of road.

"Drop further back," Rudd told Kyle. "I don't want him to see us."

They slowed down to a sedate thirty miles an hour. There was very little other traffic about. A couple of cars passed them going in the opposite direction and that was all. In the gentle evening light, the countryside seemed empty and peaceful, resting quietly after the heat of the day.

"How did the interview go?" Boyce was asking.

"Quite well. Lovell didn't give much away but, then, he never does. I found out one thing, though. Two people are sharing the double bed in the best room."

"Geoff Lovell and Betty?"

"It looks like it."

"So if Ron Lovell came back and found . . ."

"Let's leave out the speculation for the moment," Rudd replied, with a warning look at Kyle's back.

"We'll need a lot more evidence before that charge can be made to stick." He glanced out of the window at the passing fields. "I wonder where he's making for and why?"

"It looks like Harlsdon," Boyce replied.

He was right. Soon afterwards they were entering the town, which began abruptly, with no intervening suburbs, the countryside that surrounded it giving way to a scattering of houses, and then they were driving through the deserted main street, the shops closed, the pavements empty of people. It was a town that had escaped the worst of modern development, although there had been changes over the years. But, at heart, it remained unaltered: a country market town that served the surrounding villages and hamlets and where the slow, local dialect could still be heard in the streets.

Ahead of them, Lovell's van was turning into the car-park of the Blue Boar, which faced the old market hall.

"Draw in at the side of the road," Rudd instructed Kyle.

With the engine turned off, the Inspector was aware of the silence of the town in which the pealing of church bells being rung for an evening practise sounded unnaturally loud and insistent on the quiet air and added to the feeling of Sabbath calm. To it was suddenly added the sharp slam of a car door and Lovell came into sight, walking quickly, his dark head bent forward, and clearly unaware of their presence for he didn't so much as glance in their direction as he went in at the front entrance of the Blue Boar.

"Give him five minutes," Rudd told Kyle, "and then I want you to follow him inside."

Lovell entered the saloon bar, where he knew Nancy Fowler was most likely to be found at that time of the evening, and noticed her straightaway, sitting at a table by herself against the far wall, an empty glass in front of her. As he walked towards her, she looked up, her face expressing astonishment and, to his embarrassment, pleasure as well.

"My God!" she exclaimed. "Geoff Lovell! After all this time. You're a bloody bad penny, aren't you?"

"Hello Nancy," he said awkwardly. "Let me buy you a drink. What'll you have?"

"The usual."

He couldn't remember what it was and, seeing the look on his face, she guessed this and laughed.

"Gin and orange, ducky. And a packet of cheese and onion crisps as well," she called after him as he turned back to the bar.

As he ordered the drinks, Lovell noticed the landlord's expression, tight-lipped and disapproving. He banged the change down on the counter, ignoring Lovell's outstretched hand, and Lovell could guess the cause of it. Nancy was on the loose again.

Well, it doesn't matter, he told himself. I'll be out of the place in half an hour at most.

Carrying the drinks over to the table, he sat down opposite her, taking in the details of her appearance for the first time. She had changed a lot since the last time he had seen her; coarsened and put on weight. The thin summer dress she was wearing revealed plump arms and too much of her breasts, pushed up high and close together so that the cleft between them showed as a dark crack. Her hair was a different colour, too, from what he remembered; reddish and unnaturally stiff so that when she moved her head it remained curiously static; more like a hat than real hair. She was sweating underneath her heavy make-up and tiny beads of perspiration had gathered across her forehead and in the folds of her nose.

"Well and how's the world treating you?" she was asking.

"All right," he replied.

"Still got the farm?"

"Yes."

He had forgotten how to talk to her and, besides, there was nothing much now that he wanted to say to her, despite her easy assumption that they could pick up the old topics as if they were back on their familiar footing.

"How are you keeping, Nance?" he asked, switching the subject away from himself.

She shrugged, her mouth suddenly going sulky.

"All right, I suppose."

"Still working at the same place?"

"No. I chucked that. I'm at the egg-packing plant now. Bloody awful hours and on your feet all day long, too."

"You're looking well, though. Your hair's nice."

He offered the compliment clumsily but she was pleased and put up a hand to touch it.

"Noticed it, did you? I've had it tinted. It's called 'Auburn Dawn.'"

"It suits you," he told her gravely.

"Well, you have to do something to cheer yourself up. You could rot in this hole and nobody'd notice."

There was a complaining note in her voice and he turned the conversation again, shifting uncomfortably in his chair.

"The boys all right?"

"Oh, Christ," she said. "Don't talk to me about those little buggers."

"I'm sorry, Nance," he said and meant it.

"What for?" she asked sharply.

He made a movement with one hand, indicating everything, and, understanding him, her face softened.

"It's not your fault," she said. "And don't take no notice of me. I'm a bit fed up, that's all. But I'll get over it. Bloody well have to, won't I?"

"I could lend you a bit of cash if it's money that's worrying you," he said humbly and she leaned forward to pat his hand.

"You're a good old sod but hang on to your money," she told him. "You need it as much as me. Betty all right?" she added unexpectedly.

The question caught him off guard and he looked quickly into her face, wondering how much she knew. But she couldn't suspect anything, he decided. Besides, her expression was the same as it always was when she spoke of Betty, politely interested and a little pitying, as if she were asking after some sick relative. All the same, it was a subject that he wanted to avoid and it was time, anyway, he thought, that he got to the point.

"She's keeping well," he said and added hurriedly, "Look, Nance, there's something I wanted to ask you."

"About Betty?"

"No. About Ron."

"Ron?" she asked quickly. "You haven't heard from him?"

"No."

He was finding it harder than he had imagined and wished now that he had taken more time to think out what he was going to say to her. He didn't want to give too much away and yet he would have to make it sound urgent enough to convince her.

"I've had the police round to see me," he explained. "They didn't say much but it's something to do with Ron. They were asking for a photo of him and, as I didn't want to get him into any trouble, I said we'd got rid of all ours . . ."

"He's in trouble with the police?" she interrupted.

"No. I don't know," he said impatiently. "They didn't go into details. But, look, Nance, suppose he is. I thought it best to come over and see you, just in case you'd got a photo of him and they came asking . . ."

"How would they find out about me?"

"I don't know. But they might. You know what they're like, snooping round, asking questions."

"I wouldn't bloody tell them anything if they did."

"But have you got any photos of Ron?" he asked, close to desperation.

He saw her face close over with the stubborn look he'd seen before.

"I might have. I don't remember. I might have chucked them out."

"Will you have a look?"

"I might."

"Will you, *please?*"

She became suddenly and unexpectedly angry.

"You and your brother make a right bloody pair!" she said, her voice rising. "Both of you drop me like a hot brick when it suits you and then come whining back when you want some bloody favour doing."

The landlord looked up and began lifting the counter flap as if to come across to them.

"Keep your voice down, Nancy," Lovell urged her. "People are looking."

"Let them bloody look," she replied, but he noticed she spoke more quietly. "Let them have an eyeful. Him and all," she added, nodding towards the landlord, who had retreated behind the bar again but was still watching them suspiciously. "Rotten, sodding old git he is. Just looking for a chance to throw me out. Well, I don't bloody care. I'll drink where I like. My money's as good as anyone else's."

"I'll make it right by you," he said quickly, seizing on the mention of money, and, getting out his wallet, he took out a five pound note and slid it across the table towards her. "For your trouble," he explained.

For a few seconds, she looked at it without speaking, her face inexpressibly sad. Then she shrugged and picked it up.

"Why not?" she said. "Ron's borrowed enough off of me in his time."

"He owes you money?" Lovell asked.

"He owes me, but not money," she replied bitterly and he was silent, not knowing what to reply.

"It's all right," she said in a gentler voice. "I don't blame you for what he did. And I'll have a look for them photos. I've got some somewhere. For, when all's said and done, I don't want to drop him into any trouble, more fool me."

"I'll come back the same time next week to pick them up, shall I?" he asked, getting to his feet. "You'll be here?"

"I'm always bloody here. Part of the fixtures, that's me."

"I'll be seeing you then, Nance," he said awkwardly and walked away, resisting the temptation to look back at her from the doorway.

Chapter 10

Rudd and Boyce watched him leave from the parked car.

"Are we going to follow him?" Boyce asked.

"No. My guess is he's only going home. We'll wait for Kyle."

Five minutes after Lovell had driven away, Kyle too emerged from the Blue Boar and got into the front seat, bringing with him the warm, yeasty smell of beer which Boyce sniffed at jealously.

"I had a pint," Kyle explained defensively. "I had to. I couldn't stand at the bar and drink nothing. It'd've looked suspicious."

"Never mind that," Rudd told him. "Did he meet anyone?"

"Yes. A woman. He seemed to know her quite well.

They talked normally for a few minutes and then she seemed to get angry and started raising her voice. The landlord didn't like it much. At one point, I thought he was going over to ask her to leave. He was watching her all the time after that."

"Interesting," murmured Rudd. "Why was that?"

Kyle flushed.

"I don't think he likes her being in there. By the look of her, she's on the game."

"Go on!" Rudd teased him gently. "What did she say when she got angry?"

"I didn't catch it all. Something about him, Mr. Lovell that i⟨, and his brother making a right b. pair."

In deference to Rudd's rank, he thought he ought to censor the swear word.

"Then Mr. Lovell calmed her down and I didn't hear any more. A bit later, though, he got out his wallet and passed something across the table to her."

"Money?" Rudd asked.

"I think so but I'm not sure. It could have been a piece of paper. Soon after that, Mr. Lovell left."

Rudd thought quickly. It seemed likely that the woman's remark about Lovell's brother almost certainly referred to Ron, and this piece of information, added to the gossip that Boyce had picked up in the village about Ron Lovell spending his evenings in Harlsdon, suggested to the Inspector that she was someone he had known in the past. He got out of the car, announcing:

"I'm going to have a chat with her."

"You can't miss her," Kyle assured him. "She's a big red-head sitting at one of the tables in the saloon bar."

Boyce's face looked up longingly from the open passenger window.

"Bring us out a drink afterwards," he begged. "My tongue's sticking to the roof of my mouth."

"If you can hang on, we might all be able to go inside later for a pint of the best," Rudd told him and, strolling over to the door of the Blue Boar, went into the saloon bar.

There was no mistaking her. She was sitting, as Kyle had said, at a table, although he doubted Kyle's assumption that she was on the game for, as he bought himself a pint and carried it over towards her table, she looked up at him with a startled and slightly hostile expression. A professional tart would have given a potential customer more of a welcome. He could understand, however, Kyle's mistake. Her low-cut dress and heavy make-up certainly gave that impression, although there was something naïve about her as well. Rudd guessed she wasn't averse to picking up men but it would be on an amateur basis and probably only when she was a bit tight. He doubted if she ever did it for money. A few gins and the fleeting illusion of love would be enough.

"Do you mind?" he asked pleasantly, putting his hand on the back of an empty chair opposite her.

"Please yourself," she said indifferently, although he noticed she shot a look across at the landlord who, pausing in the act of wiping down the counter, was watching them closely.

"Warm this evening," Rudd went on.

She ignored him and, swallowing down what was left in her glass, began gathering up her handbag as if preparing to leave. There wasn't going to be time for any preamble. Rudd would have to plunge straight in.

"Mr. Lovell didn't stay very long," he remarked.

She sat down again suddenly with a bump.

"How the hell do you know?" she demanded.

"I followed him," Rudd replied promptly and, flipping open his identification, he held it briefly towards her.

"Oh, Christ," she said in a weary voice. "The bloody police."

"What did Mr. Lovell want?"

She hesitated and then seemed to recover some of her assurance.

"Nothing. Just a chat."

"About Ronnie Lovell?"

Her eyes didn't leave his face.

"We might have mentioned him in passing."

Rudd returned her gaze and, after a few seconds, her glance wavered.

"What's your name?" he asked in his official voice, kindly but impersonal.

"Mrs. Fowler. Nancy Fowler," she replied sulkily.

"Well, it won't do, Mrs. Fowler. You'll have to think up something better than that. I happen to know Geoff Lovell and I'm quite sure he didn't drive all the way over here at this time of the evening just for a chat. So what did he want?"

She ran her tongue over her lips.

"He—he wanted to know if Ron owed me any money."

"After fifteen years?"

"Well, not just Ron. He'd borrowed a bit of cash off me himself and he wanted to pay me back."

So it was money that Kyle had seen Lovell pass across the table, Rudd thought. That bit, at least, was true. All the same, she wasn't a very good liar. Lovell was, in his estimation, too proud to borrow money from a woman and besides, even if he had, Rudd didn't believe he had come rushing over to Harlsdon on a sudden impulse to pay it back.

He leaned forward, speaking in a low and confidential voice.

"Look, Mrs. Fowler, I don't want to make life awkward for you by taking you into headquarters in a squad car to make an official statement but unless you're prepared to help us ..."

He left the threat unfinished and it had its effect. She looked alarmed.

"I don't want no trouble," she told him. "I've got my job to think of and the house. It's Council you see ..."

"They're being difficult?" Rudd asked. He switched roles quickly, assuming the sympathetic, listening air of an older relative, prepared to give good advice.

"I've got behind with the rent," she explained. Her plump, heavily powdered face had collapsed into creases like a child's on the verge of tears. "And there's been complaints about the garden being left to go wild and the telly being on too loud. Bloody neighbours."

She sniffed noisily.

And men friends calling late at night, too, I shouldn't wonder, Rudd thought.

"But I don't want to drop Ron in it," she went on.

"Who said anything about Ron Lovell being in trouble?"

Her eyes widened.

"But Geoff said . . ."

"Look, I don't know what Mr. Lovell's told you . . ." Rudd began, deliberately leaving the sentence unfinished.

"He said the police had been round asking questions about Ron and that he must be in some kind of mess."

"Then he's got hold of the wrong end of the stick," Rudd assured her cheerfully. It was clear Geoff Lovell had told her nothing about the body of the dead man being found near his farm. "Yes, it's true we'd like to find Ron Lovell and ask him a few questions but it's only about a line of inquiry we think he can help us with. As far as I'm concerned, he may be useful but only as a possible witness."

It was near enough to the truth, he thought.

"So you don't want no photos of him?" Nancy Fowler asked.

"Photos?" Rudd asked too sharply and saw that he had put her on her guard. But it was too late to retrieve the situation and he went on, "You've got some photos of Ron?"

"I might have," she said warily. "I'm not sure. I told Geoff I'd have a look."

"He wants them?"

"Yes. He said he'd come back next week to pick them up."

"I'd like to see them first," Rudd told her. "They might be a great help in our inquiry."

She still hesitated.

"If you're sure Ron isn't in no trouble?"

"No. I've already told you. We'd like to interview him as a possible witness, that's all. A photograph of him would make our job of finding him a lot easier."

"You really think you can find him?"

The eagerness in her voice and face made the situation quite clear to Rudd. Nancy Fowler was in love with Ron Lovell and, in order to have him found and possibly brought back to her, she was prepared to risk anything, even handing over evidence to the police.

"I'm certainly going to try," Rudd assured her.

She came to a sudden decision.

"All right!" she said, getting to her feet. "I'll go and look for them. Do you want to wait here and I'll bring them back?"

"I'll come with you, if you don't mind," Rudd replied. He didn't think she'd give him the slip but, all the same, it would be useful to know where she lived.

She seemed reluctant at first and then agreed, shrugging.

"Please yourself. It's not far. You'll have to take the place as you find it, though. I haven't had time to clean it up."

They left together, going out into the street where the long shadows were already falling across the pavements, Rudd matching his pace to hers, which was slow and a little uncertain, a combination of high heels, a tight skirt and a few gins.

"Turn left here," she told him, a little further down the road. At the corner, Rudd glanced back and smiled to himself. Boyce was already getting out of the car with surprising alacrity for a man of his size and was making for the entrance of the Blue Boar.

Nancy Fowler's house was one of a small and new-looking Council development, tucked away behind the shops at the end of a narrow side street that suddenly opened out into a semi-circle of raw concrete and paving-stones, the houses fanning out round it, each with its own tiny front garden enclosed in galvanised wire netting.

As Nancy pushed open the gate and he followed her up the dead-straight path to the front door, he could see what she meant by complaints about the garden. Knee-high grass and weeds, heavy with pollen and seeds, grew on both sides of the path, in contrast to the minute lawns and rose beds, edged with lobelia, of the neighbouring gardens. The sound of the television was also apparent, blaring out of the

open window where grubby net curtains stirred list-
lessly in the warm air.

They entered a tiny hall, with a stair-case rising
steeply, and then went into the living-room that
opened from it.

It was quite a large room but so crowded with furniture and so untidy that it appeared much smaller. A
dining-table and chairs were pushed together under
the window while a three-piece suite, covered with
worn, rust-coloured fabric, was drawn up round a
fire-place of mottled tiles, the empty grate of which
was littered with spent matches and cigarette ends.
Two boys, one about fourteen, Rudd guessed, the
other a year or so younger, were sprawled in the arm-
chairs watching the television set, which stood on a
shelf beside the fire-place. Both had cigarettes in their
hands and the air was blue with smoke.

Nancy, her lips compressed angrily, stalked over to
the set and switched it off.

"I've told you before, don't have that bloody thing
on so loud. And put those ciggies away. I'm not going
out to work to keep you in bloody fags."

"You're back early, ain't you?" the eldest boy asked,
lounging to his feet. "Got chucked out?"

"You mind your lip," she told him, "else you'll get a
clump round the ear-hole. I've brought a friend back
for a talk."

"Oh, yeah?" the boy asked, his eyes moving inso-
lently across to Rudd. "*Talk?*"

"So the pair of you can clear off to the kitchen," she
went on, ignoring him.

"I ain't had nothin' to eat yet," the younger boy
complained.

"I told you, there's a pork pie and some cold potatoes in the fridge. You can have those."

"Phil's eaten all the spuds."

"Oh, Christ! Trust him! Come on then, I'll have to
cut you some bread."

She hustled them out into the kitchen, where Rudd
could hear her banging about and talking in a loud,
angry voice. While he waited for her to return, he
lowered himself gingerly into one of the sagging

arm-chairs and looked about him. Signs of Nancy's housekeeping, or lack of it, were everywhere about the room. Dirty cups, plates and overflowing ash-trays stood on the floor, the sideboard and along the top of the mantelpiece while the furniture, although comparatively new, was already battered and scarred. The arms of the chair in which he was sitting were dark and tacky with dirt.

She came back into the room, red in the face and flustered.

"Bloody kids!" she said. "Look at the mess they've made of this room."

Rudd made sympathetic noises although the disorder was not a mere evening's untidiness. It had taken time to build up that rich patina of squalor. She began futilely to pick up some of the scattered comics and clothes that lay cn the stained carpet and then plumped down onto the sofa, saying in an aggrieved voice:

"I don't see why the hell I should bother."

"The photographs," Rudd reminded her gently.

"Oh, God, yes. I'll go and look for them."

She evidently didn't have to look very far for she was back in the room within a few minutes and Rudd suspected that she had known all along where they were.

"Ron had them taken soon after he went into the army," she explained as she handed them over. "I said I wanted one of him in his uniform."

They were three small photographs on a strip, cut from one of those sheets of poly-photos that Rudd remembered had been popular at the time. Despite the smallness of their size, they were clear and showed in good detail the features of the man's face.

It was the first time he had seen a likeness of Ron Lovell and Rudd studied them with interest. There was very little family resemblance, he decided. Ron was smaller-featured and more finely boned, the jaw lighter and the hair-line further back from the forehead, although like Geoff he had dark hair and eyes and well-defined eyebrows. But the face lacked the heavy, brooding quality of his older brother. In all three photographs he was smiling with a cocky, self-assured expression and a bold, almost flirtatious look straight into the camera, as if he were chatting it up.

It was a mistake, Rudd knew, to read too much of a man's character in a photograph and yet he felt these three small portraits told him something about Lovell as a person. The Inspector had met his type before: self-confident, breezy, relaxed in his relationships with women, good-humoured, even generous when things went his way but basically the sort who thinks that life owes him a living, a permanent adolescent, and therefore quick to take advantage of anyone who was fool enough to let him get away with it. Nancy Fowler, too, he guessed.

He examined them for a second time, wondering if McCullum would be able to find anything in them to use in the making of a life-size enlargement. There was nothing in the way of a background and all three were only head and shoulder studies, two full-face, one slightly turned towards a three-quarter profile. In all of them he was wearing a uniform battle-dress top and was bare-headed, except for the last one in which he had on an army beret, worn at a more rakish angle than regulations permitted.

Well, McCullum will have to do his best, Rudd decided. He's the expert.

Nancy Fowler had come to stand behind his chair and was also looking at the photographs over his shoulder.

"They're a good likeness?" he asked, turning round to her. He saw her expression had softened and there was a sadness in her face.

"Oh, yes. They're the spitting image of Ron."

She pointed to the centre photograph.

"I like that one the best. I wanted him to have an enlargement done and he promised he would but he never did."

He noticed she was holding a piece of paper folded up small in one hand and he nodded towards it.

"Another photograph?" he asked. "May I see it?"

She hesitated before handing it over.

"You can look if you like. It's not such a good picture of Ron, though."

As he opened it out, he saw it was a newspaper cutting, old and well-handled, the paper already turning yellow, that contained a photograph of Ron and Betty Lovell on their wedding day. It was three-quarter length and showed them standing in what appeared to be a doorway, Ron wearing army uniform, Betty in a short-sleeved dress and a little hat, carrying a bunch of flowers in one hand while with the other she was clinging to his arm and leaning towards him, perhaps in order for both of them to be in the picture, her hair, shoulder-length and softly curled, touching his sleeve.

He could understand why Nancy Fowler had not thought it a good picture of Ron. He was unsmiling this time, staring out of the photograph with a surly look, more like his brother Geoff. Betty Lovell's face, younger, prettier, wore a nervous half-smile.

The caption below it read, "Local Girl Weds Soldier." It was followed by a short account of the wedding that Rudd read through quickly.

"Miss Elizabeth Mary Walsh was married on Saturday to Sapper Ronald Lovell, stationed locally with the Royal Engineers.

"The bride, who wore a dress of blue-flowered nylon voile, with a matching hat, and carried a bunch of pink carnations, was given away by Mr. Terence Bright, manager of the White Hart Hotel where Miss Walsh worked as a waitress.

"After a reception at the White Hart, where the bridal pair were presented with a canteen of cutlery by the staff, the couple left for a short honeymoon in Devon."

It was evidently a cutting from a Dorsetshire newspaper and Rudd asked curiously, "How did you get hold of it?"

"It just arrived by post one day," she replied, her mouth twisting wryly. "No letter with it but the envelope had a Dorset postmark so you can guess who sent it."

"Ron?" Rudd asked quietly.

"Hadn't the bloody nerve to write and say he'd got married so he sent the cutting instead. Do you think she's pretty?" she added unexpectedly.

Rudd studied the photograph with apparent seriousness, aware he was on dangerous ground.

"In a way, yes, I suppose she is," he admitted but with the right show of reluctance.

"A bit washed-out looking, if you ask me," Nancy said in a hard, positive voice. "One of them pale blondes, but he always was a sucker for fair hair. She hooked him, mind."

"Did she? How?"

Rudd looked interested.

"How do you think?" Nancy asked scornfully. "The usual way. Got pregnant so he had to marry her. I could have caught him the same way, if I'd wanted to, but I was only seventeen at the time and my dad would have beaten hell out of me. A right sod, my old man was. It's different today, though, isn't it? Bits of kids sleeping around, having babies. It's all wrong."

There was a moralising tone in her voice that was genuine enough.

"She hasn't got a child, has she?" Rudd asked sharply, wondering if this was another secret of the Lovell household that he hadn't yet uncovered.

"Miscarried," Nancy told him. "Had a couple more misses, too, after that one. They took her into hospital with the last and did something so that she couldn't have any more." She made a vague, embarrassed gesture in the region of her own stomach, indicating an operation. "Said it'd kill her if she did. Ron told me. Mind you, I felt sorry for her in a way. She was only a kid herself and Ron wasn't much help. He'd started drinking again. 'You ought to be home looking after her,' I told him. But he wouldn't listen. It wasn't long after she'd had the operation that he cleared out. 'I've had about bloody enough,' he said, 'what with her sick half the time and Geoff ordering me about. I'll write,' he said. But he never did."

"So you don't know where he went?"

"If I did, I'd've gone after him," she said promptly.

"It was me he should have married, anyway, not her. I'd've seen he kept out of trouble."

"Trouble?" Rudd asked. "Was there some sort of trouble?"

"Oh, nothing much. He got drunk a few times, that's all. Being young, he didn't know how to hold his drink. And he got put on a couple of charges when he was in the army, once for having a punch-up with another soldier. He was quick-tempered, see. But he'd've been all right with me. I understood him."

It was said with the absolute assurance of a woman who believes in the reforming power of love.

"'Stead of which," she went on, "he marries *her* and I marry someone who clears off and leaves me with a couple of kids to bring up on my own and no money. Still, that's life, I suppose."

"You've never met her?" Rudd asked.

"No and I don't want to."

Rudd said nothing, although he understood her feelings. In Nancy Fowler's eyes, Betty Lovell had done the inexcusable thing of taking away her man. He thought of Betty, exhausted, her face drawn down to the bone, and saw the irony of it all.

"Still," Nancy Fowler was saying with a triumphant air, "he left her, too, in the end, didn't he?"

"Yes," Rudd agreed. "He did."

He had suddenly had enough and he got to his feet. There were other questions he wanted to ask but they could wait until another occasion.

"If I may keep the photographs for a few days, Mrs. Fowler?" he asked, deliberately using formal, official language.

"If you like. But what do I say to Geoff when he comes for them?"

"I'll see that they're returned to you before then."

"Well, you know where to find me; either here or round at the Blue Boar."

"I'd be grateful if you didn't say anything to Mr. Lovell," he went on. "There's no need for him to know at this stage."

She shrugged.

"Please yourself. I'll just hand them over, then, and keep my mouth shut."

She saw him to the door.

"You'll let me know when you find Ron?" she asked, with the same eagerness that she had shown before.

"Of course," he assured her blandly.

"He might . . ."

She laughed suddenly, looking young and happy, but she didn't finish the sentence.

Come back to her, Rudd supposed she meant.

As he thanked her politely for her trouble, he saw her colour up with pleasure. It was probably the first time for years that anyone had shown her that kind of courtesy and, as he walked away, he felt something of the same compassion towards her that he felt for Betty Lovell, the other woman in Ron's life.

Chapter 11

All the same, the interview with Nancy Fowler had left a sour taste in his mouth, and later, when he joined the other two in the saloon bar of the Blue Boar, he was relieved that Kyle's presence made it impossible to discuss the interview at length with Boyce, except for a brief and hurried explanation in the few moments while they were alone at the table when the constable lingered at the counter buying cigarettes.

Rudd was still feeling angry and obscurely guilty. Angry with her for the mess she had managed to make of her life; the dirt and confusion that surrounded her; the futility of it all. Angry with Ron Lovell, who had walked into her life and out again with no thought of the damage he was doing. Angry with himself for reacting in so personal a way.

He found the guilt less easy to rationalise, except he felt he had used her and, quite unwittingly, raised her hopes that Ron Lovell might one day come back to her. But even that exasperated him. It had all the ingredients of cheap, romantic fiction and he knew that the reality would be very different from the dream.

Kyle joined them at the table and the talk shifted to other matters. Rudd began slowly to recover his good humour and, by the time they returned to headquarters, most of the oppressive effect of Nancy Fowler's personality had lifted.

"There you are!" he said with a triumphant air, spreading the photographs out on the desk for Boyce's inspection. "Ron Lovell!"

"And you got them off that woman Geoff Lovell met in the pub?" Boyce asked, picking them up to look at them.

"Yes. Nancy Fowler. Evidently an old flame of Ronnie's. In fact, she was hoping he would marry her but he married Betty instead."

He pointed to the newspaper cutting.

"There's a picture of them on their wedding day. Read the bit underneath and see if you can find anything odd about it."

Boyce read it through, muttering every third word aloud to himself. When he had finished, Rudd asked, "Well?"

"Nothing much that I can see," Boyce replied, "except it strikes me it was a bit rushed. 'Short honeymoon spent in Devon.' It doesn't sound exactly lavish. *He* doesn't look too pleased, either," he added, indicating Lovell's sullen face.

"Shot-gun wedding," Rudd explained briefly. "Betty Lovell was pregnant. She lost the baby later and couldn't have any more."

Some of the angry pity he had felt earlier in the evening returned to him and he broke off suddenly. Boyce, unaware of this, was saying, "In that case, it's safe for her and Geoff to have an affair, if that's what they're doing. There'd be no risk of her having a child."

"That's true," agreed Rudd. "But to get back to the cutting—there's nothing about it that seems odd?"

Boyce shook his head.

"No mention of her parents," Rudd explained, "even though it says 'Local Girl Weds Soldier' under the photograph. And she was given away by the manager of the hotel where she worked."

"Perhaps her people didn't approve, especially if she was pregnant," Boyce said, without much interest. "I've known it happen—to a girl I went to school with. Her parents washed their hands, as they say. Didn't turn up at the church and her mother used to pass her in the street and not speak. Daft."

"It could be like that, I suppose," Rudd replied. "I'll ask Nancy Fowler when I take the photos back. She may know something. From what she said, I gather she knew Ron before he went into the army and started seeing him again after he came out, although by that time he was married to Betty. According to her, he was fed up with the way things were going on the farm; fed up with his marriage, too, and told her he was clearing out, although she denied knowing where he went. And I've got good reason to believe her. She'd've gone with him if she'd known. She did let drop one interesting piece of information, though, and I'd like you to check on it tomorrow. In fact, if I'd had my wits about me, I might have tumbled to it before, from the gossip we've already picked up about Ron Lovell. It's possible he'd been in trouble with the police. Nancy said he'd been drunk a few times. So get hold of the records, will you, and see if he's ever been booked? She also mentioned he'd been put on a couple of charges while he was in the army."

"I've sent for his army records," Boyce put in. "They're not through yet."

"Right. There's something else, too, that's worth following up. When I see McCullum tomorrow, I'll get him to make an extra copy of one of the photographs to send up to the Yard for the *Police Gazette*, together with a description. Some other force may have him on their books and recognise him. If he was in trouble with the law down here, the chances are he may have been picked up since. It could be a way of finding out where he went after he left the farm. Besides, it might explain why he came back, if that's what he did; a point we haven't considered yet. We've got a pretty good idea why he left. He was tired of the farm, his marriage, the life he was leading. Given those reasons, why did he come back? He couldn't have expected anything would be drastically changed. But supposing the police somewhere were looking for him? That could have been enough to force him home. It was the excuse, too, that Geoff Lovell gave to Nancy Fowler when he asked for the photographs—that Ron was in trouble with the police and he didn't want them falling into our hands. There might be some truth in it."

"It shows one thing," Boyce pointed out. "Geoff Lovell has something to hide. He was damned quick off the mark in trying to get his hands on the photographs before we did."

"Oh, yes," Rudd agreed. "The man's no fool. I think I'll pay him another visit tomorrow. We've obviously got him worried and I think the time's ripe to stir things up a bit more. I'd like you to come with me this time. It'll make it look more official but leave the talking to me. I want you to keep your eyes open, though. We'll tell him we want to measure the distance from his farm to the field where the body was found. How does that strike you as a reason for calling on him?"

"Feeble. It's something a couple of constables could do on their own."

"Good. That's just what I hope Lovell will think, too, so we may get him even more rattled. By the way, I don't want the photos mentioned. He's not to know I've seen Nancy Fowler and borrowed them from her."

He gave them a final glance before putting them away in the drawer.

"Let's shut up shop, Tom. We've done all we can for today. Tomorrow, I'll get McCullum to look them over and, with a bit of luck, we might be a step nearer proving who it is we've dug up."

The next morning, as he spread the photographs out again for McCullum to examine, Rudd tried to conceal his impatience as the man bent his long body over them, studying them intently through a powerful magnifying glass that he had taken from the bulging pockets of his jacket.

"Any good?" Rudd was forced to ask at last.

McCullum merely grunted and went on looking. Presently he put the glass down and said grudgingly:

"The newspaper photograph is out; the definition's too poor. But the smaller ones are not too bad. I should be able to make a decent enlargement from one of those."

"A life-size one?" Rudd asked, trying not to sound too eager.

McCullum pursed his lips doubtfully.

"Well, now, that depends. There's not a lot of detail in any of them that I could use to make exact measurements."

"What about the clothing?" Rudd persisted, determined not to be put off by McCullum's lack of enthusiasm. "The battle-dress would be standard issue. Couldn't you measure something on that? The collar, for instance, or the shoulder tabs?"

"Not one that would stand up as exact evidence and I take it that's what you're looking for? We're dealing here with two different dimensions, you understand; the flat, two-dimensional photograph and the living, three-dimensional man. Look at your own jacket," he added, taking Rudd by the lapels. "I could take, say, the width of the collar and then measure it again with you wearing it, but I very much doubt if the two measurements would be exactly the same. You get me?"

"Yes," Rudd replied, sounding subdued, "I get you. So there's nothing in any of the photographs that you could use?"

"I didn't say that," McCullum snapped, with the obstinate expression of a man who doesn't like to have his decisions made for him. Picking up the magnifying glass, he resumed his study and Rudd, realising he would take his time, waited in silence.

"What regiment was he in?" McCullum asked suddenly.

The question was so unexpected that, for a moment, Rudd couldn't remember what Geoff Lovell had told him. Then he recalled it.

"The Royal Engineers."

"Then I could have good news for you," McCullum went on, permitting his face to break into a slow smile. "See the last photograph? The one in which he's wearing the army beret? You get me a Royal Engineer's cap badge and I might be able to make you that blow-up. The detail in the photograph is quite good and if I used a lay head to get the exact angle, it might work. Lighting it will be tricky though," he added, lapsing into his usual melancholy at the thought of it.

"That is good news," Rudd replied, subduing his jubilation. "Mind if I have a look?"

McCullum handed him the glass and Rudd held it over the photograph. The badge leapt forward in amazing detail. He could make out the wreath of leaves that surrounded it and the crown that surmounted the central motto. Fascinated by this new, enlarged dimension, he moved the glass across the rest of the face, seeing the eyes and then the mouth in single, disembodied close-up. He turned it next on the newspaper cutting and saw at once what McCullum meant by poor definition. The individual grey and black dots with which the picture was composed became, under the powerful lens, too enlarged and broke up the outlines of the features. Betty's face became a mere chiaroscuro of shaded circles in which the details were lost. Holding the lens further away, he tried to adjust the magnification so that the nervous half-smile, diffident and shy, was in better focus.

Suddenly he stopped.

"McCullum," he said quickly, "take a look here."

McCullum took the glass from him and bent over the cutting.

"The girl's neck," Rudd explained. "What's she wearing round it?"

"Looks like a chain of some sort," McCullum replied, after a maddening pause.

"Can you see what's on the end of it?"

McCullum moved the lens down a fraction of an inch.

"No. Whatever it is, it's hidden below the neck of her dress."

"Damn!" Rudd said softly.

McCullum looked up.

"Something important?"

"It could be. Remember that crucifix that was found in the grave? Could it be the chain to that?"

McCullum shrugged.

"It could be. I wouldn't like to commit myself, though."

"It's gone up to forensic in London for a detailed examination. They'll send photographs of it once it's been cleaned up. Any chance you could make an enlargement of the chain the girl's wearing for comparison?"

"I could certainly enlarge it but if you're hoping to prove they're the same by comparing the links, you're out of luck. The definition's too poor for me to raise that sort of detail."

It was exactly what Rudd had been hoping for, although he kept the disappointment out of his face. It was expecting too much. But at least it proved that Betty Lovell had possessed a chain. Whether or not a cross had hung on the end of it was another matter.

McCullum had put away the magnifying glass and was gathering up the photographs.

"If that's all I'll get started on the enlargement as soon as I get the badge. Anything else you want done with them?"

"I'd like several copies made of all of them—I've got to return the originals—and an extra one to send up to the Yard for the *Police Gazette*. It had better be one of the full-face photos. I'll leave the choice to you. How soon can you let me have them?"

"On your desk by lunch-time?" McCullum replied. "The life-size blow-up will take longer, say a couple of days."

At the door he added, "I'll do my best with the chain but I'm not promising anything."

He went out, almost colliding with Boyce, who came bustling in, looking pleased with himself and announcing:

"I've checked with the Harlsdon police. Lovell *was* picked up by them, three times altogether; twice for being drunk and disorderly; once for riding that motor-bike of his without due care and attention. He was fined on all three occasions. So you could be right about him being picked up by the police since."

"It's worth a try," agreed Rudd.

"What did McCullum have to say?"

"There's a good chance he can make a life-size enlargement for us, using the cap badge in one of the small photos. So get hold of Kyle and send him out to borrow a Royal Engineers badge from somewhere. The local army recruiting office ought to have one. After that, when McCullum's finished making them, I want him to take a copy of one of the photos up to the Yard for the *Gazette*. I'll draft out a description to go with it. That's one line of inquiry we can put into operation straightaway. The life-size enlargement won't be ready for a couple of days. But, as soon as it is, we can start work on the crucial issue in this case—proving whether or not it is Ronnie Lovell's body."

Boyce looked at Rudd covertly, aware of a peevish air about the Inspector that he couldn't account for. After all, with the investigation at last showing signs of getting off the ground, he ought to be more pleased.

"Something bugging you?" he asked tentatively.

"Yes, blast it, there is!" Rudd replied with more warmth. "The question of the crucifix has cropped up again." He explained briefly how he had noticed a chain round Betty Lovell's neck in the newspaper photograph. "Not that McCullum holds out much hope of enlarging it so that we can compare it with the chain found in the grave," he added.

"Well?" Boyce asked, puzzled why this small detail should cause the Inspector so much uneasiness.

"I still don't see where it fits in," Rudd explained.

It was only part of the truth, the rest of which he was reluctant to admit even to himself. Now that the case had begun to move out of the area of mere speculation and theory into the possibility of proof, he found himself in the unusual position of wishing to hold back. It was quite irrational, he told himself. He had no business to feel this way. And yet, their faces kept rising up in his mind to disconcert him: Betty's peeled down to the bone; Lovell's dark with a weight of brooding unhappiness that Rudd could only guess at.

"Did you ask Betty Lovell if she's owned a cross and chain?" Boyce was asking.

"No, I didn't," Rudd replied snappily. At times he found Boyce's literal-mindedness a source of exasperation. "I only saw her alone for a few minutes. I'll make a point, though, of asking her this afternoon."

"I still don't think it's got any bearing on the case," Boyce went on, hoping mistakenly that by playing down its importance he might put the Inspector in a more cheerful frame of mind.

"Why not?" Rudd asked.

"Well, look at it logically. In the first place, there's no proof that it is a cross and chain she's wearing in that photograph, let alone the same one. Women wear all sorts of things round their necks—those pendant do-dahs, for instance. Secondly, it wasn't found on the body, only near it. And what the hell was a cross and chain doing there anyway? Had he pinched it, hoping to flog it? But, according to Pardoe, it's only silver-plated, so he couldn't have hoped to get much for it. Or had he torn it off her neck, in a struggle, say? Got it tangled up in his clothing? That doesn't sound very likely to me and, even if he had, it'd still be on him."

"It could have been placed there," Rudd said slowly. The impression that he had received when he stood alone in the field at dusk returned to him, only dimly, and all he was left with was a fleeting feeling of something significant that was vaguely connected with death and darkness, ritual and sacrifice, that was gone as soon as he tried to analyse it.

"By her?" Boyce asked.

"I don't know. By one of them."

Boyce sniffed disbelievingly.

"Why?"

"As a token."

"Of what?"

Rudd felt exasperation rising.

"I don't know. Love. Family feeling. People bury their dead with all sorts of keep-sakes—rings, love letters, locks of hair."

"From what I've heard of him, I can't see Ronnie Lovell inspiring that kind of devotion," Boyce objected.

"But we don't know," Rudd pointed out. "He was, after all, Betty's husband and Geoff's brother. They must have felt something towards him. Or it could be meant for what it is, a Christian symbol. We've got good reason to believe that somebody went to the trouble of laying the body out."

He offered the explanation reluctantly, knowing Boyce would have little sympathy with it.

"But they're not religious, are they?" Boyce demanded. "They certainly don't seem to be church-goers or we'd've heard about it from someone. Instead, all we *have* heard is that they keep themselves to themselves and don't mix in the village."

"That doesn't mean the crucifix had no significance," Rudd replied. He began to feel he was arguing intangibles. "Look, I'll tell you what we'll do. We'll drop in at Stebbing's farm first and ask Wheeler. He might know if Betty ever wore a crucifix."

But later that afternoon, when they called at the farm, Wheeler wasn't much help. He had been sent for from the fields and obviously resented this and Rudd's renewed inquiries into what he considered a trivial matter.

"No, I ain't seen her wearing one," he said. "Is that all you've got me back here to ask?"

"You're sure?" Rudd pressed him.

"I've told you, ain't I? She never wore nothing in the way of jewellery, except for her wedding ring."

It was said with an air of angry certainty and yet

Rudd wasn't convinced. Wheeler didn't strike him as the type of man who would notice that kind of detail about a woman's appearance. Something of this doubt must have showed in his face for Wheeler went on:

"I made a point of looking, see? My mother left some bits and pieces, a couple of rings and stuff like that. I was going to ask her . . ."

He broke off and shot Rudd a furious glance, aware that he had said too much in his eagerness to prove himself right. Rudd kept his face bland as he asked the next question.

"Did any of the Lovell family ever go to church?"

"How the hell should I know?" Wheeler retorted and began stumping away across the yard, shouting back over his shoulder, "Ask Stebbing. He'll be able to tell you."

Rudd went to look for Stebbing and found him hanging about in one of the barns, having been politely but firmly excluded from the interview with Wheeler. He came forward eagerly as Rudd approached, putting the Inspector in mind of a large dog bounding up, tail wagging, for a little attention.

"You wanted me?" he asked.

"It's only a small point," Rudd replied. "Wheeler said you might be able to help. It's this—do any of the Lovells attend church?"

"I can see why Wheeler suggested you ask me," Stebbing replied, looking serious and important. "I go regularly to church myself. Never miss a Sunday if I can help it. After all, when you come to live in a small community, like a village, it's as well to join in, make yourself known. Not that I believe it all, mind. Funnily enough, I was discussing that very point with the vicar only the other day . . ."

"But have you ever seen any of the Lovells at church?" Rudd interrupted him.

"No," Stebbing admitted, reluctant to come to the point. "No. I can't say I have."

"Thank you, Mr. Stebbing," Rudd replied in his formal voice, walking away. Even then the man couldn't resist following him across the yard and, planting himself in front of Rudd, he announced with anxious officiousness, "I've been in touch with Mr. Rose. He's back in my field, with that society of his, digging. That's all right, isn't it? You did say I could tell him."

"Yes, that's quite all right," Rudd assured him and was about to side-step round him when he heard distinctly on the hot, still air the far-off sound of a dog barking savagely. He stopped and cocked his head inquiringly.

"That's Lovell's dog, isn't it?" he asked Stebbing.

"Sounds like it," Stebbing agreed. "I've got used to it so I don't take much notice when it starts up. It carries on like that two or three times a day sometimes. It's a good job there's a fair distance between the two farms or it could be a damned nuisance."

"Two or three times a day?" Rudd asked. "But the Lovells can't have that number of people calling at the farm?"

Stebbing shrugged.

"I shouldn't think so. Maybe it just likes barking its head off from time to time. Some dogs are like that. Anything'll set them off. A bit of paper blowing past. A bird. A door slamming. Mind you, they're not much good as guard dogs in my opinion."

Rudd made no reply, except to wish Stebbing good-bye, and walked on to meet Boyce, who was waiting in the car.

"Any luck?" he asked, as Rudd got into the seat beside him.

"Not on the cross and chain. Wheeler was quite adamant he'd never seen Betty Lovell wearing one and I've got good reason to believe him. He was thinking of offering her some of his mother's pieces of jewellery and, cautious man that he is, he had a good look first to see what she owned herself before thinking of parting with them. And Stebbing, who evidently likes to think of himself as a pillar of the community, hasn't seen any of them in church, so that's a dead end."

Boyce, leaning forward to start the engine, tried unsuccessfully to keep a smug, I-told-you-so expression off his face.

"There was one odd little incident, though," Rudd went on. "Did you notice it?"

"Only the look on Wheeler's face when you were talking to him," Boyce replied with happy malice. "That man hates your guts."

"I know," Rudd replied equably. "I've rumbled his secret and he knows it. No, I was referring to something else. Did you hear Lovell's dog barking?"

"Can't say I did," Boyce replied indifferently, turning the car into the narrow lane. "What of it?"

"You'll see in a minute. I'm going to try a little experiment. When we pull up at Lovell's farm, I want both of us to stay in the car for a couple of minutes."

"All right," Boyce agreed. "I don't see the point but . . ."

"You will," Rudd promised him.

They were approaching the entrance to the farm and, at Rudd's directions, Boyce drew the car off the road, bumping it up onto the grass verge, and then, switching off the engine, remained seated behind the wheel.

"Hear anything?" Rudd asked.

Boyce listened. There was no sound except for the faint soughing of a light wind in the top-most branches of the trees and the piercing song of a lark somewhere out of sight in the dazzle of the sky.

"Not a thing," Boyce replied.

"Come on," Rudd told him and, getting out of the car, slammed the door hard shut behind him. Again he stopped to listen but there was still no sound. Smiling, he beckoned to Boyce and began walking towards the gate. The sergeant followed, feeling a bit of a fool and wondering what all the pantomime was about.

At the gate, they paused, looking down into the yard. The concrete was blindingly white and almost shadowless in the sun; empty, too, apart from the black Labrador that, with ears erect and scruff already rising, was beginning to stalk, stiff-legged, up the driveway towards them, its lips drawn back in a silent snarl.

Rudd watched it carefully and then, putting his

hand on the gate, shook it so that the chain and padlock rattled. The next instant, the dog broke into a
frenzy of barking and came racing towards them to
fling itself against the bars.

"Christ!" exclaimed Boyce, stepping back in alarm.

"See what I mean?" Rudd shouted above the din.
"The dog didn't bark until I touched the gate and it
looked as if I were coming in. But, according to Stebbing, it sometimes barks two or three times a day. So
I ask myself, why?"

Boyce was about to shout back an answer when the
figure of Geoff Lovell emerged from behind the barn,
walked into the centre of the yard and, having sur-
veyed them deliberately for a few seconds, his hands
on his hips, began walking slowly towards them.

"Awkward devil," Rudd said happily and Boyce
looked at him in surprise at the note of admiration in
his voice. Now that the inquiry was under way, the
Inspector had lost any sense of a special sympathy for
Lovell, although he watched him with lively interest
as he approached them.

"Take your cue from me," Rudd added quickly but
Boyce had no time to reply, except to give a brief nod
of agreement, before Geoff Lovell was at the gate,
looking at them over it with a surly expression.

Chapter 12

"What do you want this time?" he asked.

"If you'll call the dog off, I'll explain," Rudd replied.

At first, Lovell seemed reluctant to agree, glancing back at the house as if to assure himself of something and then, seizing the dog by the collar, he began dragging it down the slope towards the barn where he fastened it to its chain. He seemed as if he were about to walk back towards them to speak to them over the gate but Rudd had already forestalled him by climbing nimbly over it and, dropping down on the other side, walked forward to meet him, leaving Boyce to follow more cautiously.

"Had visitors already this afternoon?" Rudd asked Lovell pleasantly as they met in the yard.

"What do you mean?" Lovell replied belligerently.

"I heard the dog barking a little earlier."

"My dog?"

"It must have been. There's no other dog along this lane, is there?"

Lovell didn't reply and Rudd cocked his head expectantly. At last, Lovell said slowly, "Oh yes, I remember. It started up barking when Charlie took the tractor out. Something fell off the back of the trailer."

That's a lie for a start, Rudd thought. If I heard the dog barking, I'm damned sure I'd've heard the tractor as well. Besides, it's not likely that something would fall off the back of it two or three times a day.

But, at least, it told him where Charlie was and Rudd suspected that Lovell had deliberately sent him out to the fields in order to get him out of the way in case Rudd returned to ask more questions. Lovell, then, had glanced back at the house to make sure that Betty Lovell was also safely out of sight.

By this time, Boyce had joined them and Rudd introduced him.

"Two of you this time," Lovell remarked with a sneer. "Well, what do you want?"

"To measure the distance from your yard to Stebbing's field," Rudd explained.

"Is that all?" Lovell demanded angrily. "Couldn't you have got it off an ordnance survey map without bothering me?"

It was a shrewd question and Rudd silently applauded the man's quick-wittedness.

"It's the time it would take to walk it rather than the actual length I'm interested in," he replied, improvising quickly. "So, if you don't mind, Mr. Lovell . . ."

As he was speaking, he began walking towards the end of the yard where a gate separated it from the adjoining field, giving Lovell no option but to follow. At the gate, Rudd paused and ostentatiously looked at his watch, jotting down the time in a small notebook that he took from his inside pocket. Lovell watched these official-seeming proceedings with a sardonic smile but Rudd thought he saw a look of alarm in his eyes.

The gate was not padlocked and Rudd unfastened it and walked on, up the gradient of the field that led away from the farm, Boyce at his heels and Lovell, after a final backward look, following after them, although halfway up the slope he caught up with Rudd.

"It must have been quite a job, carrying a dead body up here, if this is the route it came," Rudd remarked to Boyce over Lovell's head.

The sergeant, already out of breath, grunted a reply. Lovell, too, made no comment, although his face took on a heavy, obstinate look.

"Quite a view, too," Rudd went on, pausing at the top, as if casually, to glance back.

The farm lay below them, cradled in its surrounding trees, the old tiles on the house and the barns a warm red in the full sunlight. Through a gap in the trees, Rudd caught sight of a woman moving in the kitchen garden behind the house. She stooped, picked something up at her feet and then held her arms above her head. A white oblong appeared above her. She stooped again and lifted her arms and another white oblong appeared alongside the first. Betty Lovell was pegging out sheets on a washing line.

Rudd made no comment but, turning away, went on into the second field where the slope gradually flattened out so that, although they were still walking uphill, the going was easier. It was pasture land in which a few cows were grazing over to their right. Ahead of them ran the boundary hedge that separated Lovell's land from Stebbing's and, as they drew nearer, figures could be seen working in the adjoining meadow, Hollowfield. It was Rose and his archaeological society back on the job, as Stebbing had already informed Rudd.

It hadn't taken them long to resume their dig, he thought, although he could understand Rose's anxiety to finish excavating the site in the limited time he had available.

The field, busy now with people and activity,

presented a different scene to the one when Rudd had stood alone in the centre of it, with the light fading. A couple of brightly coloured tents, one orange, one blue, had been re-erected at the far side, near the copse, while in the middle distance men and women were at work again in the area where the post-holes had been discovered, shovelling soil and wheeling it away in barrows. Closer to the hedge, the oblong of exposed earth showed the site of the grave. Rudd noticed that no-one was working on the test trench that ran along the bottom of it.

"Hard work," Rudd commented to Boyce.

"Must be," the sergeant replied.

Lovell still said nothing but stood awkwardly, a little to one side of them, like an outsider who has been excluded from a conversation.

"It'd need a pick to get started on ground like that. Wouldn't you agree, Mr. Lovell?" Rudd went on, turning suddenly to address him. "A spade wouldn't touch it. The earth's as hard and as dry as a bone."

He stamped with one foot and they heard the parched soil ring with a dull, hollow sound under his heel.

Lovell's face had gone dark, the angry flush extending down his throat into the open neck of his shirt. But when he spoke, his voice was cool enough, almost drawling.

"I wouldn't know. I've never had any call to dig in this field. Nor in Stebbing's either," he replied.

Top marks for nerve, Rudd thought. He certainly doesn't rattle very easily.

"Somebody did," he pointed out. "Somebody dug a grave there. You know, ever since the body was found, it's puzzled me why that particular field was chosen. Have you any idea why it was?"

Lovell scowled.

"Why should I? If you ask me, it's a bit of rough, old pasture, not worth bothering with."

"But I understand Mr. Stebbing thinks it's worth bothering with. He's going to plough it up in the autumn."

He watched Lovell's face closely for his reaction to

this particular piece of information but Lovell only shrugged.

"More fool him, then. It's not worth it. He'll have trouble getting the water off it for a start. Still, if he's willing to spend money putting in land drains, that's his business."

"He's obviously spent money on fencing it off," Rudd said, pointing to the new-looking posts and barbed wire.

"Probably thought my cattle might stray," Lovell replied. His voice held a note of amused contempt and he was more relaxed now that the conversation had shifted on to farming matters.

I'll get him to loosen up a bit more before I have another go at him, Rudd decided.

"The fence been up long?" he asked casually.

"A year. Eighteen months."

"And before that there was just the hedge and the trees?"

"And a bit of a ditch," Lovell added.

"Not very deep, I gather, for Mr. Stebbing had it dug out on his side."

"Could be," Lovell conceded grudgingly.

"You hadn't bothered much with it?"

Lovell scowled, as if angered by this apparent slur on his farming efficiency.

"It isn't so much a question of bothering," he replied, "it's time. I've got more important things to do about the place than clear out ditches."

"Of course," Rudd agreed. "There's only you and Charlie while Stebbing's got quite a lot of farm help."

Lovell didn't reply and, after a pause, Rudd picked the subject up again himself.

"So, until a year or eighteen months ago, the two fields were separated by a ditch, not very deep, and a hedge that had quite a few gaps in it?"

If Lovell saw the point in the question, it didn't show in his face. He merely lifted his shoulders indifferently.

"Yes. I reckon it was."

"Rough pasture," Rudd went on musingly, looking

again at the adjoining field. "Good land for growing crops would you say?"

"No. Like I said, I wouldn't bother with it. He'll have to spend a packet on fertilizer to get it back in good heart. But then, he's got the cash, hasn't he?"

By "he," Rudd took it Lovell meant Stebbing.

"Poor soil?" he asked.

"Clay under a spit of top-soil."

"So I noticed," Rudd said promptly, feeling it was time he closed in. Lovell was now sufficiently off guard. "It couldn't have been easy, could it, digging that grave? Perhaps that's why it was relatively shallow. Only four feet deep instead of the usual six, although there were signs that someone had gone to a lot of trouble to lay the body out decently. Strange that."

He assumed his listening stance, head on one side, a bright, interested look on his face, but Lovell wasn't to be drawn. Instead, he countered with a question of his own.

"I thought you wanted to find out the time it took to walk here?" he asked in a jeering voice. "I haven't seen you look at your bloody watch since we started out."

It was quick thinking on his part and even quicker on Boyce's, who interrupted to remark, "I've kept a note of the time, Mr. Lovell. It took us exactly twenty-eight and a half minutes."

Rudd smiled broadly as he took out his notebook and wrote it down. He was thoroughly enjoying himself. The quick thrust and parry of the encounter was something he met only too rarely. It was more often a matter of plodding through an interview, question by question, trying to elicit facts.

"Longer, of course," he couldn't resist adding, as he stowed the notebook away, "if you're carrying a dead weight."

Lovell looked from one to the other of them. For a moment, Rudd thought he was going to lose his temper. The broad barrel of his chest rose against the thin cotton shirt as he drew in huge lungsful of air. The Inspector watched him warily. The fire that he suspected burnt under that heavy, brooding exterior seemed about to break through. But the expected outburst didn't come. Lovell subsided slowly.

"If you've finished," he said in his usual surly voice, "I've got better things to do than stand about yattering with you two."

They walked back across the fields in silence, Lovell a little ahead of them, moving with a deliberate and yet not clumsy gait. Rudd watched his back with interest. The broad, muscular shoulders rose and fell with a steady rhythm, his feet were planted with a heavy and yet easy assurance on the ground, as if he were familiar with every inch of the earth he trod on. There was a fine physical balance in his whole body and the kind of economy of movement that a man, used to hard, outdoor work and heavy lifting, learns to assume.

Yes, Rudd thought, he'd manage a dead body all right. He'd sling it over his shoulder like a sack of grain.

He pondered, too, the relevance of the information he had picked up that afternoon in conversation with Lovell.

First of all, as he had suspected, the fence had been put up and the ditch dug out fairly recently, probably since the body was buried, which meant that carrying it from Lovell's land into the field on Stebbing's side of the boundary would have been comparatively easy, if that was the way it had come. That much seemed fairly conclusive.

Whether Lovell had known that the field was due to go under the plough he was not so certain about, although it seemed unlikely, in view of the strained relationship between the two men, that Stebbing had told Lovell of his intentions. It followed, then, that Lovell could have believed that the field would remain as it was: rough pasture. He certainly didn't himself think it was worth cultivating.

The third point he had to consider was Lovell's knowledge that the field consisted of clay covered by a spit of top-soil, although he had denied ever digging in it. But wasn't it possible that he'd know that anyway? After all, he was a farmer. It would be his business to know what lay under his fields and the land that ran adjacent to his wouldn't be all that different from his own. As far as evidence went, that point was inconclusive.

The relationship between Lovell and Stebbing also intrigued him. The deepest animosity seemed to be on Lovell's side and Rudd wondered whether there was more to it than mere exasperation towards an overfriendly neighbour. It could be jealousy, of course. Lovell wouldn't be human if he didn't feel some envy of Stebbing, who, although a relative newcomer to the district, had capital to invest in his land while Lovell was struggling to keep his run-down farm going.

And yet Rudd wasn't convinced that this was the main reason. Envy is a mean emotion and Rudd was certain that, whatever else Lovell might be as a man, he wasn't a mean one. No, Stebbing had touched something deeper and stronger in Lovell than mere jealousy and Rudd thought he knew what it was: his pride. Had Stebbing suggested, as Rudd had done, only in stronger terms, that Lovell wasn't much good as a farmer? Or had he antagonised Lovell in some other way? Knowing Stebbing, with his officiousness, his know-all air and his superb lack of tact, and Lovell with his moody touchiness, it wouldn't take much for Stebbing to catch him on a raw spot, without possibly even being aware of it.

But one thing Rudd was sure of, if Lovell had killed his brother, it had been under extreme provocation. Rudd had deliberately driven him pretty far that afternoon, almost to the edge of losing his temper, and yet Lovell had held himself in check.

He was sure, too, that if murder had taken place and Lovell had carried the body to that field to bury it, it was for some perfectly sane reason. Lovell wasn't mad, not in any sense of the word, and the choice of the grave site would have been a rational one. But what it was Rudd was no nearer to finding out.

By now they had crossed the pasture and, as they approached the slope above the farm, Rudd could see

Betty Lovell still busy in the garden behind the
house. The line of washing had extended, now taking
up more than half its length but, as they jogged down
the last field, the angle of view changed slightly and
she disappeared from sight behind the massed foliage.

In the yard, the dog, which had been lying asleep
in a small patch of shadow against the wall, rose to its
feet suspiciously, the chain clinking behind it. But it
didn't bark. Presumably now they were on the prem-
ises and in Lovell's company, it accepted their
presence.

Lovell stopped in the centre of the yard.

"You're off now?" he asked. "You've seen all you
want?"

He seemed eager to see them go.

"Not quite," Rudd replied. "There's one small question I'd like to ask Mrs. Lovell."

Lovell shot a backward look at the house.

"I don't know that she's in," he muttered.

"She's in the garden behind the house and I want a
word with her," Rudd said in his official voice.

Lovell turned back slowly to face him. The anger
had burnt away, leaving him resigned and subdued.

"I've told you before, I don't want her bothered,"
he said quietly.

"I shan't bother her," Rudd assured him. Without
wanting to, he found himself responding to Lovell's
mood. His own exultation had died down and he felt
his compassion for the man return. "You can be
present when I speak to her, if you want to."

Lovell looked at him, searching his face with troubled eyes.

"All right," he conceded reluctantly and they
tramped round the side of the house to the garden at
the rear.

It was a long, narrow garden, surrounded on three
sides by trees and hedges that formed a close, leafy
background, the back wall of the house enclosing it
on the fourth and presenting a curiously blank
façade, the steep slope of the roof sweeping down to
only a few feet above ground level, and windowless
except for the small dormer casement of the landing

and a skylight, set in the roof and propped open, presumably to let air into the attic.

Looking about him, Rudd remembered Wheeler saying that Betty Lovell took care of the garden, as well as the poultry. He could see her influence on it. A path divided the garden into two plots, both of which were carefully tended. There was not a weed to be seen between the neat rows of vegetables. Soft fruit trees at the far end had been swathed in old net curtains to keep off the birds and the edges of the path were planted with herbs, among which Rudd recognised chives and parsley.

A washing-line ran the length of the garden, slung between poles, on which pairs of pillowcases, sheets and shirts were hanging, hardly stirring in the hot, still air.

Betty Lovell, unaware of their approach, was in the act of pegging up another shirt that she had taken from a bright red, plastic laundry basket at her feet, shaking out the sleeves as she hung it up and smoothing out the cuffs with the palm of her hand. Rudd remembered his mother doing the same, in order to remove as many creases before the shirt dried to make the task of ironing it a little easier.

"Betty!" Lovell called when they were still some distance from her and she turned swiftly towards them. She was startled. Every line of her body expressed tension and alarm. Rudd studied her face as they walked towards her. She looked more haggard and exhausted than the last time he had seen her, the shadows under her eyes more pronounced. The blue dress she was wearing accentuated her pallor, and her hair, tied back for coolness, gave her face a scraped, bony look. A few loose tendrils hung damply on her forehead.

Rudd remembered the young, pretty, tentative girl, clinging closely to the arm of her husband in the wedding photograph, and knew that, as a man, he wasn't going to find the interview easy. As a policeman, though, every nerve in him was alert to observe the smallest nuance of voice and expression.

He noticed her eyes went immediately to Lovell's

face as they halted in front of her on the path. There was an unspoken question in them. He wasn't quick enough to catch Lovell's answering look but whatever it was there must have been something reassuring in it, for her own became more composed.

They make a pair, Rudd thought. They don't need words to speak to one another.

And yet he was aware, too, of an undercurrent of something else between them. At first he thought it was hostility until he realised it was more complex than this. It was more a clash of wills and he wasn't sure that, despite her fragility and seeming docility, Betty Lovell hadn't got the upper hand. Lovell's stance had subtly changed as he stood in front of her. His shoulders were a little rounder, his head held a little further forward, as if, by his mere bodily presence, he was trying to placate her. He was, however, quick enough to get in the first word, as if warning her.

"The Inspector'd like a word with you, Betty."

"Yes?" she asked quickly, turning towards Rudd. There was a blind expression in her face, rigid with taut nerves.

"It's a very small point," Rudd said soothingly, trying to calm her down so that the question, when it came, should have the maximum impact. "Have you ever owned a cross and chain, Mrs. Lovell?"

For a second, the blank expression remained and then every muscle in her face jumped. It was an alarming experience, even for Rudd, who had seen many people on the verge of breaking down. It was as if the whole structure of her face was falling apart, every plane of it twitching into disintegration.

Then Lovell spoke.

"No. She's never owned one."

Damn him to hell! Rudd thought furiously.

"Let her answer for herself," he told him. But the damage had been done. Betty Lovell had been given the time to recover. Her face tightened up again.

"No, I've never owned one," she said in a voice that was barely audible. It was almost an exact repetition of Lovell's words.

"What's all this about a cross and chain anyway?" Lovell was asking. He was angry but he seemed genuinely nonplussed by the question and Rudd was sure he knew nothing about it, just as he was equally sure that Betty Lovell did.

"Just a line of inquiry we're following up," Rudd replied.

"Sorry we can't help you," Lovell said with heavy irony. "Is that the lot? Or have you any more damn fool questions you want to ask?"

There was an elated, confident air about him as if he knew he had got the better of Rudd.

"For the moment, yes," Rudd replied.

He looked round for Boyce, who had wandered off to the end of the garden, where he was sauntering about, his hands behind his back, looking at a row of currant bushes with a bored expression. Catching his attention, Rudd beckoned and the sergeant strolled back in their direction.

"We'll be off then," Rudd announced. "I'm sorry we've taken up so much of your time, Mr. Lovell."

Lovell didn't bother to answer and there was nothing Rudd could do except walk away, followed by Boyce.

As they reached the yard, the dog stirred again, rising at their approach. It seemed to know Lovell wasn't with them, for it began to growl, only tentatively, as if it wasn't sure how it was expected to react under the circumstances. All the same, they gave it a wide berth as they passed and walked up the rutted drive towards the gate.

"Funny bloke," Boyce commented as they got into the car.

"Funny lot altogether," Rudd replied. "And damned close. Lovell's not going to give anything away in a hurry, not even the time of day, if he can help it. And Betty Lovell may be a bundle of nerves but there's a will of iron under it. Were you there when I asked about the cross and chain?"

"No, I'd wandered off," Boyce replied negligently but there was a suppressed air of excitement about him that didn't register with Rudd at first.

"She denied owning one but I'm convinced she knows something about it. If Lovell hadn't shoved his oar in . . ."

He broke off, aware of the look on Boyce's face.

"What's up with you?" he asked. "You look like the cat that's got the cream."

"Just this," Boyce replied, grinning broadly, and, getting out his wallet, he opened it to reveal five fragments of paper, the largest no bigger than a postage stamp and all of them charred along at least one edge.

"Where did you find these?" Rudd asked.

"At the bottom of the garden, behind some bushes. There's a kind of rubbish dump there; mostly kitchen waste, old potato peelings and the like, but someone had lit a fire on top of it recently. Most of it was too charred to be recognisable but it had burnt into oblongs, if you get my meaning, like letters or postcards. A few bits near the edge hadn't burnt through and while you lot were talking I picked up what I could reach."

Rudd touched the fragments gingerly. Two were blue with faint lines on them and one still retained part of a shape written in ink.

"These could be bits of letters," he said. "It looks like lined writing paper."

He bent to examine the other pieces. The paper was different in quality and texture, thicker and with a glossy surface that he could feel when he rubbed his finger across them.

"Photographs?" he suggested.

"That's what I reckon," Boyce agreed. "And quite a collection of them, too, judging by what was left. Some snapshots, I'd say, and some bigger in size than that, more like studio portraits. One at least had been properly mounted. I saw a bit of deckle edging like the backing card a professional photographer would use but it was too far over for me to reach it."

"You know what this means?" Rudd asked.

"Geoff or Betty Lovell deliberately got rid of them."

"Yes, and my guess is quite recently, since the last time I called and asked for photographs of Ron. Then

Lovell must have realised Nancy Fowler might have some so he rushed over there to get his hands on those as well. And I've no doubt he would have burnt those too, if I hadn't got there first."

"Destroying evidence," Boyce pointed out. "You must admit it looks suspicious."

"Of course it does!" Rudd snapped. "The whole damned business looks suspicious. And yet . . ."

He bit furiously at his thumb-nail.

"Something's not right about it, Tom. It doesn't quite add up, although I can't put my finger on it."

"What doesn't add up?" Boyce asked. "It all looks straightforward enough to me. In fact, what we've found out this afternoon about the burnt photographs would support the theory—Ron Lovell comes home, finds his wife and brother are having an affair, there's a quarrel . . ."

"I'm not sure they *are* having an affair," Rudd broke in.

"But I thought you said the two of them are sharing a bed," Boyce protested.

"They may be sharing a bed but that doesn't necessarily mean they're lovers."

It was too subtle for Boyce, who looked both puzzled and outraged.

"I don't get your meaning," he replied heavily. "In my book, if two people are sleeping together, it only means one thing. But maybe I'm old-fashioned."

"It's more complex than that," Rudd tried to explain. He thought back to the scene in the garden, the three of them standing on the path, under the hanging sheets and pillowcases, drooping like flags, and tried to recapture the interplay of reaction that had passed between Geoff and Betty Lovell. There was something else, too, about the setting and he frowned with the effort of trying to recall it in all its detail.

Betty Lovell. He could focus in on her quite easily, standing against a background of runner beans, growing rich and luxuriant on their supporting poles. Her blue dress. The red laundry basket at her feet. Nearby something low and dark green growing along the edge of the path, only he couldn't quite see what it was. Then his memory sharpened. Of course! Parsley. The clump of dense, serrated, curled-back leaves came vividly to his mind.

He switched back to her face, changing swiftly in expression from alarm to rigidity and through the white terror of jumping nerves back to the taut mask of immobility again; her eyes flickering across to look at Geoff Lovell, a more shadowy figure in Rudd's mind and one that he couldn't recall in anything like the same detail, only as a heavy, dark presence, oddly humble, oddly shy, quite unlike the man who had walked with such easy, physical assurance down the slope of the field. And yet a spark had jumped across the gap. There had been understanding and intimacy that was oddly mixed with something else.

No, Rudd decided. He had been wrong to think of it as hostility but he was hard put to it to describe exactly what it had been. It was as if she had drawn a circle round herself, a space, which Lovell was not allowed to enter and from the centre of which she spoke to him.

But before he could frame the idea properly, his mind had darted off again, ridiculously, to the line of washing above her head and he found himself counting along it. Shirts, sheets, tea-towels, pillow-cases . . .

"Well?" Boyce was asking.

The scene vanished and Rudd struggled to return to the present moment.

"Well what?"

"You were saying something about their relationship, Geoff and Betty's, being more complex and then you went off into one of your trances."

"Oh, yes. What I meant was, whatever they may have been to each other in the past, there's a feeling of tension between them now."

It was only a very rough approximation of what he really meant but he couldn't explain it more exactly.

"Guilt," Boyce said promptly. "If they killed Ronnie Lovell, it'd be bound to come between them."

"Yes," said Rudd, appearing to agree, and Boyce, satisfied, started up the car and drove away.

Lovell heard the car and guessed they had been sitting in it, talking. He guessed, too, what about. The business with the cross and chain. The whole interview troubled him but this particular part of it he could make no sense of at all.

What the hell was all this about a cross and chain? That damned Inspector seemed to think it was important and Lovell hadn't liked the look on Betty's face when Rudd asked about it. For a moment, she seemed as if she were going to pieces.

As soon as Rudd and the sergeant left the garden, he had turned to question her himself but she had pushed past him and run back to the house, shouting at him, "Leave me alone, for God's sake!"

Baffled and hurt, he remained behind, brooding on it, going over and over in his mind what had been said. Rudd had seemed very sure of himself. There had been an alert, watchful air about him all afternoon; at times, almost jubilant. He knew something, of course, and suspected a great deal more, but how much evidence did he have? Not much, Lovell suspected, or he would have been more open in his accusations. The reason he had given for calling, to time the walk to the boundary hedge, was only an excuse. And why had the sergeant come as well? Apart from a few remarks, he had said very little. In fact, when Rudd had been questioning Betty about the cross and chain, Lovell couldn't remember where he had been. He certainly hadn't been present.

He had a sudden recollection of seeing him strolling up from the bottom of the garden when Rudd was about to leave.

Oh, God! The bonfire! He hadn't thought of that. Could the sergeant have been nosing about round there?

He set off at a run down the path and, squatting down in front of the remains of the fire, examined it carefully. It looked all right. There were no obvious signs that anybody had been poking about in it and yet he couldn't be sure. The fragments of charred letters and photographs seemed to be as he had left them, although he was aware, for the first time, of unburnt scraps that remained, untouched by the fire. But they were too small surely to be recognisable.

All the same, to be on the safe side, he brought his foot down in the centre of them, crushing the brittle flakes of paper, churning them to dust under the heel of his boot.

Christ! he thought, as he felt them powder into oblivion, if only the whole, bloody, terrifying, crazy situation could be got rid of in the same easy way.

Chapter 13

For two days after the visit to Lovell's farm, the case seemed to come to a standstill. There was nothing Rudd could do except wait: for the Yard to send a report on the forensic evidence; for McCullum to produce the life-size enlargement; for someone to see the photograph and description in the *Police Gazette* and come forward with more information, if there was any.

The only positive action he could take was to return the original photographs and newspaper cutting to Nancy Fowler, now that McCullum had finished making copies of them. He had been hoping for a chat with her in which he might learn more about the Lovell family background but, as he walked into the lounge bar of the Blue Boar the following evening, it was clear Nancy was embarrassed by his presence and unwilling to talk as freely as she had done on their first meeting.

Had she regretted her outspokenness? Rudd wondered. She certainly seemed relieved to get the photographs back and stuffed them quickly into her handbag, snapping the catch shut with a quick, decisive movement, as if that were the end of the incident.

"Ta," she said briefly.

He had bought her a gin and orange which she drank furtively, keeping an eye on the landlord.

"I can't stay chatting tonight," she went on. "I'm meeting a gentleman friend later."

It was said defiantly but Rudd was inclined to take it as an excuse to get rid of him as quickly as possible. He had noticed her as soon as he entered the bar and before she had seen him, sitting by herself, a closed, sulky look on her face; the look of a woman drinking alone and not expecting company. All the same, she couldn't pass up the opportunity to ask:

"No news of Ron yet?"

There was the same desperate eagerness in her voice that he had noticed the first time.

"Sorry, no. Not yet," he replied. "We're still making inquiries."

"What do you want him for?"

"I told you, as a possible witness."

"Witness to what?"

So she still hadn't heard about the body being found near Lovell's farm, Rudd decided with relief. There had been a short paragraph in the local paper that morning, giving very little information, except for the fact of the discovery and its whereabouts. Either she hadn't read it or hadn't made the connection between the village, which was named, and Rudd's interest in the Lovell family.

"Just a line of investigation," he said vaguely and added quickly, to draw her away from any further questions about the case, "How did you come to meet Ron in the first place?"

She seemed more inclined to talk, now that the subject had switched back to her relationship with Ronnie Lovell, and she said, with a little laugh:

"He used to come here of an evening, drinking with his mates."

"Here? You mean the Blue Boar?"

"Yes, only they met in the public bar in them days; played darts; had a few rounds and a few laughs, that sort of thing. I don't use the public myself anymore, being on my own. It's nicer in here."

It struck him as an extraordinary example of her loyalty that she should go on drinking in the same pub, in spite of the obvious hostility of the landlord. Did it make her feel nearer to him? Or nearer, perhaps, to the green days of her youth when the future had seemed full of bright promise?

"And Geoff?" he asked. "How did you come to meet him?"

It was mere curiosity that prompted the question.

"Oh, him. Well, Ron had a few too many one evening and couldn't get himself home on his bike. One of his mates went over to the farm and Geoff came out in the van to pick him up. Talk about laugh! We had Ronnie out in the car-park, trying to sober him up but he kept falling about, singing and trying to take his shirt off."

Her face brightened at this recollection of high revelry.

"On good terms were they?" Rudd asked.

"Who, Geoff and Ron?" She looked surprised at the question. "Yes, all right, I suppose. They're brothers, aren't they?"

As if blood relationship explained all and excused all.

"And Geoff came back to see you after Ron left to ask if you knew where he'd gone?"

"That's right. Like I said, I couldn't tell him 'cos I didn't know."

She paused and gave Rudd a sly, almost coquettish look.

"As a matter of fact, he hung about for a few months. I'm not saying he really fancied me but I got the feeling if I'd taken a bit more trouble . . ."

She left the sentence unfinished, shrugged and laughed.

"Not that he was my type. Too bloody gloomy, for one thing. No chance of a laugh with him; not like Ron. And always on about that farm of his. I got fed up listening to it. Anyway, he stopped coming after a bit."

Rudd was silent, thinking over the implications of what she had told him. Without realising it, Nancy Fowler might have given him a clue to another possible motive for murder, and a powerful one at that, if he was right. Sexual jealousy. It seemed likely that Geoff Lovell had harboured a grudge for years against his younger and more attractive brother who, unlike himself, had no difficulty in picking up women. His own fumbling attempts at trying to establish some kind of relationship with Nancy might indicate this. Now that his brother had gone, she was free and Ronnie had already shown him that she was sexually available. Then he had stopped seeing her. Why? Because he realised his attempts were futile? That Nancy Fowler didn't fancy him? Or had he already turned to the other woman whom Ronnie had loved and abandoned: Betty Lovell? Not that Geoff's relationship with her could be compared in any way with the hankerings he might have had for Nancy. Rudd had seen them together and had realised that, whatever Betty's feelings for him were now, his affection for her was genuine enough. It struck him that there was something deeply tragic about a man who could only approach the women his brother had discarded, as if he doubted his own powers of attraction.

And then, if Ronnie came home . . .

Nancy Fowler's voice broke into his thoughts.

"If that's all," she was saying, looking pointedly at the clock over the bar.

"Just one more question," Rudd said, rousing himself. "I was a bit curious about the newspaper cutting of the wedding."

Her face went sulky again at the mention of Ron's marriage.

"Well, what of it?"

"Betty was given away by the manager of the hotel, not by her father, and there's no mention of her parents being there."

"No they wouldn't be 'cos she didn't have none. She was brought up in a children's home. Ron told me. It was one of the reasons he felt he had to marry her. She had no-one else and no where to go. It was a living-in job, see, at the hotel and she'd've been chucked out if they knew she was pregnant. 'She got me in a corner,' he said. Those were his very words."

"I see," Rudd said thoughtfully.

It explained why Betty had stayed on at the farm after Ron had left her; a small point but one loose end, at least, that had been satisfactorily tied up.

He finished his beer and got ready to leave.

"Thank you, Mrs. Fowler."

"That the lot?"

"Yes. I don't think I need trouble you again."

It was the wrong thing to say. Her expression hardened.

"You said you'd let me know . . ."

"Of course," he put in quickly. "I haven't forgotten. I'll be in touch the minute I know anything."

"He'll turn up," she said with an air of quiet conviction that had an odd quality of bitterness in it. "He always does, like a bad bloody penny, borrowing a few quid when he's short, pissing off again when it suits him."

I've underestimated her, Rudd thought. There's no false sentimentality in her attitude to Ron Lovell. She knows him for what he is and yet she's still prepared to have him back.

As he rose to go, he looked at her with renewed respect. The heat had caked her powder and her eye make-up had been amateurishly put on, too heavy on one side, giving her face an uneven, lop-sided look, as if one side of it was in sharper focus than the other. Ridiculous. Comic. Pathetic, even. But Rudd saw none of these qualities. He recognised, instead, a kind of courage and gallantry and a tough instinct for survival.

Apart from this one encounter, there was no other

activity. Rudd finished the paper-work, read over the reports already written, fidgeted about the office. He hated these periods of waiting in the middle of a case. They made him fretful and bad-tempered. Boyce, knowing this, kept well clear of him, to the cowardly extent of sending Kyle along to the office with the completed list of missing persons, aware that none of them were relevant.

Rudd read it over with disgust. Only five were manual workers who approximately fitted the description and had been reported missing during the past two years and all of them were vouched for by next of kin. Therefore none could possibly be Ron Lovell, who, whatever life he had made for himself after he left the farm, certainly couldn't be traced back more than fifteen years.

Kyle scuttled out of the office as soon as he decently could, leaving Rudd to bung the report into a file with the morose thought that the gods seemed to be conspiring against him.

The following morning, however, things began to move at last. The forensic report arrived from the Yard and, seeing the envelope lying on his desk as he entered the office, Rudd felt his spirits rise. Peeling off his jacket and throwing open the window, he sent for Boyce before settling down at the desk to read it.

The report was detailed; pages of it, in fact; a lot of it medical evidence which he skimmed over quickly with a practised eye, lifting out the guts of the information before Boyce's arrival.

The first few paragraphs largely tallied with the facts that Pardoe had already given him. The man had been dead for approximately two years. He was five feet ten inches. Medium build. In his early forties. Hair dark brown beginning to turn grey.

There was more detail on the dental evidence but in substance it amounted to Pardoe's comment: the man had had most of his teeth removed and those that were left were badly neglected.

The new information concerned the clothing that Pardoe hadn't been able to examine in detail. The man had been wearing cheap quality underwear of a cotton and nylon mixture; grey nylon socks; a blue-and white-checked cotton shirt, collar size fifteen; dark brown Terylene trousers; a wool jacket of dark brown and green mixture, with leather patches on the elbows; leather boots, size eight, with metal studs on the soles, showing signs of wear.

The scraps of fabric that had covered the body were pieces of a grey woollen blanket.

He turned the page. More forensic information in greater detail under separate headings: the bones; the stomach; the tissue. Nothing much here to interest him, although it was all good medical stuff. One detail, however, caught his eye. The man had evidently suffered from early symptoms of rheumatism, discernible in the knee joints, suggesting he might have worked out of doors or in damp conditions. Otherwise there were no distinguishing features; no signs of old fractures or scars; no warts or moles. No chance of finger-prints either, as Pardoe had warned him. "The tissue on the finger-tips is in too advanced a state of decomposition," the report stated laconically.

Boyce entered at this moment, a little cautiously, wondering what the Inspector's mood would be, just as Rudd, running his eye further down the page, caught sight of the phrase "possible cause of death." Raising a hand in warning that he didn't want to be interrupted, he bent over the type-written sheet, reading with concentrated attention, while Boyce creaked his way across the room to a vacant chair.

It came in a paragraph with the general heading "The Heart," which went on to state:

"Although the heart was also decomposed, it was in a better state of preservation than the other internal organs and there was sufficient muscle tissue left intact for the following facts to be established:

"(1) The heart had been punctured by a wound in the left ventricle of sufficient depth to cause heavy if not massive bleeding and, although in the absence of other evidence it cannot be categorically stated, it was of a serious enough nature to be a possible cause of death.

"(2) The wound was caused by an implement,

weapon or blade at least four inches in length and
varying in width, being broadest at the point of entry
into the muscle tissue, viz. approximately 3/16 of an
inch in width, tapering to a point approximately 1/8
of an inch. The implement, weapon or blade also had
a downward curvature. It is, however, important to
note that, because of the decayed condition of the
heart, precise measurements could not be taken.

"(3) There were signs that a second penetration
had been made into the chest wall approximately six
inches to the right of the wound in the heart and possibly of the same nature and depth, although no
measurements were possible in this wound because of
the advanced state of decomposition of the surrounding tissue."

But Rudd needed no careful hedging of the facts to
convince him of the evidence.

"Stabbed!" he said out loud.

"Who's been stabbed?" Boyce asked, getting out of
his chair and coming over to the desk.

"Our corpus delicti," Rudd told him, handing him
the report. "Read it for yourself. Last paragraph but
one."

"It certainly looks like it," the sergeant agreed,
when he had finished, "once you've picked your way
through the three-syllable jungle. Wordy lot, aren't
they, these experts? Why can't they say it straight
out—the bloke was stabbed in the heart, because
that's what it amounts to?"

"Stabbed, certainly; and twice by the look of it, although whether stabbed to death is another matter. I
can understand them being cagey about that one. He
might have been dead or dying from other causes."

"Odd weapon, though," mused Boyce. "At least four
inches long and tapering off to a point. *And* curving
downwards. I can't think off-hand of any knife that's
shaped like that. A stiletto's got a long, narrow blade,
but it's straight, not bent down."

"That would depend on which way this particular
weapon was used," Rudd pointed out.

"I don't get you."

"Then I'll show you," Rudd replied and, taking a

sheet of typing paper from the drawer, he folded it over several times into a narrow strip about half an inch wide. "There's the blade. I know it's not tapering but that doesn't matter for this experiment. Now look."

He bent the last two inches of the paper strip so that it was pointing downwards.

"And now I shall proceed to stab you with it," he went on and lunged at Boyce's chest, bringing his arm down from the shoulder. "Result—one wound with a downward penetration. Get it?"

"I get it," Boyce replied with a so-what-anyway expression on his face.

"I now turn the blade over so that the curve is pointing upwards and stab you again. A different action this time, you'll notice. I have to drive it in from below, leaving a wound with an upward penetration. Two different wounds but the same blade, depending which way round you hold it."

"Yes, I see that," Boyce replied in a slightly disparaging tone, "but I still don't see how it helps us to identify what sort of weapon it was. It's not any kind of knife you'd find, say, in a kitchen. But could it be a farm implement? Assuming it's Ronnie Lovell we've dug up, then it's likely he was killed on the farm and more than possible with something that was lying about to hand. It's no good asking me what exactly. The sum total of what I know about farming could be written down in large capital letters on the back of an envelope . . ."

He broke off to add:

"You look as if that rings a bell."

"Not for the weapon itself," Rudd admitted. "I'm as much in the dark about that as you are. But it could tie in with something I noticed the first time I visited the farm. I asked Geoff Lovell about any tools that had gone missing. I meant something like a spade that could have been used to dig the grave. He reacted oddly to the question, I thought; denied it very positively, as if it had upset him in some way."

"Guilty conscience?" suggested Boyce. "He could

have used a farm tool to kill his brother and then got rid of it afterwards."

"Possibly, but I don't want to read too much into it, not at this stage. I wish to God McCullum would come up with that life-size enlargement! Until he does and we've got positive proof it's Ronnie Lovell's body, we're working with our hands tied." He paused and added, "Let's have another look at the description of the wound. We may get an idea."

He took the report from Boyce and began re-reading it. Suddenly he stopped and, turning back to the first page, started to scan it eagerly. Boyce, aware that he had found something important, leaned forward to ask:

"What's up?"

"Something I should have noticed the first time I read it. It says here 'heavy if not massive bleeding' and yet there's no mention of blood found on the clothing."

"Could he have been naked when he was killed?" Boyce put in.

"It's possible but I think there's a more likely explanation. There were signs that the body was laid out. Somebody had taken the trouble to fold the arms and wrap the body in a blanket. I think the same person also stripped it of its blood-stained clothing and dressed it in clean clothes before it was buried."

"Crazy," said Boyce.

"No, not crazy. Anything but that. Whoever did it had a perfectly sane and logical reason; the same sort of motive that was behind the choice of that field for the grave site . . ."

The telephone rang at this point and Rudd stretched across the desk to pick up the receiver. A man's voice, deep and with a Midlands accent, asked:

"Detective Inspector Rudd? I'm Detective Chief Inspector Mullen, stationed at Mill Edge. I saw the photograph and description in the *Police Gazette* this morning and I'm fairly certain that I recognise the man."

"You mean Ronnie Lovell?" Rudd broke in.

"That's not the name we know him by. The man

we're looking for is James, or Jimmy, Neal, who went missing three years ago."

"Three years!"

That didn't fit in with the facts but there was no time to discuss the point for Mullen was continuing:

"Over three years, as a matter of fact. We put out a 'wanted' on him at the time."

"And the charge?" Rudd asked, signalling urgently to Boyce.

"Attempted murder."

Cupping his hand over the mouthpiece, Rudd said hurriedly to Boyce, "James Neal. Wanted for attempted murder. Over three years ago."

Boyce raised his eyebrows and then, picking up the internal telephone, began giving instructions to someone at the other end.

Rudd, meanwhile, was asking Mullen, "Are you sure it's the same man?"

"Fairly certain," Mullen replied. "But I'd like to discuss it with you. Any chance of your coming up here? I'm anxious to get this case closed."

And so am I, Rudd said to himself.

"If you left now," Mullen went on, "you could be up here soon after mid-day. It doesn't take all that long on the motorway."

"Mill Edge, you said?"

"That's right. It's about twelve miles south of Manchester. If you take the M1 and then the M6 and turn off at intersection nineteen, you'll find Mill Edge well signposted from then on. The police station's in the centre, in a turning beside the town hall." He paused and then added, "You haven't any more recent photographs of this man—what's-his-name—Lovell, have you?"

"Sorry, no. I'll bring what I have."

"Right. We'll compare notes when we meet," Mullen replied and rang off.

"A constable's bringing the 'wanted' file," Boyce said as Rudd replaced the receiver.

"No time now," Rudd replied, grabbing up his jacket. "You check it out for me. I'm off to Mill Edge.

The Inspector there thinks he recognises Ronnie Lovell."

"On an attempted murder charge?" Boyce asked, as Rudd made for the door but the Inspector waved a dismissive hand.

"Can't stop now. I'll see you later. I should be back by late afternoon, early evening. Stir McCullum up meanwhile," he added, over his shoulder. "Tell him things are moving and I'll want that blow-up."

He went, slamming the door behind him and creating a small draught that stirred the pile of papers on his desk.

Once he got onto the motorway, Rudd found the drive rapid but boring. The three-lane highway sliced its way north, busy with fast-moving traffic that gave the impression it was fleeing from some major catastrophe. Or feeling towards it, perhaps, for the cars and lorries on the south-bound carriageways were travelling at the same manic speed. Sunlight splintered off windscreens and chrome and glared back from the surface of the road. Alongside it, the countryside flickered past, anonymous fields for the most part, that looked as if they had come complete with the motorway, bought up as a job lot by the Ministry of Transport ready for rolling out beside the miles of sterile concrete.

Rudd was glad to get off it, into the comparative sanity of the ordinary roads in the built-up area, where traffic moved at a more reasonable speed and where there were shops and houses and people, going about their everyday lives.

Mill Edge merged with it, part of the great, sprawling conurbation of Manchester, joined to it by miles of industrial suburb and yet managing to preserve something of its own separate identity. Rudd drove into it slowly, noticing the grimy rows of terrace cottages. Two up and two down, run up cheaply in the last century to house the mill-workers; and the mills themselves, grim, flat-faced, many-windowed buildings which, with their massive gates and sunless yards, put him in mind of Victorian prisons.

The town centre was a little gayer, tricked out with

concrete tubs of flowers and coloured awnings. There
was even a floral coat of arms with a grass border
outside the town hall.

He took the turning beside it and drew up outside
the police station, where he was shown upstairs to
Mullen's office. Mullen, a large, grey-haired, baggy
man, came forward to shake hands, adding with a
smile:

"Fancy a beer and a cheese sandwich? Or have you
eaten?"

"Yes to the first. No to the second," Rudd replied.

"Come on then. There's a pub round the corner
that's got a snug where we can talk."

It was a genuine snug, with a brown Lincrusta
dado, an ornate plaster ceiling and mahogany
benches upholstered in worn, buttoned, red plush.
Mullen ordered beer and sandwiches at the tiny section of the counter that served it, the other side of
which they could hear the roar and clatter of the
public bar.

"Always peaceful here," Mullen commented, as
they carried the plates and glasses over to a round,
marble-topped table. He drank deeply and then said,
without any preamble:

"Jimmy Neal. Well, as I said on the phone, we're
looking for him on an attempted murder charge. I'll
give you his story, what I know of it, and you can see
how well it fits in with the man you're looking for.
Neal turned up in this area about eight years ago, as
far as we can make out, and worked for a time at a
factory assembling washing-machines on the outskirts
of Manchester but left after a row with the foreman.
We don't know what he was up to for about eighteen
months after that. The next we heard of him, he'd
been taken on as a mechanic at a garage and repair
shop not far from here, out at Westbridge, run by a
man called Maguire, Pat Maguire. Neal was there for
just over a year and then there was a quarrel between
the two men over Maguire's wife, Babs, who worked
on the cash desk for the petrol pumps. Evidently
Maguire thought Neal was being a bit too friendly
with her, and not without good reason as it turned

out. Anyway, Neal got the sack. A few weeks later, Maguire's garage was raided and he was arrested on a receiving charge. I had a chat with the Inspector in charge of the case out at Westbridge. He told me the place was stuffed full of stolen spare parts and he'd been tipped off, although by who he wouldn't say. 'Acting on information received. Blah. Blah.' But we can guess who grassed."

"Neal?"

"I reckon so. It was his way of paying out Maguire for giving him the push. Anyway, Maguire got sent down, although that's neither here nor there, and Neal meanwhile turned up here, in Mill Edge, with Babs Maguire in tow, calling herself Mrs. Neal by this time, and they installed themselves in a flat over a launderette just off the High Street, Babs working downstairs in the shop. Neal was in and out of jobs, mostly out, but when he did work it was usually in some small engineering firm or work-shop. I gather he was quite a good mechanic when he wasn't quarrelling with someone and either getting the sack or asking for his cards."

He paused and looked quizzically at Rudd.

"It fits so far?"

"It fits," Rudd agreed.

As Mullen had been talking, he had been mentally ticking off the points that related to what he knew of Ronnie Lovell; the fact that the man had turned up in the area, without anything previously known about him; his mechanical skill; his tendency to stick at nothing for very long; the quarrelsome, belligerent character; the use he made of women, all coincided.

"Did he drink?" he added.

Mullen nodded.

"Yes, heavily at times. It was his drinking that first got him noticed by my lot. Nothing much to start with; mostly shouting matches with Babs Maguire late on a Saturday night when he'd had a skinful. The neighbours called the police out a couple of times but there's not much we can do in a domestic. There was one brawl in a pub for which Neal and the other man involved got fined. And then we come to the night in question; four years ago come next New Year, as a matter of fact. They'd been to a New Year's Eve booze-up and got back to the flat in the early hours. Soon afterwards, there was a violent row over another man, I gather, and Neal clobbered her with a chair. The police were sent for but by the time the patrol car arrived, Neal had skipped out, leaving Babs Maguire lying in the kitchen with serious head injuries. He was damned lucky he didn't kill her. We've been looking for him ever since."

He took a photograph out of his pocket and laid it on the table.

"That's the only picture we have of him."

Rudd picked it up and studied it. By the look of it, it had been taken by flash-light at a party in somebody's house. Three men and two women, all of them looking a little drunk and dishevelled, were standing in front of a sideboard, holding up their glasses in boozy salutation. But, despite the poor quality of the photograph and the intervening years, Rudd had no difficulty in picking out Ron Lovell. He was the man in the centre of the group, tie loosened, hair flopping on his forehead, older and thinner-faced than in the photographs of him that Rudd had got from Nancy Fowler, but unmistakably the same, still eyeing the camera with that bold, swaggering, come-on look and the same confident smile.

He laid the three copies of the photographs that McCullum had made beside it.

"Royal flush, I think," he said.

Mullen examined the four photographs for a moment before commenting wryly:

"A handful of knaves, if you ask me."

He pointed to one of the women in the group picture.

"That's Babs Maguire, if you want to know what she looks like. The man on her right is her husband."

It was the woman who interested Rudd the most. Blond, plump, already showing signs of coarsening, with an incipient double chin and small belly showing beneath a too-tight, shiny silk dress, she put him in mind of Nancy Fowler; the same type, busty

and well-fleshed, but with a harder, city gloss to her.
He gave only a cursory glance at the husband, who,
wearing a paper hat, his mouth foolishly open,
seemed to be propped up against Ron Lovell, who
was standing next to him.

"No doubt in your mind?" Mullen was asking.

"None," Rudd replied with conviction. "It's the
same man all right."

"And you're looking for him too?"

"I think we may have found him," Rudd said and
went on to explain briefly the discovery of the body
and what he knew of Ron Lovell's life before he left
home.

"So your theory is he was on the run, with an attempted murder charge hanging over him, returned
home and was killed in a quarrel with his brother?"
Mullen asked, as Rudd finished. "It fits. He was a violent man; the type who was likely to end violently. I
can't say I'm surprised. You'll probably find he started
the fight himself."

"The only snag is the time factor," Rudd pointed
out. "The man we've found has been dead for about
two years. But your man, Jimmy Neal, skipped out
over three years ago. That leaves about eighteen
months unaccounted for."

"Could be he spent the time somewhere else," Mullen replied, "under another name. It's obvious he was
using false papers—a National Insurance card, for instance—when we knew him. He could have pushed
off, assumed another false identity, perhaps even got
into more trouble with the law before finally deciding
to go home."

"It's possible," agreed Rudd, although he didn't
sound too happy with the idea. It was another loose
end to be tied; another unsatisfactory part of the case
that would need resolving.

He glanced at his watch.

"I'd better be pushing off myself. McCullum may
have come up with that life-size enlargement which
will clinch once and for all the question of identity.
I'll let you know as soon as he does."

"Thanks," Mullen said. "But I don't think you need

to worry on that score. The description, everything, fits too neatly. I bet you a pound to a penny it's Ronnie Lovell, alias Jimmy Neal, you've got there and I for one won't be sorry. I shall close the file on him with a happy heart."

But his confidence was to prove misplaced. Later, when Rudd, hot, tired and suffering from the slightly disoriented feeling of a man who has driven too far and too fast, walked into the office to find Boyce and McCullum waiting for him, he knew by the looks on their faces that the news wasn't good.

McCullum put it into words:

"I'm sorry but there's no question of doubt, according to the photographic evidence. That body you've got is definitely not Ronnie Lovell's."

He had spread the photographs out on the desk ready for the Inspector's examination and in silence Rudd crossed the room and bent down over them. The life-size enlargement of Ronnie Lovell's face, under its jaunty beret, smiled up at him in what now seemed to be triumph. Beside it lay a transparent sheet on which the outlines of a face had been drawn in black ink. McCullum, in a subdued voice, like a man present at a sick-bed, began explaining.

"I had the features of the dead man sketched out from the measurements Pardoe took when he first examined him; length and width of skull, the position of the eyes and ears . . ."

He broke off, seeing the expression on Rudd's face.

"But I won't go into the details now. The point is, it's accurate. Now see what happens."

Lifting the transparent sheet, he laid it over the photograph, without speaking. No words, in fact, were needed. The evidence spoke for itself. At no point did the features of the dead man correspond to those of Ronnie Lovell. Eyes, nose, mouth were all differently spaced. Even the jaw-line ran at a sharper angle.

Rudd rested his hands on the surface of the desk and leaned his weight on them. He felt tired down to the marrow of his bones. Behind him, he heard Boyce stir and clear his throat.

"I'll send out for tea," he announced. He, too, spoke in the hushed tones of someone addressing a patient who needed gentle handling.

Suddenly Rudd was angry; not with Boyce, but with himself. It had been so damned easy to accept the obvious, to drift along with the comfortable and facile theory that had so conveniently seemed to fit the facts. Well, let that be a lesson to him!

He stumped over to the door and, flinging it open, said loudly, "I'm going out!"

Boyce and McCullum exchanged startled glances.

"What for?" Boyce asked tentatively.

"What the hell do you mean—what for?" Rudd snapped back. "To start again, of course."

Banging the door shut behind him, he felt a certain furious satisfaction at the rightness of the decision that he had made in anger on the spur of the moment.

To start again was the only answer. And where better than the place where it had all begun: that scrappy bit of rough pasture that someone had chosen as a grave site for an unknown man; where he had stood alone and felt the first stirring of understanding; and where he knew he must now return—Hollowfield.

Chapter 14

He had expected the field to be empty, as it had been
when he stood alone in the centre of it and felt close
to the heart of the place. Instead, as he climbed over
the gate, he saw Rose and a few of the younger members of the society still at work on the rectangular site
where the post-holes had been discovered.

Damn! Rudd thought. He had forgotten they would
be there.

He stood irresolute, wondering whether to turn
back and yet reluctant to retreat. There was nothing
else he could do towards the case except return to the
office and go over the files once again and he was
tired of reports and all the formal routine of investigation.

Besides, it was a beautiful evening. The sun was

low on the horizon and the day's heat was dying with it, leaving only a gentle warmth and a promise of later coolness. After a day spent largely driving along motorways, it would be pleasant to wander about, with his hands in his pockets, while he tried to recapture the mood of that first day of the inquiry, before his mind had been cluttered up with all the useless theorising and the irrelevant detail that still lingered in his thoughts.

In the event, his mind was made up for him. Rose, glancing up, saw him and came forward to meet him, his face expressing both welcome and concern.

"Good evening, Inspector," he said. "I do hope you're not going to ask us to leave again just when we're so near to finishing our dig. Two or three more days should see it completed."

There was nothing Rudd could do except put a pleasant face on it.

"No. I just happened to be passing and I thought I'd look in and see how you're getting on," he replied, lying agreeably.

"How very kind!" Rose said in his precise voice, his face flushing with pleasure. "I shall be delighted to show you round."

As they began walking towards the main excavation site, Rudd remarked, "You're doing overtime, I see."

Rose gave his high, pinched laugh.

"Unpaid, I'm afraid, Inspector! But we try to keep going while the light lasts. As you can see, we're making very good progress."

They had reached the edge of the site, which was now almost completely cleared, showing lines of circular post-holes in the clay, forming a rough box shape; the size, Rudd reckoned, of an average room.

Rose was looking at him with a proud and slightly roguish expression.

"Now that you see it uncovered, can you make a guess as to what sort of building it was?" he asked in the teasing manner of a schoolmaster who, while knowing the answer himself, is determined to obtain the maximum scholastic amusement out of the situa-

tion by getting his pupils to make their own fatuous
suggestions first.

Although exasperated not only by Rose's manner
but by his presence there at all, Rudd decided to go
along with the game for a little while before making
an excuse to escape. Besides, despite his impatience,
he was genuinely interested in the findings of the excavation.

He studied the post-holes in silence for a few moments and then said thoughtfully, "It's not big enough
for a farm-house. It could, I suppose, be a cottage or
a small barn."

"Wrong!" Rose announced triumphantly. "Quite
wrong! It's something much more interesting than either of those."

"Then I'm afraid I have no idea," Rudd said firmly.
"You'll have to tell me."

Although disappointed that the Inspector had given
up so quickly, Rose was nevertheless determined to
get the best effect out of his final revelation. Walking
to the centre of the rectangle, with the absolute assurance of a man who has no idea that he might be running the risk of making a fool of himself, he lifted up
his arms in a gesture that had a touch of theatricality
about it. Behind his glasses, his eyes were shining
with enthusiasm. Rudd watched him with amused admiration, wondering how this style of instruction
went down in the class-room. It was certainly more
riveting than the average school history book.

"Imagine it as it was!" Rose was exhorting. "The
spaces between the posts filled in with wattle and
daub to form the walls and rising up to support a
thatched roof; sunlight filtering in through the cracks
in the walls and through the open doorway to fall
across the floor of beaten clay; outside a crowd of
people, murmuring together in soft voices, some of
whom had possibly come for miles to bring their
offerings . . ."

"Offerings?" Rudd asked quickly. Something more
than just mere interest began to stir in his mind. He
thought of the body, laid out with its arms crossed,
the signs of ritual. . . .

Ignoring his question, Rose turned to call in his normal schoolmasterish voice to one of the young men who was pushing a barrow-load of earth past the end of the site.

"Neil, be a good lad will you, and pop over to my tent and bring me my little box?"

Neil, a strapping six-footer who looked mildly amused at being called a good lad, nodded and began walking towards the camp site.

"Offerings?" Rudd repeated.

"You'll see, all in good time," Rose replied, with an air of maddening secrecy. "As a matter of fact, we only fully realised the significance of the place this morning when we found . . . But you'll see. I shan't spoil it by telling you."

The young man had returned carrying a box which he handed over to Rose, who, opening it, took out three small objects from its cotton-wool-lined interior and gave them to Rudd. He examined them carefully as they lay in the palm of his hand. They were tiny metal figurines, crudely fashioned into naked female shapes, with well-developed breasts and protuberant bellies.

"Bronze votive offerings," Rose was explaining. "We found them scattered about the site. Of course, there were doubtlessly other objects that haven't survived; offerings of food, for example; possibly wooden figures, too. We've found some clay pieces that may be parts of similar shapes but we'll have to re-assemble them before we can be sure. But what we are certain about is that this place was once a place of pagan worship, almost certainly to a local goddess. The name of the field bears that out—Hollowfield; a corruption, of course, of the Saxon word 'halig,' meaning 'holy.' Isn't it fascinating how far place names go back into history? Never ignore them," he added, wagging an admonishing finger at Rudd as if he had been found guilty of such an omission. "They can be vital clues to the origin of a site. Take the name of the lane that runs past the farms—Hallbrook Lane, another word that has Saxon origins, from 'hael,' which meant 'health,' suggesting a stream or brook that had healing powers, which may give us the reason why this place was considered sacred. Pilgrims would come to drink or bathe in the magic water and offer up gifts to the goddess of the place, here, on this very spot where we're standing now, where possibly the spring bubbled out of the ground. Interesting, isn't it?"

Before Rudd had time to reply, Rose had plunged on.

"Then came Christianity; for the second time, as a matter of fact, although that's neither here nor there in our present study of the place. But the people didn't give up their old gods willingly. Do you know the story of the Saxon warriors, forced by their king to accept baptism and driven en masse through a river while a Christian bishop blessed the water upstream, holding their sword arms high above their heads so they wouldn't be weakened by what they considered an effeminate religion that told them to forgive their enemies and turn the other cheek? The same attitude was found in many others. They clung to their old beliefs which, in fact, haven't entirely died out even today. There are still people about who worship the horned god of their ancestors. Indeed, Essex is supposed to be one of the counties where his worshippers are particularly flourishing." He giggled deprecatingly. "Not, of course, that I have first-hand knowledge. The Eucharist is the nearest I've ever been to ancient ritual and that's a long way from a Sabbat. But I'm digressing. The point is, faced with a pagan people who wouldn't readily accept a monotheistic religion, the Christian missionaries, rather cleverly I think, adopted some of the old gods and goddesses as their own saints and converted their shrines to churches, which is clearly what happened here."

He took another object from the box and passed it to Rudd, adding:

"Evidence, Inspector. You'll appreciate the importance of that I'm sure. Indeed, you might say that you and I are in the same line of country, piecing together facts in order to arrive at the truth. *That* was found only this morning but it's enough to prove that the site continued to be used as a place of worship into the Christian era."

He had handed the Inspector a piece of bone, jaggedly broken and dirt-stained, that had been carved with what appeared to be the letters X and R enclosed in an intricate, circular border. As he ran his fingers over it, Rudd had the sensation that he was holding part of the key to the mystery in this broken fragment. It hadn't been a sense of death that the field conveyed to him, in spite of the anonymous grave and the heaps of excavated earth; nor a mere feeling of the past. He realised that now. But could he have been instinctively aware of its sacred and magic powers that had inspired all that past veneration and worship?

Another idea, too, began to take form at the back of his mind but Rose's voice over-rode his thoughts.

"The Chi-Rho monogram, an early Christian symbol," he was saying, coming close to point at the carved letters. "It's been broken off but that's undoubtedly what it was; the first two letters of the Greek word for Christ, set in a circle. Notice the border; a typical Saxon design with an interlaced ribbon pattern. It's a pity it's so damaged because we may never know what it was part of, unless we're lucky enough to find the other pieces; a crucifix, perhaps, or the decorative top to a staff or some other ritual object."

"A crucifix, did you say?" Rudd asked.

He was thinking of the other crucifix that had been found in the field; the cheap, silver-plated cross and chain that had been lying in the man's grave.

Sacred ground, of course. Holyfield. At last, that part of it made sense.

Rose had started to reply but Rudd didn't wait to listen. He was eager to pursue his own particular, over-riding interest.

"Could it still be known locally that this field had once been a place of worship?" he broke in.

"Strange that you should ask that," Rose answered. "The site must have been abandoned a long time ago, certainly before the wooden building was replaced by something more permanent in stone. Why, we don't know. Possibly the spring dried up. But some folk memory of the place must have lingered on. I was talking to one of Stebbing's men only yesterday and he told me that he remembered, as a boy, people saying that herbs picked in this field had particular healing power and that carrying an acorn in your pocket from one of the oak trees growing over there along the hedge was supposed to ward off rheumatism."

"Was the man called Wheeler?" Rudd asked with rising excitement.

Rose pursed his lips doubtfully.

"I'm afraid I can't recall his name."

"What did he look like?"

"A small man, in his fifties, I'd say. Rather—well—sly, if you know what I mean, and not very eager to give away much."

"Wheeler!" said Rudd.

Handing back the piece of carved bone, he added hurriedly, "Thank you very much, Mr. Rose. You've been more help than you can possibly imagine."

"Have I?" asked Rose, sounding bewildered but gratified, as Rudd turned away and began walking rapidly across the field towards Stebbing's farm.

It fitted. It had to fit. There was no other possible explanation. And now that the question of the choice of the field for a grave site was explained, other details made sense as well; the tidiness of Lovell's house; the gun propped up in the corner by the fireplace; the dog turned loose in the yard. He remembered, too, the scene in the kitchen garden when he had questioned Betty Lovell under the washing-line, and the significance of what he had seen then, which had eluded him at the time, now sprang into sharp focus and, with that realisation, the last piece of the puzzle dropped into place.

He found himself in Stebbing's yard without being aware of making the journey there and, banging loudly on the door, he brought the farmer out onto the step.

"I want to use your phone," Rudd told him, cutting

short any possibility of time-wasting social prelimi-
naries. "And I'd like to talk to Wheeler."

"He's knocked off work for the day," Stebbing replied.

"Could he be sent for?"

Even Stebbing seemed aware of a sense of urgency.

"I'll get the car out and fetch him myself," he offered with surprising decision. "The phone's through
here," he added, showing Rudd into a small room
opening off the hall and evidently used as an office,
for it contained a desk and filing cabinets. As he ushered Rudd inside, he couldn't resist asking, "Something turned up?"

"Possibly," Rudd said shortly and waited until Stebbing had left the room before reaching for the telephone.

He made three calls altogether. The first was to Detective Chief Inspector Mullen at Mill Edge, whom
he was lucky to find still at the office. It was a short
conversation, consisting of two questions and Mullen's
replies to them, and, when he replaced the receiver,
Rudd had a look of quiet satisfaction.

Next, he rang Harlsdon police station and spoke to
the sergeant on duty.

"Yes, I know Nancy Fowler, sir," the man said,
sounding amused. "What's she been up to now to interest headquarters?"

"Nothing. I want to talk to her, that's all. Can you
get her to ring me here as soon as possible?" Rudd replied, giving Stebbing's telephone number. "You know
where to find her?"

"Yes. She'll be round at the Blue Boar at this time
of the evening. I'll send a constable to bring her in."

"Plain-clothes," Rudd said quickly, remembering
the landlord's hostile interest. "I don't want her harassed. You understand?"

There was a tiny pause in which Rudd imagined
the sergeant raising his eyebrows. But when he spoke,
his voice was deferential. "Very good, sir."

While he waited for Nancy Fowler to telephone,
Rudd made his last call, to Boyce.

"I was just about to go home," Boyce said. "What's up?"

"A whole lot," Rudd replied. As he spoke, he saw Stebbing's car turn into the yard and Wheeler get out of the front passenger seat. He began to walk reluctantly towards the house, his whole body expressing hostility, while Stebbing fussed round him, attempting to hustle him along.

"I can't explain now," Rudd continued hurriedly, "but I want you to meet me at Lovell's farm as soon as you can get there. It could be important."

"Christ!" exclaimed Boyce. "You don't mean you've got something definite on Lovell? But, surely, now we know the body isn't his brother's . . . ?"

"I'll explain it when I see you," Rudd replied and hung up just as the door opened and Stebbing ushered Wheeler officiously into the room. He refused to come too far and stood just inside the threshold, regarding Rudd with open dislike.

"I'd just started my bloody supper . . ." he began.

"I'm sorry, Mr. Wheeler," Rudd replied briskly, "but there are a few questions I must ask you straightaway. I believe you talked to Mr. Rose yesterday about the field where they're making the dig?"

"What of it?" Wheeler asked belligerently. "There ain't no law. He'd come to fetch drinking water from the house and it was him who kept me chatting in the yard."

"And you told him," Rudd went on, ignoring his reply, "that there's a local story about herbs picked in that field having special healing powers. Am I right?"

Wheeler gave a slow, contemptuous smile.

"Yes and he believed it and all."

"It's not true?"

Wheeler shrugged.

"Maybe," he said cautiously.

"Do other people know of these stories about the field? Mr. Lovell, for instance?"

Wheeler watched the Inspector carefully. He was unsure of the purpose behind the questions and didn't want to commit himself.

"Does he?" Rudd persisted.

"How the hell should I know? I never talked to him about it."

"Or Mrs. Lovell?"

A bright, knowing look passed across Wheeler's face and was gone in an instant, but not before Rudd had glimpsed it. He pounced quickly.

"You discussed it with her?"

"Maybe."

"Not maybe, Mr. Wheeler. I want a straight answer for once. What did you say to her about that field?"

Wheeler hesitated before saying in an off-hand manner, "Nothing much."

Rudd felt his temper rising and it was with difficulty that he kept his voice level as he replied, "I haven't got the time for games, Mr. Wheeler. I want to know exactly what you told her."

It was Wheeler who became angry.

"All right, I'll tell you, since you're so bloody bent on finding out but what good it'll do you, don't ask me," he said, his voice rising and two ugly, red patches appearing on his bony cheeks. "She had a headache one day, see, and I told her to pick a dock leaf from up that field and hold it to her forehead and that'd cure it. I was having her on, like," he added, trailing off and sounding embarrassed and Rudd guessed that, like a lot of country people, Wheeler had an ambivalent attitude to folk lore, part belief, part scepticism.

"Did you explain why?" he asked.

But Wheeler set his mouth stubbornly.

"I don't remember," he said flatly and turned away.

Stebbing, who had been hanging about near the open doorway during the interview, bustled forward.

"If you'll go through to the kitchen, Len," he said, "and ask Mrs. Stebbing to pour you a glass of beer, I'll drive you home in a few minutes."

As Wheeler walked away down the hall, he added to Rudd, "A glass for you as well, Inspector, or are you on duty?"

His face was alive with curiosity and Rudd parried

the inquisitiveness behind the innocent-seeming question by saying vaguely, "I've got a few calls to make later."

To forestall any further questions from Stebbing while he waited for Nancy Fowler's call, he turned to a chart that was pinned up over the desk, detailing the fields belonging to the farms, with their acreage and crops marked in and commented, "That shows good organisation. Your idea, is it?"

"My son's," Stebbing replied with pride. "He's the expert round here; went to agricultural college and picked up all sorts of modern, farming know-how. Me, I'm just an ordinary working farmer." He laughed deprecatingly. "As a matter of fact," he went on in a confiding tone, "I'd got my eye on Lovell's place for him. It's been neglected, mind, and it'll need money spending on it but I reckon we could run the two farms jointly and make it a going concern. No chance of Lovell moving out, I suppose?"

The remark seemed harmless enough but Rudd guessed the implied meaning behind it. Like Boyce, Stebbing had jumped to the conclusion that the case against Geoff Lovell was building up and was hoping that, whatever move Rudd seemed about to make, it might benefit him. Rudd now understood, too, why Lovell had so disliked the man, in spite of his professed neighbourliness. Behind it lay the same self-seeking motive that must have angered Lovell more than it angered Rudd.

"I have no idea, Mr. Stebbing," he replied shortly and was spared further conversation with him by the ringing of the telephone.

"If you don't mind going outside," he added and, showing Stebbing out into the hall, shut the door on him before picking up the receiver.

Nancy Fowler's voice, loud and breathy, vibrated in his ear.

"The police said you wanted to talk to me. What's it about?"

"There's a query you might be able to help me with," Rudd said quickly, before she could get on to the inevitable question. "You remember you told me that Betty Lovell had been brought up in a children's home? Do you by any chance know whether it was Catholic?"

"Yes, it was. I know 'cos Ron said that's why she'd never divorce him. She'd been brought up by nuns and she didn't hold with it. But how did you guess?"

"I just wondered," Rudd replied but added to himself that it was a fact he should have realised, if not on the first occasion when he visited the farm and the neatness of the living-room had struck him, then at least on the second when he had spoken to Betty Lovell in the kitchen where she was mending shirts. Only Catholic sisters could have taught her that exquisitely fine needlework.

It explained, too, a lot more about the case that had puzzled him at the time; not only the reason why, as Nancy Fowler had said, Betty Lovell had never divorced her husband but the other details concerning the burial of the dead man.

"Is that all?" Nancy Fowler was asking, sounding surprised.

"Just one more question," Rudd added. "Has Geoff Lovell been to collect the photographs yet?"

"No but he should be calling round soon. He said a week. Have you found . . . ?"

"Thank you, Mrs. Fowler," Rudd broke in. "I'm sorry you've been troubled."

He rang off guiltily. There was nothing he could do to shield her from finding out the truth eventually but not now, he decided. Not at the end of a telephone with a policeman standing at her elbow. Later, he would break it to her himself.

He could do little to protect Betty Lovell but she, at least, knew the truth and had known it all along. The burden of it had worn her down. Her pale face with the bones showing through the thin skin rose in his mind but he thrust it quickly to one side. There was no room for sentiment. Not even for her. The process of justice that he would soon have to put into motion took no notice of the tragic circumstances of the individual and it was right not to do so. He would have to make the arrest.

Besides, he comforted himself, as he made for the door, there was that steely centre to her that he had recognised. She would bend but she would not break.

Chapter 15

As he bumped the car up onto the grass verge by
Lovell's farm and switched off the engine, Rudd was
aware of the silence. There was no wind. The trees
were quite motionless. Even the long grasses that
grew along the bottom of the hedge held themselves
erect and still.

Getting out of the car, he was acutely conscious of
the sharp snap of the door, even though he closed it
quietly, and the sound of his feet crunching on the
surface of the road as he walked towards the gate.

As usual, it was padlocked. Below, the yard lay in
the last rays of sunlight that fell in sections between
the long, peaked shadows cast by the roofs of the outbuildings. The dog lay in one of them, motionless on
its side, its head stretched out in an attitude of exhausted sleep.

Rudd laid his hand on the top bar of the gate, expecting the dog to spring immediately to its feet and come racing up the track towards him. It didn't move.

Surprised, he shook the bar, making the chain and padlock rattle. Still the dog didn't stir. At the same time, some fleeting impression of movement made him glance towards the house. But whatever he had seen—a curtain momentarily lifted, a face appearing briefly at a window—was gone in an instant. The house presented the blank façade, its door closed, its chimneys smokeless, of an empty building.

Cautiously, he began to climb over the gate, keeping his eyes on the dog, which still lay in its patch of shadow, and finding its silence more menacing than its normal ferocity. Dropping almost without sound onto the dusty ruts of the drive, he reached the grass edge in one long stride and stopped again.

He now had the house and the dog in plain view. It was possible to watch both without turning his head. The house presented the same lifeless appearance although he noticed, for the first time, that the windows of the upper storey were set open, so someone must be at home.

The dog remained where it lay and something about its stretched attitude struck the Inspector as strange. The legs were stiffly extended, the head bent back at an uncomfortable angle, as if the creature had been arrested in mid-howl.

He began to walk rapidly forward, his footsteps softened by the grass, keeping his eyes fixed on the dog.

It was dead. He realised that before he reached the end of the drive and, stopping at the entrance to the yard, saw the darker blotch of blood spread out in the shadow of the barn. He could make out the huge wound in its head, round which the flies were greedily clustering.

At exactly the same moment, a shot rang out to his left, from the direction of the house, its report so loud that he felt as much as heard it, like a physical blow, even though the bullet passed a few feet in front of him and thudded into the barn wall, blasting a hole in its wooden cladding.

For a terrible instant that seemed endless, he remained standing, confused and deafened, while, at the same time, another quite clear and logical part of his mind told him that if he stayed where he was he presented a perfect target and the second shot might not miss.

The next second, he found himself falling face downwards on the grass and then scrambling on all fours, with an alacrity he didn't know he possessed, back along the verge towards the gate.

Above him, rooks, startled from the trees, circled in a wide sweep, cawing loudly, and through their frightened cries came Lovell's voice:

"Get back, you bloody fool, unless you want your head blown off!"

The shout and the birds' clamour followed him as he made for the gate, still keeping low, out of the line of fire. Reaching it, he hesitated, not daring to climb over it, knowing that, once astride the top bar, he would be in full view of the house.

The hedge beside it was thick and well grown but, with his arms shielding his face, he broke through it, his hair and clothes full of pieces of broken leaf and twig, just as Boyce's car drew up alongside. The sergeant's face appeared at the driver's window, which he was furiously winding down, at the same time shouting through it, "What the hell's going on? Wasn't that a shot I heard?"

"Get back to Stebbing's farm," Rudd ordered him between gasps for breath. "Use his phone. I want some men here as soon as possible. As many as can be spared. A couple of marksmen, too. While you're there, see if you can borrow a hacksaw, anything, to cut through the chain on that gate. We'll have to get it open for a clear view of the house. And keep Stebbing away at all costs!" he added, raising his voice as Boyce reversed and turned the car, its engine racing.

"I'll arrest him if he so much as pokes his nose near here," he added aloud to himself as the car tore away up the road.

Meanwhile, there was nothing he could do except wait. Squatting down on the grass verge in front of the gap he had torn in the hedge, Rudd contemplated what he could see of the house. It was silent again now. The windows, catching the last light of the sun as it slanted over the roofs of the outbuildings, glittered golden, allowing him not even the smallest glimpse of any movement inside. The body of the dog was no longer visible either, lying hidden from sight below a dip in the ground.

It occurred to him then to wonder exactly when it had been killed. Not during the last hour certainly, when he had been talking with Rose in Hollowfield. The farm was less than a mile away and the sound of a shot would have been easily audible at that distance. So it must have been fired sometime earlier, before he arrived, and he wondered what had happened at the farm-house to precipitate this sudden violence.

He wondered, too, who was inside the house. Lovell, of course, and presumably the others as well, although there had been no sign of any of them at the windows. But if one of them had managed to get away, the alarm would have been raised and that hadn't happened.

Were they dead?

The thought struck him like a blow and he leaned forward to peer anxiously through the gap, focussing his attention on the blank, golden windows that gave nothing away.

Should he shout down to them? Or would that only make matters worse? Better, perhaps, to wait until the others arrived and he could have the place surrounded. That, at least, would give him a psychological advantage. Alone, there was little he could do.

He cursed himself for not having tumbled to the truth earlier and yet he knew he was being less than just to himself. There was no way he could have guessed at what had happened until this evening, when the full significance of the site chosen for the grave had been revealed to him, unwittingly, by Rose and, with that difficulty removed, the other details had begun to make sense.

Boyce's car slid almost silently to a halt beside him and the sergeant got out and came to squat beside him.

"I've spoken to the chief," he said quietly. "The men are on their way. Fifteen of them. And Rogers and Wylie, who'll be armed. Davies will send on more later, as you need them, and any special equipment you want, like listening-in devices, in case it looks like being a long-drawn-out siege."

"I hope to God it doesn't come to that," Rudd said with feeling.

"And I borrowed these from Stebbing," the sergeant continued, flourishing a pair of huge, long-handled wire clippers. "They should cut through that chain. Shall I get started on it?"

"Keep your head down," Rudd warned him. "I'll put you in the picture while you do it."

Boyce crawled across to the other side of the gate where the padlock and chain hung and, as he worked to cut through it, Rudd explained briefly.

"And that's what I reckon happened," he concluded, "although the proof of it's down there, in that house, and there's no chance of getting anywhere near it at the moment."

"Do you think he'll give himself up quietly?" Boyce asked.

"I don't know," Rudd admitted. "He may do once he realises it's useless to hold out but I'm not too happy about that dog being killed. It shows he's pretty near the edge."

"Stebbing mentioned hearing a shot earlier this afternoon," Boyce broke in. "About five o'clock, he reckoned."

"Then why the hell didn't he say something about it to me?" Rudd asked bitterly. "I nearly walked into his line of fire. A few more feet and I'd've got it in the head too."

"Said he thought it was Lovell out after rooks," Boyce grunted. He was kneeling upright in the soft dust at the gate opening, trying to get a purchase on the wire cutters, the sweat standing out on his fore-head.

Suddenly the link gave, the chain and padlock fell away and the gate began to swing slowly open, Boyce giving it a final push with his foot before scrambling back to the cover of the hedge.

They now had an uninterrupted view of the house at the bottom of the slope. It still presented its blank, silent face but, as they watched, a slight movement on the back slope of the roof caught Rudd's attention. At first, it was no more than a flash of brightness as glass reflected the light of the sun.

"The skylight!" Rudd said urgently, pointing.

A few seconds later, the head of a man appeared, dwarfed by the distance, a mere dark blob against the steep incline.

Boyce opened his mouth as if to shout but Rudd silenced him by grasping his arm.

"God, it's Lovell!" he said softly. "He's going to try to make it down the roof. Don't move, Tom. Don't even breathe. If he loses his grip . . ."

He fell silent, watching, absorbed, as the figure struggled like a fly on the precipice of tiles that glowed a warm, deep red in the last rays of the sun.

Lovell was unaware of their attention. Having pushed the skylight open with his shoulders, he rested for a moment, breathing heavily, his whole weight carried on his forearms, which were braced across the wooden frame. He could feel the muscles in them jumping convulsively and he knew that he had, at most, a few seconds in which to force his body up-wards, over the edge of the skylight, before their strength gave out. Below him, the steep slope of the tiled roof seemed to avalanche downwards to a dis-tant view of the garden, strangely and dizzyingly diminished at that unaccustomed height. But he daren't think of that. Kicking with his legs, he slowly drew himself upwards until he could feel the frame biting into his chest. He leaned forward gratefully, taking the strain from his arms, and then painfully drew first one leg and then the other through the narrow opening, until he was lying bunched up on his side, his knees touching his chin.

He waited, trying to listen for sounds below him in the house but the heavy rasping of his own breath and the pulsing roar of blood in his head and ears covered all other noises.

Clutching the frame with both hands, until his knuckles cracked and whitened, he let his legs swing over and down with their own weight, at the same time altering his grip on the edge of the skylight, so that he was now lying face downwards and fully extended, only his grasp on the frame preventing him from sliding down.

He could feel the tiles, warm and hard, pressing into his chest and could see, in close-up, those that lay immediately under his face, in one of those dazzling moments of complete perception in which every detail of their colour and texture was absorbed in an instant. He saw, too, the round blobs of grey-green moss with which they were patched and their coarse, porous, animal surface, like skin seen under a microscope.

The next second, almost without making a conscious decision, he had loosened his grip on the frame and was slithering rapidly down the pitch of the roof. He felt the edges of the tiles catch and tear, first at his clothes, then at the bare skin on his chest as the thin fabric of his shirt was ripped away but, although he was aware of warm blood trickling down and a burning sensation in his finger-tips as his hands scrabbled for any hold, however small, to slow up the falling rush of his body, he was not conscious of any pain, only of the sense of speed and the rough, bumping motion as he glissaded downwards.

Strangely, there was no fear either, until he felt his feet drop away into space and knew he was within inches of the edge of the roof.

It was not far to the ground but a concrete path ran along the back of the house and Lovell knew that, if he dropped onto it at the speed he was falling, he would be lucky to escape with just broken legs.

Bracing his knees and hands against the tiles, he

thrust himself away from the roof, at the same time tensing his muscles to turn and spring for the softer earth beyond the path.

All the same, he fell awkwardly and heavily, one shoulder striking the concrete before he was able to roll to safety. For a moment, he lay stunned and winded. The next, he was on his feet and, bent double, one hand clutching his shoulder, was making for the far side of the garden where a belt of trees and bushes separated it from the road.

He broke through it, in the same way Rudd had done higher up the lane, shielding his face with one arm, before collapsing onto the grass verge.

Rudd and Boyce, who had lost sight of him behind the trees when he was halfway down the roof, ran forward to where he lay on his side. At first sight, his condition looked serious. His shirt and the knees of his trousers were torn to ribbons and through the rents Rudd could see long lacerations and grazes from which blood was trickling.

"Get an ambulance," he said to Boyce but Lovell struggled to sit up, shaking his head.

"Not hospital," he gasped. "I'll be all right. Just let me get my breath."

"Those cuts must be cleaned up," Rudd told him briskly and added to Boyce, "There's a first-aid kit in my car. Fetch it, will you? And then get back to the gate. Keep a watch on the house and report to me the second anything happens."

As Boyce ran back to the car, Lovell made an effort to speak again.

"Betty and Charlie . . ." he began, his mouth shaking.

"We'll get them out," Rudd assured him. "I don't think he'll do anything to harm them."

"You know about him?"

"I guessed. Only this evening, unfortunately, otherwise I might have done something sooner."

Boyce had returned with the first-aid kit, which he handed to the Inspector before moving away to take up his watch on the house, while Rudd, ripping open Lovell's shirt, began dabbing his chest with antiseptic lotion, covering the worst of the cuts with gauze and plaster. His shoulder, Rudd noticed, was badly bruised but not, he thought, broken, as Lovell seemed to be able to move it without too much pain.

"I fell on it when I came off the roof," he explained and added urgently, "Ron . . ."

"Don't talk," Rudd told him. "Get your breath back. I'll tell you what I think happened and you put me right if I get any of it wrong. Ronnie came back nearly four years ago and expected you to take him in."

He didn't add, as he could have done, that Ronnie had, at the same time, resumed his rights as Betty's husband. Had he known of the relationship that existed between his wife and his brother? Possibly not. But if he had, Rudd couldn't see that he would have cared. Ronnie's attitude to women was one of sexual exploitation. Even after eleven years' desertion, he would have expected Betty to share his bed again. As for her, Rudd could understand her feelings. A Catholic upbringing that denied her the possibility of divorce must also have instilled into her a deeply held sense of her obligations as a wife. Besides, Rudd had recognised in her a rigid and unbending quality, perhaps an overdeveloped sense of shame, that was apparent in the excessive, almost obsessive, tidiness of the house. Whatever love she had felt for Geoff Lovell had been denied out of guilt. Rudd remembered the occasion when he had seen them together in the garden and had been aware of the space she was deliberately creating between them that held him back from any real contact.

How Lovell had taken it, Rudd could only guess, but the weariness and defeat that the Inspector had seen stamped deeply into his face on that first visit when Lovell had stood on the doorstep of the house in the sunlight had been eloquent enough. He had been forced to accept the situation because there was nothing else to do; because legally he had no rights; because she was stronger willed than he was; because, like her, he felt a deep sense of guilt and shame; but, ultimately and tragically, because he

loved her too much, with that humble and self-effacing devotion that accepts all and forgives all.

Lovell raised his head, which he had been resting
against his knees. His face was ravaged.

"How did you guess?" he asked.

"Something I noticed," Rudd replied. "Only at the
time I didn't realise its significance."

It had been that same afternoon when he had seen
her hanging out the washing in the garden. Afterwards, his mind had kept reverting to the scene when
he was talking to Boyce in the car, only he hadn't
then been able to make the connection. Four pillow-
cases, hanging in pairs on the line, when there should
have been only three. A small, domestic detail but
one he ought to have taken account of. It was a vital
clue to the number of people who were sleeping in
the house. And the gun, too, of course. That also
should have registered more positively on him as a
symbol of violence; Ronnie's signature on a room that
otherwise contained only the signs of Betty's well-or-
dered routine.

"Yes," Lovell said bitterly. "He came back, after
eleven years when we hadn't heard a word from him,
expecting to be looked after and sheltered, as if none
of it mattered."

"Did you know what the charge was against him?"

"No, not then. He said he was broke and in trouble
with a gang for informing against them and he was
afraid they'd come looking for him. I believed him.
He was afraid of being seen. But there was something
else about him, too, that was different. He was
harder, almost vicious. He'd always been wild and
quick-tempered but there'd always been part of him
you couldn't help liking, even though he was out for
himself most of the time."

"Yes, I can imagine that," Rudd replied, thinking of
Nancy Fowler, who had gone on loving him. Even
Tidyman, who ran the local garage, had had a good
word for Ronnie Lovell as he had been in those days.
"Of course," he went on, "he'd been drinking heavily
for years."

"Yes," Lovell agreed, with a wry twist of his mouth and then fell silent.

"And so you got the dog?" Rudd asked.

"What?" Lovell asked blankly. His thoughts seemed to be far away.

"You got the dog and let it run loose in the yard so that no-one could come near the house without you knowing it?"

"It wasn't meant to be like that," Lovell answered. "I'd kept a dog before, a collie, only she'd died. The idea was to get another and keep it chained up in the yard during the day, like we'd done with Bess. Ron wanted it, as you said, to give him warning of anyone coming to the gate and, anyway, we'd been used to having a dog about the place. Only . . ."

He broke off and Rudd took up the sentence for him.

"Ronnie turned it into a guard dog."

I should have guessed that, too, Rudd thought. It wasn't in Geoff Lovell's nature to allow a dog to become so fierce. He understood animals and, as a farmer, he'd know the value of having a well-trained dog, not a savage animal that would attack anything or anybody.

"He said he'd train it. Like a fool, I said yes. I thought it'd give him something to do. He'd been giving me a hand with the farm machinery but that's about all. He'd never cared for farming. Anyway, I got the dog to please Ronnie but he didn't know how to treat it. It was young and needed proper handling. If it didn't do what he wanted, he used to hit it. In the end, of course, it turned on him. He couldn't go outside the door without it starting to bark at him."

Which accounted, Rudd said to himself, for the fact that Stebbing had heard it two or three times a day on occasions.

"Ron had let it run loose," Lovell was continuing. "I tried keeping it on the chain for at least part of the day but it only made Ron more tensed up, knowing someone could come through the gate without him being warned. This frightened him and, when he's frightened, he takes it out on other people. It was

Betty and Charlie who used to feel it most, so I gave in and let the dog run loose and padlocked the gate. It made for a bit of peace, at least where Ron was concerned."

"Until Maguire turned up," Rudd pointed out.

"You found out about him?" Lovell asked quickly.

"Only today," Rudd admitted, "and even then the story didn't register with me. It wasn't until this evening when I knew without doubt that it wasn't Ronnie's body that had been found in the field that I realised it must be someone connected with him and Maguire seemed the most likely person. How did he find out where Ronnie was hiding? After all, he'd changed his name. There was nothing to trace him to this place."

"He knew Ronnie had been carrying on with his wife while he was still working for him at the garage, somewhere up in the Midlands. I got the story out of Ron after it all happened. It seems Maguire guessed, from one or two things that Ron let slip when he'd been drinking, that there was something about his past that he was covering up. Then one day Ron left his jacket hanging up in the office and Maguire went through his wallet. Like a fool, Ron had kept his old driver's licence, with his name and this address on it, so Maguire knew where to come looking for him when he came out of prison."

"He knew Ronnie had shopped him?"

Lovell gave a short, hard laugh.

"What do you think? He guessed as soon as the police raided the garage. In fact, I've often wondered since if that story Ron told about a gang being after him didn't have some truth in it; only it was just the one man who'd be out for his blood—Maguire; not only because Ron had tipped off the police but for what he'd done to Maguire's wife."

"So after Maguire came out of prison, he came here looking for him?"

"Yes. It was two years ago, next October, about late afternoon. I was out ploughing when Betty came up the field to fetch me. She told me a man had come to the gate and Charlie had taken him down to the house. He was asking for Ron and didn't believe her when she told him that we hadn't seen Ron for years. When I got back to the house, Maguire was in the kitchen. I could see he was spoiling for a fight. I tried to get rid of him by repeating what Betty had already told him—that we hadn't seen Ron since he'd left home fifteen years ago, but he didn't believe me either. He said he knew he was somewhere in the house and he wasn't leaving until he'd searched every room to find him and then give him back what he'd given to his wife."

Lovell shuddered.

"I could see he meant it, too. He'd picked up the poker from the fire-place and was waving it about, shouting obscenities about Ronnie and what he'd do to him. God! It was terrifying! Charlie was crying like a child and saying over and over, 'I didn't mean it! I didn't mean it!' He knew he shouldn't have let anyone in without asking one of us first."

"Was that the first time you knew about the attempted murder charge against your brother?" Rudd asked.

"Yes," Lovell replied in a quiet voice. "Until Maguire turned up, I swear I didn't know Ron was wanted by the police."

"Go on," Rudd told him. "What happened then?"

"Ron was upstairs. He'd heard Maguire's voice in the yard, when Charlie brought him to the house, and he'd managed to get away without being seen. He was in my bedroom, the one at the end, over the kitchen, listening to what was being said. The ceilings aren't all that thick and, anyway, Maguire was shouting so loudly he could hear every word. When he heard Maguire threaten to search the house, he decided to try to make a run for it. He came down the stairs and across the yard towards the barn, only Maguire saw him through the window and went charging off through the house after him. I followed. I knew there was going to be a fight and I thought there was something I could do to stop it but, by the time I got there, it was too late.

"Ron had gone up into the hayloft. God knows

what was in his mind, because once up there he was trapped. As I ran into the barn after Maguire, I saw Ron standing on the edge of the loft with a pitch-fork in his hand."

He rubbed his own hand over his eyes as if to erase the memory.

"I can't describe the look on his face. I knew then he was mad; crazy not just with fear but with the rage you see in a savage animal when it's been cornered. I'll never forget that look. He yelled something; what I don't know. All I can remember is standing there, thinking Christ! he doesn't look human. The next moment, he'd flung the pitch-fork like a javelin and Maguire fell backwards with it sticking out of his chest, the handle of it still vibrating."

Rudd was silent. He understood now why his inquiries about tools missing from the farm had provoked such a sharp response in Lovell at the time. He also realised the significance of the nature of the wounds described in the forensic report. It hadn't been a double stabbing as he and Boyce had thought but a single blow from a pitch-fork with a sharp, curved, two-pronged head.

"He must have died almost at once," Lovell was saying in a flat, exhausted voice. "One of the tines had got him through the heart. He didn't have a chance. I got Ron back to the house and locked up the barn. I was in a daze and couldn't think what the hell to do. Charlie kept asking where the man had gone and Ronnie told him he'd sent him away. But Betty knew it wasn't the truth. She kept looking at me and I could see it in her eyes. Later, I sent Charlie out to shut up the animals for the night and got her on her own in the living-room and told her what had happened. Ron was in the kitchen, drinking. He was on whisky. I used to go out in the evenings round the pubs and off-licences where I wasn't known to buy it for him. He couldn't give it up and that way he wasn't too much of a nuisance."

Did he mean to Betty? Rudd wondered. Drunk, Ronnie could be put to bed, his sexual demands diminished. It was probably the lesser of two evils.

"I had to tell her the truth," Lovell continued. "She'd guessed it anyway, when we came back to the house without Maguire. And, besides, I had to get her to agree to what I was going to do—turn Ronnie over to the police. I couldn't see any other way out of it. He'd murdered Maguire and nearly killed his wife. We couldn't go on harbouring him, knowing that.

"In the middle of it, Ron came out of the kitchen. He was drunk all right but there was more to it than that. There was a sort of glitter to him; I can't describe it in any other way. He stood leaning in the doorway, with my shot-gun over his arm, and he said, 'If you think I'm bloody well going to stand by while you hand me over, you'd better get one thing straight. I won't give myself up without making a fight of it and I don't bloody care who gets it; you, her, or Charlie, or one of the bleeding fuzz who comes to arrest me. But I can promise you this—one of you'll cop it with me. So what's it to be? Make up your mind.' What could I do? I had to agree not to send for the police. I knew by then he was mad enough to do anything he threatened if he got pushed far enough, and he knew it, too. It was like a game of dare that kids play, only in Ronnie's case we both realised it could be for real. It wasn't a risk I was going to take, not with other people's lives.

"After that he made damned sure there was either Betty or Charlie in the house or nearby to act as a sort of hostage. That's why I didn't dare risk warning you when you came to the house. Ron was upstairs, listening in to everything that was said and he always had one of my guns handy, either the shot-gun or the rifle, and I knew that, even if you brought more men with you, by the time you got inside the yard, he'd've turned the gun on someone."

The risk was real enough, as Rudd had to admit to himself. With the dog loose in the yard, there was no chance of anyone approaching the house without Ron being aware of it. He realised, too, how close he might have been to death when he searched the upstairs rooms in the farm-house. Ronnie must have been only a few yards away, in the one bedroom he didn't have time to examine.

"Whose idea was it to bury the body?" he asked. "Ronnie's?"

Lovell nodded.

"That was later, after we'd sent Charlie to bed. I said, 'We can't leave it in the barn. What are we going to do?' 'Get rid of it,' he said. 'Dig a hole. No-one'll miss him.' "

He had been right, Rudd thought. No-one had reported Maguire missing. It was one of the questions he had asked Mullen when he had telephoned him earlier; that, and the date of Maguire's release from prison; a date that coincided too closely with the length of time the body had been buried for Rudd to be any longer in doubt as to its identity. Maguire had few friends. His business had gone bankrupt. His wife had moved away from the area after her discharge from hospital. Those who knew him had assumed he had moved on himself in search of her. Even Mullen had come to that conclusion when Maguire had dropped out of sight in the district.

"And then," Lovell was continuing, "Ronnie said something that started the whole bloody, stupid business off. 'While you're at it,' he said to Betty, 'say a few prayers over him. He was a bloody R.C. the same as you.' He meant it to be sarcastic. He'd always made fun of her religion. She'd stopped going to church years before but, deep down, she'd never really ly given up believing."

"So she laid the body out and asked you to bury it in Stebbing's field because she'd heard from Wheeler it was sacred ground?"

"You know about that?" Lovell asked.

"There had to be some logical reason why that field was chosen. I only tumbled to the truth myself this evening, after I'd spoken to Rose and Wheeler. It was then it began to make sense."

"She stuck out on that. Even Ron couldn't make her change her mind. 'All right,' he said, 'Bury him where you bloody well like. There's no chance anyone's going to dig him up again.' He knew the field and there

didn't seem any likelihood anyone'd bother to culti-
vate it. It had never been anything else except rough
pasture." He laughed shortly. "But he didn't reckon
with Stebbing."

"Go on," Rudd said quietly.

Lovell eased his shoulder, which was evidently giving him some pain, by cupping his hand under his elbow to take the weight. He was visibly tiring and
there was a hoarse note in his voice as he took up the
account again.

"I'll never forget the next couple of hours. We took
a lantern out to the barn and I helped her wash and
lay out the body. He was about the same height and
build as Ron and we put some of his clothes on him.
Then she asked to be left alone with him. I could
guess why. As I went out, I turned and looked back.
She was kneeling on the edge of the blanket I'd
spread out on the floor. Later, when I went back,
she'd wrapped the body up in the blanket and fastened it together. I carried the body up to Stebbing's
field. . . ."

"Was it your idea you should bury the body?"
Rudd broke in to ask.

Lovell looked at him with a flash of his former bel-
ligerency.

"What the hell do you think? No, it bloody wasn't
but with Betty and Charlie in the house and Ron sitting in the kitchen, with the gun across his knees and
half drunk, I wasn't going to argue with him. It was
getting light by then and I didn't dare stop too long,
so I didn't have time to dig the grave very deep. I
laid him in it and put the earth back."

"And the cross and chain?" Rudd asked.

"I only found out about it later, after you'd been
here that day and questioned Betty about it. I could
tell by the look on her face that she knew something
about it and, afterwards, she told me. It'd been given
to her by the nuns for her first communion and she'd
always worn it until she married Ronnie. He'd never
liked her wearing it because, like I said, he hadn't
any time for religion. Besides, I think she felt she'd
lost all right to wear it. She'd sinned by marrying him

in the first place; he wasn't a Catholic. I don't understand it all. We talked about it a few times and she told me her priest had tried to explain that the church wouldn't reject her but she felt, because she'd sinned, she didn't have any right to forgiveness. I can't put it clearer than that."

He didn't have to, Rudd thought. He could perfectly well understand how Betty Lovell, with her strong sense of guilt, coupled with a masochistic streak in her personality, could persuade herself that she was unworthy of forgiveness, not just for marrying Ronnie, but for committing what in her eyes would be the sin of fornication, a fact that Lovell, with an innate sense of discretion, had omitted to mention.

"Anyway, it seemed she'd kept the cross and chain and, before she wrapped the body up, she put it between his hands. It must have slipped out when I laid the body down to dig the grave and got mixed up with the earth when I threw it back," Lovell concluded.

So that was the explanation, Rudd thought. Simple enough, although at the time it had puzzled him.

"And this evening?" he asked. "What happened to bring things to a head?"

"It was the dog. I told you it had taken against him for the way he treated it. It went for him again this afternoon when he was crossing the yard. He'd got to the stage, anyway, where the smallest thing got him angry. Not being able to leave the farm was bad enough. That'd been going on for over three years. Then you started coming to the house, making inquiries about the body. I used to dread your visits. He always drank more heavily after you'd been here and it was Betty who suffered most. . . ."

No wonder Lovell had been so anxious to get rid of him, Rudd realised.

"Then, this afternoon when the dog went for him, something seemed to snap inside him. He came raging into the house for the gun and shot it before anyone could stop him. I was up the top field so I didn't see what happened but the minute I heard the shot, I came down to the house. As soon as I got inside, he bolted the door after me. He'd got them in the living-room. Charlie was terrified. He'd always been afraid of Ron. Betty was trying to calm him down. Ron was sitting by the fire-place with the gun across his knees and the same look on his face that I'd seen when he killed Maguire. After a bit, though, he seemed to go quieter. Betty started talking to him, trying to persuade him to let Charlie go out and see to the cows. I knew what she was thinking of—if she could get Charlie out of the way, it might be easier for us to get Ron to put the gun down. There were times when she could talk him round, if he wasn't in too much of a rage, because, in a funny way, I think deep down he trusted her. He seemed ready to listen and then we heard your car arrive."

"And that finished it?" Rudd asked.

Lovell nodded.

"He made us go upstairs to the bedroom he shared with Betty. I know why. From there, he had a clear view up the yard. He told us to sit on the bed while he stood at the window watching. He must have seen you coming because he put the gun to his shoulder . . ."

"He missed," Rudd pointed out. "What happened?"

"I managed to get across the room and knock the gun to one side. Then I shouted to you. You heard me?"

"Yes, thank God. I was within feet of getting my head blown off."

"There was a bit of a scuffle," Lovell went on. "Ron lost his balance and while he was on the floor, I ran for the door and through to the far bedroom where there's a ladder leading up to the attic. I didn't know what the hell else to do. He still had the gun and at the time I had no idea you knew about Ronnie. I wanted to come and warn you. I was scared you'd come back with more police and try to rush the place and I knew what that might lead to, Ronnie turning the gun on Betty or Charlie or on one of your men."

He passed a hand over his mouth to hide its trembling.

"Maybe I should have stayed. I might have been able to get the gun off him in time, or, at least, talked him into letting Betty and Charlie go. They're alone with him now and God alone knows what he'll do."

"Nothing for the moment," Rudd replied with more conviction than he felt. "The men should be arriving any minute now and . . ."

"For God's sake, don't let him see them!" Lovell broke in hoarsely. "He'll really go berserk if he thinks he's surrounded. I know him. He'll feel trapped."

"All right," Rudd assured him. "I'll make sure they're not seen."

He walked back to the gate where Boyce was still squatting under cover of the hedge, keeping watch on the house.

"Nothing's happened so far," the sergeant began.

"Never mind that now. Something more important's come up. Lovell thinks Ron may blow his top if he knows we've sent for more men and we've got to go along with what he says. He knows his brother and the state of mind he's in. So what I want you to do is to walk along the lane and stop any cars or vans from coming too near. If the sound of my car set Ronnie off, God knows what the arrival of fifteen coppers will do to him."

"Right," Boyce said, getting to his feet. "And what then?"

"I don't know," Rudd confessed. He looked back at the figure of Geoff Lovell, sitting on the verge, his knees drawn up and his head resting on them, in an attitude of total exhaustion. "Maybe he'll come up with a bright idea. At the moment, though, I'm inclined to leave things as they are. Given time, we may be able to wear Ron down into giving himself up or, at least, letting the other two go. You'd better be on your way, Tom. Tell the men to approach on foot and they're not so much as to open their mouths."

As Boyce walked away down the lane, Rudd took up his position at the gate, peering down the drive towards the house. As Boyce had reported, all seemed quiet. The house still presented its silent façade, although the sun had moved round so that the windows no longer glittered golden. He was relieved to see they were still open.

Would it be possible to make use of them? he wondered. Get into the house through the front while Ronnie's attention was diverted to the back? Using the front door was out. Geoff Lovell had said Ron had bolted it, but he might be able to smuggle one of the police marksmen through the window at the far end.

Meanwhile, if he could persuade Ron to come to the landing window that overlooked the back garden, he could have already placed some of the men there out of sight. There was plenty of cover. The rest of the men could be positioned near the front of the house, hidden in the sheds and barns that faced it.

He looked towards them. Plenty of room there to hide as many men as he wanted. But could he get them inside without Ronnie seeing them? They'd have to be brought in through the back, out of sight of the house. He'd have to consult Geoff Lovell on that point. He'd know if there were any doors or windows facing away from the house that they could get in by.

The subdued tread of feet distracted his attention. Turning his head, he saw Boyce approaching up the lane, along the grass verge, followed by a long line of men in single file.

Rudd got to his feet and began walking towards them, lifting his arm in a signal for them to stop.

What happened next occurred so quickly that there was no time, after all, to plan out any moves.

As the men drew to a halt, and Boyce stepped forward to speak to Rudd, the sound of a car coming up fast behind them made the sergeant pause and then step rapidly into the road, waving his arms at it. It swerved, hooted violently and screamed to a stop.

Rudd had only a second in which to glimpse the driver's face but it was enough.

Stebbing!

Chapter 16

He hardly had time to register this fact when two shots rang out in quick succession from the direction of the house. As if jerked into action by the double report, Geoff Lovell was on his feet and was running past Rudd, shouting something incoherent as he ran. Cursing Stebbing out loud, Rudd turned and pounded after Lovell towards the gate. At the entrance, he paused momentarily to look down again at the farm.

In the short time since he had last seen it, the scene had changed completely from its former blank, empty stillness. In the middle distance, Lovell was sprinting down the drive, running awkwardly, holding his injured arm against his body with his other hand to prevent it from swinging, the tattered remnants of his shirt flying out behind him.

Beyond him, from the upper window of the bedroom that Ron and Betty had shared and where he now held her and Charlie hostage, thick smoke was pouring, behind which Rudd could see the bright flicker of flames.

Pausing only long enough to shout over his shoulder for someone to send for an ambulance and the fire brigade, Rudd set off down the drive in pursuit of Lovell, who had now reached the front door and was throwing himself repeatedly against it in a futile effort to burst it open.

"The window, man!" Rudd yelled.

He saw Lovell's face turned towards him, twisted with pain and that unseeing, unhearing desperation of a man who is acting out of blind impulse.

It was Boyce who, coming up behind Lovell, smashed the glass with his forearm and reached in to open the latch. Rudd scrambled through, aware as he did so that the other men were running into the yard.

As he ran towards the door, he found himself straining for any sounds from the room upstairs. The sound of flames crackling, with a leisurely crunching noise like wheels moving slowly across gravel, was clearly audible and he thought he heard someone moaning quietly as well but he couldn't be sure for, as he slid the bolts open, the door was thrown back and Lovell had flung violently past him and was making for the stair-case door, his feet clattering and skidding on the polished boards.

Rudd followed only a few steps behind him, Boyce on his heels, with the two marksmen and four other plain-clothes men whom Rudd had ordered to accompany them crowding up the narrow staircase at their rear.

"I've sent five men to cover the back of the house," Boyce announced, already out of breath.

Rudd merely nodded. There was no time to reply. They had reached the tiny landing where Lovell was in the act of bursting open the bedroom door. There was not even time to shout a warning to him that Ron might still be armed and could fire on him at close range for, without hesitating, Lovell had plunged into the smoke that was pouring out of the open doorway.

In the event, no warning was needed for Rudd, already on the threshold, could see what lay beyond inside the room.

The body of Ron Lovell was lying just inside the door, sprawled face downwards on the bedside rug, the end of which was buckled under, the gun caught under him with its barrel close to his head. Used as he was to violent death, even Rudd averted his eyes from what was left of the side of Ronnie's face.

A little distance away, Charlie lay huddled, curled up on his side as if asleep, except it was a sleep from which he would not awake. From the doorway, Rudd could see the wound in his chest from which the blood was still trickling to gather in a dark pool on the floor.

The only moving figure was Betty Lovell's, crawling towards them, her face raised, out of the heart, it seemed, of the smoke and flame of the fire that was burning behind her under the window.

Lovell gave a great cry that sounded as if it had been torn out of him and, gathering her up in his arms as a father might a child, his dark face brilliant with an expression of such fierce love that it was transfigured, shouldered his way roughly through the group of men that was now crowding into the room and carried her down the stairs.

Rudd let him go without comment and, turning away, began rapping out orders for the fire to be extinguished. It was not a large conflagration, consisting mostly of bedding that had been piled up in a heap under the window, with a few smaller articles of furniture placed on top of it, but it was well alight and, as he and Boyce crossed the room towards it, they saw the flames touch the edge of the curtains and run quickly up them, transforming them in seconds into fiery pennants.

As they tore them down and stamped on the flames, some of the men were already returning with buckets and bowls of water with which to douse the fire and, in a few minutes, nothing remained except the smouldering debris of wood and fabric which they flung through the open window into the yard below and a patch of charred floor boards from which faint wisps of smoke were still rising.

Rudd left them to it and crossed the landing to Charlie's room where he stripped the bed of sheets, returning to lay them over the two bodies. Curiosity sent him back, when this was done, to examine the further bedroom where Ronnie had lain in hiding, listening to what was said in the kitchen below, and where Geoff Lovell had slept alone.

It was a sparse, bleak room, simply furnished, like Charlie's, with a single bed and a deal chest of drawers. A few books were lined up on the window-sill, mostly farming magazines and manuals. The only novel among them was *Lorna Doone*. Intrigued by the title, Rudd opened it and saw pasted on the inside cover a plate announcing that it was a school prize awarded to Geoffrey Kenneth Lovell for good attendance. Why had he kept it? Had it been his only success? Or had he been drawn to its theme of violence and forbidden love?

It was a matter of pure speculation that had no relevance to the present investigation and yet, as Rudd replaced it on the window-sill, he felt inexplicably close to Lovell and to the lonely and taciturn child that he felt he recognised in the man.

His attention was caught next by a ladder, screwed to the wall, that led upwards to an opening in the ceiling, the wooden cover of which had been removed. Climbing up, Rudd stuck his head above the opening. A large attic, with a boarded floor, ran the length of the roof space, much of which was taken up with the miscellaneous objects that most attics accumulate: trunks and boxes, discarded furniture, old belongings no longer used but which their owners can never quite bring themselves to throw away. There was a smell, too, of dust and hot, close air, trapped beneath the tiles, and the sweet, decaying scent of stored apples.

In the centre, an up-ended crate stood beneath the open skylight, through which an oblong patch of sky, purpling into dusk, was visible. Rudd scrambled up into the loft and, mounting the crate, looked down, as Geoff Lovell had done, at the roof sloping steeply away to the darkening garden. It was, he decided, a very brave and desperate man who had made his escape by that route.

As he stood there, he heard in the distance the double warning bells of an ambulance and fire-engine approaching at speed from the main road and, closing the skylight, he went down the stairs to meet them.

The next few hours passed rapidly. Betty Lovell, unconscious but suffering only from shock, was taken away in the ambulance, Geoff Lovell accompanying her. The firemen tore up the square of smouldering floor boards and extinguished the last remnants of the fire. In the ravaged bedroom, stinking of smoke and wet, charred wood, Pardoe examined the bodies, McCullum photographed them, Boyce and Kyle marked their positions on the floor and, finally, the last mortal remains of Ron and Charlie Lovell were carried awkwardly down the narrow stairs and taken away.

In the middle of it all, some enterprising constable made tea, which they drank standing up in the kitchen. Rudd, holding the cup between two hands, had a free moment at last to look about him. It was dark outside now and, through the uncurtained window, he could see the headlamps of the parked cars shining on the façades of the out-buildings, giving them the unreal, theatrical intensity of brilliant highlights and dense shadows. It seemed a fitting backdrop to the night's activities.

Inside, the kitchen still managed to preserve, at least for him, some of Betty's ordered influence, despite the crowd of men who stood about talking and drinking tea. The blue and white mixing bowl stood on a shelf near the saucepans, which had been his first glimpse of her world. Some newly washed shirts, neatly folded down and waiting to be ironed, lay in the red plastic laundry basket in one corner.

He had seen her briefly, lying on the sofa in the living-room, Geoff Lovell squatting on his heels beside her, holding her hand; on guard, it seemed to Rudd, for he had allowed no one near her except Pardoe and the ambulance men. Not that Rudd hoped to get a statement from her; she was in too deep a state of shock.

A little later, they carried her out to the waiting ambulance, Lovell still holding her hand as he walked beside the stretcher, his head bent, his feet slurring on the ground. Watching him leave, Rudd realised how close he was to exhaustion.

The night wore on. Most of the men, their tasks completed, went away. McCullum departed, as did Pardoe. Soon there were only Rudd, Boyce and a few plain-clothes men left who were making a search of the house.

It was dawn before they finally finished. Rudd, standing at the window on the planks that had been laid across the charred hole in the floor, saw the first streaks of light lifting the darkness beyond the trees in the direction, he realised, of Hollowfield. There was, he felt, something symbolic about this, although what exactly his tired mind could not define.

"We're through with the search," Boyce announced, coming up behind him, his face streaked with dirt and rough with a night's growth of stubble. "Are you ready to leave?"

"No, not yet," Rudd replied. "I'll make my own way back. You go on ahead, Tom."

"If you want me to stay . . ." Boyce began but Rudd shook his head.

He had a desire to linger, as he had done in the field after the body of the man he now knew was Maguire had been taken away. Was it morbidity? he wondered. Or sentimentality? Or a desire to try to come nearer to an understanding of what had happened?

After all, there was nothing much left to see. In Maguire's case, there had been a heap of earth and a tarpaulin-covered hole. Of Ron and Charlie even less remained: just two shapes on the floor boards, outlined in white tape.

Boyce and the other men tramped off down the

stairs. He heard the front door close behind them and then their voices and footsteps as they crossed the yard and made their way up the slope towards the gate in the faint morning light.

After their departure, the house seemed to settle back into silence, to contract and close in on itself once more, as if thankfully resuming its old secretive habits.

Rudd remained standing at the window, his back to the room and the taped outlines on the floor, watching the light spread across the sky, confirming the outlines of barn and tree-tops, restoring colour to the leaves and grass. A few birds stirred and called, anxiously at first and then with growing confidence as the day widened, until their song rose up in a paean of triumph across the waking fields.

The sight of Geoff Lovell's figure trudging slowly down the track towards the yard did not surprise him. It was as if he had been expecting him and it seemed perfectly natural to Rudd to walk down the stairs and open the door to welcome him in. Nor did Lovell appear startled by the Inspector's presence in an otherwise empty house. He nodded briefly before stepping inside and the two men went, by common, unspoken consent, into the kitchen, where Lovell filled the kettle and put it on the stove to boil.

"I got a lift back from the hospital," he explained briefly. "I started walking and then this lorry stopped."

His injured arm was in a sling and he was wearing a jacket that someone must have lent him. It was slightly too small for him and was strained across his broad shoulders. His face was heavy with exhaustion, the features blurred as if lack of sleep had robbed them of their outlines.

"I spoke to Betty for a little while," he went on, setting out cups one-handed. "She came round and the doctor let me in to see her."

He was silent for a moment, frowning down at the table and the arrangement of china as if he felt there was something amiss with it. "She told me what happened."

Rudd, seated at the table, looked up but did not speak. He was himself in that state of tiredness when action of any kind is an effort and it is easier to remain silent and passive. Later, he would pick up the threads of the inquiry again, visit the hospital, take an official statement from Betty Lovell. But, for the time being, he was content to sit and listen while Lovell told it in his own way.

"She said, after I went, Ron tried coming after me," Lovell continued in a voice that had very little expression, "but he must have realised it was a waste of time because he was back in a few seconds, bringing with him the little paraffin heater from my room that we put up in the loft in the winter to keep the pipes from freezing. He was furious, she said, and started pulling the clothes off the bed and piling them up on the floor under the window, with some of the furniture. Then he poured the paraffin out of the stove on top of it and told them, 'If anyone tries to rush the house, I'll set light to the bloody lot.' Charlie was frightened and kept crying and this made Ron even more angry. He was shouting to Charlie to shut up and waving the gun about. Betty said she thought he was frightened, too. He was as white as a ghost and shaking and he kept looking towards the door as if he was thinking of making a run for it."

The kettle boiled and Lovell broke off to make the tea. The smell of it, fresh and aromatic, was very strong in the clear, morning air.

"If I'd been there, I might have talked him into it," Lovell went on. His face in profile as he bent over the stove had a haunted, brooding look. "At least, it might have saved Charlie's life. Then Stebbing arrived, making all that bloody racket." A paroxysm of rage twisted his mouth. "Goddamn that man to hell!"

Rudd shifted slightly in his chair but still didn't speak and, after a few seconds, Lovell recovered and took up the account in a calmer voice.

"It was enough to set Ron off again. He was standing at the window, smoking, when they heard the car and he jumped back and threw the cigarette down on the pile of bedding. The lot went up in a few seconds. There was a sheet of flame as the paraffin caught. It frightened all of them; Ron, as well. He probably didn't realise it would catch fire so quickly."

It fitted, Rudd thought, what he knew of Ron Lovell, and others like him he had had dealings with; men who had never properly grown up, who acted on impulse like children and then were aghast at what they had done. But what must it have been like for Betty Lovell, shut up in a room with two terrified men, neither of whom were capable of rational behaviour?

"Charlie began screaming and ran across the room towards Ron. Betty's not sure what happened next. She doesn't think Ron intended to fire but Charlie was hysterical and going at him with his fists and the next thing she knew the gun had gone off and Charlie fell on the floor."

He stopped abruptly and Rudd spoke for the first time.

"What happened to Ron?"

Lovell pulled himself together with a visible physical effort, straightening his shoulders and then clasping the damaged arm with the other hand as the bruised muscles contracted. But the pain seemed to steady him.

"She's not sure. It was all muddled and confused. There was the noise of the gun going off, and the smoke and flame from the fire and Ron shouting. Anyway, she ran forward to help Charlie and Ron pushed past her as if he was making for the door. The next thing she knew, she heard the gun fire a second time and when she looked round, Ron was lying by the bed. So she doesn't know whether he meant to kill himself or if it was an accident."

The position of the body, with the gun lying under it, suggested to Rudd that it was more probably an accident. In a panic, Ron had been running for the door, had tripped on the edge of the rug and fallen onto the gun. But it was only a theory. They would never positively know what had happened in those last terrifying minutes.

Lovell pushed his chair back violently from the

table and left the room, returning in a short time with a bottle of whisky and two glasses, which he banged down on the table.

"That's the last of it," he said. "I used to keep a couple of bottles in the house for Ron; hidden away so he wouldn't find it and drink it too quickly. He won't need it now."

Suddenly a spasm crossed his face, twisting and jerking his mouth and, with a muttered exclamation, he put his head in his hands.

"Get this down you," Rudd ordered, splashing whisky into one of the glasses and pushing it across the table towards him. He poured another for himself and drank it quickly, feeling the spirit run like a warm stream through his body. Lovell drank his covertly, turning his head away.

"What'll happen now?" he asked, when he had drained his glass. He still kept his face averted.

"You mean to you?" Rudd asked. Lovell nodded. The Inspector, watching his profile closely, decided it was better to tell him the truth.

"A report will have to go to the Director of Public Prosecutions to see if there's a case to answer," he said quietly.

"It must look bad," Lovell replied, in a voice as subdued as Rudd's. He turned to look directly into the Inspector's face. "I kept him on here, knowing he'd killed Maguire and after I'd found out he was wanted on an attempted murder charge. I should have handed him over to the police."

This was true but Lovell had good reason not to do so, Rudd admitted only to himself. It wasn't his place to act as judge and jury but he already knew what would figure in his report: Lovell's escape down the roof, which might have led to death or serious injury, in order to warn him; and the second time he had risked his life by bursting into the bedroom before he knew Ron was dead. It might be enough to persuade a judge, if the case ever came to trial, to give him a suspended sentence or, at most, a short term of imprisonment.

"You knew I burnt Ron's photos?" Lovell was

asking, his eyes fixed on Rudd's face. He seemed to want to admit to all, confess everything, and Rudd understood the reason behind it. Lovell must be accusing himself bitterly of being the cause of their deaths by not staying behind. But, in doing so, he was being unjust to himself. Betty's life had been saved and so possibly had been the lives of some of Rudd's own men; for God alone knew how Ronnie might have reacted had they been forced to close in on him. If anyone was directly to blame it was Stebbing.

"I understand why you did it," Rudd replied. Lovell had got rid of them in order to stop the inquiry from going ahead, knowing the state of Ronnie's mind and the danger Rudd himself was in every time he called at the farm. As it was, he had escaped death only by Lovell's prompt action in knocking the gun to one side, another fact that he intended mentioning in his report.

"Would you have given him up eventually?" he asked.

"I don't know," Lovell said slowly. "We were living from day to day. I hoped, though, that sometime Ron would be less on his guard or get so drunk that I could take the guns off him without risking anybody's life."

Rudd nodded but made no reply. He felt Lovell was speaking the truth. The man was too exhausted and too beaten by what had happened to be capable of lying.

"What will you do eventually?" he asked, changing the subject. "Will you stay on here?"

"No!" Lovell replied positively. "Not now. Not after this."

"Stebbing would buy it," Rudd remarked. "He'd pay a good price, too."

"I know," Lovell said bitterly. "He's been after it ever since he came here."

"Would you sell?"

"What's it to you?" Lovell demanded, with some of his old, jeering manner.

"Partly nosiness," Rudd admitted. "Partly real concern. I'd like to feel . . ."

This time it was his turn to look away, embarrassed by Lovell's direct gaze that was fixed on him. There was a silence in which Rudd felt there was nothing he could do except mumble some apology and take his leave. Then he heard the chink of glass and the sound of whisky being poured.

"I know what I'd do, given the chance," Lovell was saying slowly, in the low voice of a man confiding a dream. "I'd set up somewhere else on a smaller scale. Market gardening mostly. Early lettuces. Tomatoes under glass. That sort of thing. Perhaps a few chickens as a side-line."

Rudd picked up his glass, resting his elbows comfortably on the table. He was strangely touched by Lovell's confidence.

"It might still be possible," he said.

"Maybe. I don't know. It's too soon. Anyway, I'll have to see what happens to me first. But I had this idea. . . . Just the three of us . . . Charlie helping . . . Betty, as well. She likes plants. . . ."

"I know," Rudd said. "I saw the kitchen garden."

"And now Charlie's gone. And Betty . . ."

"Give her time," Rudd told him.

Lovell looked at him with a wry smile in which Rudd recognised that Lovell understood his own knowledge of their relationship.

"You reckon?" he asked.

"I'm sure," Rudd replied. He didn't add, as he could have done, that there was nothing else she could do except come back to Lovell in the end. She had no-one left now, only him. It wasn't much on which to build a marriage but it was more than a lot of people had. And perhaps the strength of Lovell's affection for her would carry them through.

He liked to think so. He wanted to imagine a happy ending for them, although Christ! he thought, I'm falling into the same sentimental trap that I thought Nancy Fowler had got caught in: the pap world of the happy-ever-after. Maybe, as she had recognised, it wouldn't work that way.

I must go and see her, he added, his thoughts veering off. Tell her what happened. We've found Ron for you with a bloody great hole in his head. Sorry, but he won't be coming back anymore.

He began to put on his jacket and do up his tie.

"You're off?" Lovell asked. He seemed to regret the Inspector's departure.

"I've got things to do," Rudd told him with a briskness he didn't feel.

"And so have I," Lovell replied, accompanying him to the door. "The cows have been out all night. I'll have to get them in and milked."

At the gate, Rudd paused for the last time to look back. The sun was fully risen now, although the front of the house was still in shadow. As he watched, he saw Lovell come out of the house and cross the yard, walking into the sunlight, towards the gate that led to the fields beyond.

Unlike Rudd, he didn't stop to look back. His dark, square-shouldered figure mounted the slope at a steady pace and presently disappeared from sight behind the trees.

ABOUT THE AUTHOR

JUNE THOMSON's previous Detective Rudd novels include *The Habit of Loving, Death Cap, Case Closed* and *The Long Revenge*. She lives in the beautiful Essex countryside outside of London.

INSPECTOR RUDD
Books by June Thomson

June Thomson is a highly praised British mystery writer whose series of books features Inspector Rudd, a likeable policeman who cleverly but without a great deal of flash, investigates and solves unusual murders in English towns. The following are the first American paperback appearances of Ms Thomson's books.

DEATH CAP

In the quiet Essex village of Abbots Stacy, Detective Inspector Rudd of the local CID becomes involved with murder—someone has slipped a poisonous mushroom in Rene King's food. Rudd is at his wits end until he discovers a piece of village gossip that had long ago been swept under the carpet.

THE HABIT OF LOVING

This time Inspector Rudd's case involves a bizarre triangle —Maggie Hearn, a middle-aged spinster who has befriended handsome young Chris Lambert and Jess Lambert, a beautiful young girl who has a date with death.

A QUESTION OF IDENTITY

When the local archaeological society asks permission to excavate a meadow they hope to find bones. They do. However they are the badly decomposed remains of more recent vintage. The only clue is a corroded cross on a chain. Rudd's investigation leads to a man who had disappeared several years before.

Read these Bantam Books by June Thomson, available wherever paperbacks are sold.

WHODUNIT?

Bantam did! By bringing you these masterful tales of murder, suspense and mystery!

☐	10706	**SLEEPING MURDER** by Agatha Christie	$2.25
☐	13774	**THE MYSTERIOUS AFFAIR** **AT STYLES** by Agatha Christie	$2.25
☐	13777	**THE SECRET ADVERSARY** by Agatha Christie	$2.25
☐	12838	**POIROT INVESTIGATES** by Agatha Christie	$2.25
☐	12458	**PLEASE PASS THE GUILT** by Rex Stout	$1.75
☐	13145	**TROUBLE IN TRIPLICATE** by Rex Stout	$1.95
☐	12408	**LONG TIME NO SEE** by Ed McBain	$1.95
☐	12310	**THE SPY WHO CAME IN** **FROM THE COLD** by John LeCarre	$2.50
☐	12443	**THE DROWNING POOL** by Ross Macdonald	$1.95
☐	12544	**THE UNDERGROUND MAN** by Ross Macdonald	$1.95
☐	13789	**THE BLUE HAMMER** by Ross MacDonald	$2.25
☐	12172	**A JUDGEMENT IN STONE** by Ruth Rendell	$1.95

Buy them at your local bookstore or use this handy coupon for ordering:

Bantam Books, Inc., Dept. BD, 414 East Golf Road, Des Plaines, Ill. 60016

Please send me the books I have checked above. I am enclosing $_____ (please add $1.00 to cover postage and handling). Send check or money order —no cash or C.O.D.'s please.

Mr/Mrs/Miss_____

Address_____

City_____State/Zip_____

BD—4/60

Please allow four to six weeks for delivery. This offer expires 10/80.

THE MYSTERIOUS WORLD OF AGATHA CHRISTIE

Acknowledged as the world's most popular mystery writer of all time, Dame Agatha Christie's books have thrilled millions of readers for generations. With her care and attention to characters, the intriguing situations and the breathtaking final deduction, it's no wonder that Agatha Christie is the world's best selling mystery writer.

☐	10706	**SLEEPING MURDER**	$2.25
☐	13262	**THE SEVEN DIALS MYSTERY**	$2.25
☐	13690	**A HOLIDAY FOR MURDER**	$2.25
☐	12838	**POIROT INVESTIGATES**	$2.25
☐	13777	**THE SECRET ADVERSARY**	$2.25
☐	12539	**DEATH ON THE NILE**	$2.25
☐	13774	**THE MYSTERIOUS AFFAIR AT STYLES**	$2.25
☐	13775	**THE POSTERN OF FATE**	$2.25